THE
PROBLEM WITH
HEARTACHE

CRAZY IN LOVE #3

THE PROBLEM WITH HEARTACHE

CRAZY IN LOVE #3

Lauren K. McKellar

ISBN: 978-0-9924524-4-5 (eBook)
ISBN: 978-0-9924524-5-2 (print)

Cover copyright © K. A. Last of KILA Designs
www.kiladesigns.com.au
Editing by Marion Archer of Marion's Making Manuscripts
www.makingmanuscripts.com
Editorial Formatting by E.M. Tippetts Book Designs
www.emtippettsbookdesigns.com

E.M.
TIPPETTS
BOOK DESIGNS

For anyone who has lost someone
Moving on doesn't mean moving away

ONе

KATE

THE PROBLEM with heartache is that you can't mourn forever. You can't walk around the streets wearing black, carrying holy water on your person in the hope that you'll stumble upon a miracle and be able to use it to bring that person back. One day, you're gonna forget that tiny vial, and you're not gonna realise until it's too late.

"Are you done?" Mum enunciated each syllable as if it weighed a ton.

"Give me a second." I threw my arms behind my back, fiddling with the straps on the bra.

A solution for heartache, however, appeared to be running. Or, it seemed to be for me. I'd been jogging in the early morning or late at night on the beach every day for six months now, and slowly but surely, I was getting better mentally, becoming able to function again.

Even if it meant that my boobs were getting smaller. Hence the new sports-bra shopping trip.

"Are you having fun?"

I cringed. Really, Mum? Fun?

My fumbling finally resulted in success and I shook the bra off, quickly shrugging my normal one over my shoulders and throwing my T-shirt on top of that. It hung loosely over my hips, the grey speckled material suiting my mood to a tee. Ha. See what I did there?

Making bad jokes to yourself: a potential symptom of heartache. Thankfully, not a symptom of Huntington's disease.

I grabbed my purse from the little seat the staff at the lingerie store so kindly provided its change-room patrons, and walked to the front of the store to the checkout area, sports bra in hand, ready to make the purchase.

"I do wish you'd get something pretty." Mum sighed, pulling at the strap of the black material. "It's hardly like you play sport."

"I just want to be comfortable." I tucked the material up in my hand. She didn't know about my nocturnal running habits. If she thought her little girl was roaming the streets late at night, she'd probably install a complex home-security system.

The guy in front of me at the counter was taking a really long time. He had six different sets of lingerie to put through. I couldn't help but check around his arm to see what. Black lace, red silk, black pleather … and was that something with fur I could see?

"Stop stickybeaking." Mum slapped my arm, and I snapped my head back to my chest.

"It's a public place," I whispered, even though glancing around revealed an empty shop. The only person there was a large guy at the door, dressed all in black, his posture alert. He looked a little like someone in security. Strange for a lingerie shop …

The transaction in front of me continued. Hopefully, underwear-fetish guy hadn't heard.

"People don't like you to look at their knickers, Kate." Mum tutted quietly, shaking her head.

"Well maybe people shouldn't buy quite so many pairs. And besides," I hissed, raising my eyebrows at her, "we don't know that he's going to wear them all at once."

"Ahem."

Of course. You whisper two fairly innocent sentences, but the one about the guy in front of you being a cross-dressing lingerie wearer, he hears.

"Sorry." I studied the ground.

The man turned around to face me. He had maroon leather shoes, scuffed, as if they'd seen better days. My gaze travelled up his black jeans, over his red-checked shirt with the triangular collar, the black scarf around his chin, covering his lips, his nose—but not his eyes.

Holy hell, did the man have eyes.

"Kate."

I blinked. What? How did this guy know my name?

"Yes?" Mum replied, and I jabbed an elbow to her ribs.

"That's me." I smiled brightly. "Sorry about the panties-wearing comment."

"To be fair, this does look a little weird," the guy said. You can say that again … "We just have this film clip tomorrow, and the stupid wardrobe guy said the models won't fit any of the … you know …" The man jerked his thumb toward the counter, indicating the underwear the checkout chick had now finished ringing up.

Cogs clicked in my head. This wasn't—

"Lee?" I silently added freaking-Collins. If he was going to the trouble of wearing a bad scarf by way of disguise, I doubted he'd be keen on me screaming his full name in a crowded shopping centre.

"Yeah?"

Silence.

"Kate's just so happy to see you, is all," Mum said. She took a step closer. "Hard to recognise behind that scarf there."

"That's kind of the point." Lee gave her a wink. I swear my mother blushed.

"Well, we'd love to have you over for dinner sometime, since you're in town," Mum was saying, her hands clasped together. She opened her mouth to continue speaking.

"But being a really busy guy, we wouldn't actually expect you to come," I overlapped.

"Well, if we invited you formally, we would," Mum said, giving me a strange look.

"I mean, I could." Lee spoke the words softly, taking a step closer. "So long as you don't tell anyone about my secret identity."

Mum giggled like a schoolgirl. Help me, God.

I looked past her, past the stands of bras and the occasional naughty dress-up item and into the shopping centre and—

Him.

I dropped the sports bra and ran, shouldering Mum as I surged forward, out the doors of the shop.

Left?

Right.

I could just make out the brown hair bobbing in the distance.

I bolted, as fast as my legs could carry me, darting around mothers with prams, old people supported by walking frames, and teenagers making their way to the food court in an achingly slow fashion.

Turning the corner, I could see the hair again, but it was still too far away. My knees rose higher, my feet hit the ground harder, and I gave it all I had. I couldn't let this chance get away. I had to take it. I had to make it.

This time when I turned the corner, he was almost within arm's reach. Ignoring the stares I was getting from the lunchtime food-court crowd, I dove, reaching out and grabbing onto the denim of his jeans as I fell.

I hit the ground, hard. Tiles smashed into my ribs, my knee, and the side of my jaw. Everything went black for a few moments, and I blinked, trying to clear my vision.

When I could focus again, I looked up. Faces hovered over me, voices yelling things, asking things I couldn't quite make out.

I need you.

Then I saw him. The blue jeans, the white shirt. The brown

floppy hair.

I blinked, and concentrated all my brainpower on focusing on his face. His face, Kate. Look at his face.

"Lachlan?"

I blinked again. An old man wearing a chocolate-coloured beret looked back at me.

Oh, God.

Lachlan's grave was located in a small cemetery just outside of town. It was one of the more popular establishments for burying the dead in the local area; people were always gathered there, remembering those they'd lost and grasping to the past. Women sobbed, men knocked back beer after beer, and the native birds sung a song of mourning, a soundtrack for all of us to grieve to.

I came here a lot. But only when I was sure no one I knew would find me.

"Hey, Lach." I sat down cross-legged in front of his gravestone. At first, that had creeped me out, until I'd remembered that Lachlan had been cremated. It wasn't like I was sitting on his bones.

I opened my handbag and brought out the little cupcake I'd packed with me. I took the candle I had in the bottom of my bag and stuck it into the pale blue icing. Resting the object on my knee, I fished around in my bag again until I found a packet of matches.

"So, I thought I'd celebrate my birthday with you." I smiled down at the tombstone. Beloved brother of Johnny. Special friend to many.

I'd been more than his special friend, but what could you say? Please, can you change the inscription to include my name? It didn't seem right. And it sure as hell wasn't fair.

I lit the candle on the cake, but instead of blowing it out, I let it burn for a few moments, the acrid smell of freshly lit match filling my lungs.

"I don't think this is going to get easier, you know," I said. "I used to think that in six months time, I'd be well and truly over … this."

The candle's flame danced in the wind, twirling from side to side like a ballet dancer.

"But I'm not. I think about you and … God, it hurts, Lachlan. It hurts." Tears stung my eyes, and salt coated the inside of my mouth, an ocean of pain I just couldn't shake. It hung heavy on me at night; it blanketed me during the day.

Six months might have passed, but the ache hadn't lessened. And I didn't know that I wanted it to. Because if the pain went away, it would mean I was forgetting. And that would cut far deeper than loss.

"I had to spend my birthday with you. Without you, it just wouldn't have been right." I leaned over and gave the gravestone a light kiss before I blew the candle out.

Happy birthday to me.

TWO

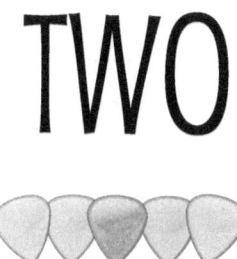

LEE

"I STILL DON'T see why you have to do this." Benny sighed, folding his arms across his chest, an action that looked entirely ridiculous since his hands barely reached the other side of his body. Instead, they rested on his bulging stomach, a hangover from his days of drinking too much beer after he was kicked out of the police force. Or, that's what he liked to tell me, anyway. He didn't know I'd seen the stash of Tim Tams he'd asked Michael's girlfriend, Stacey, to keep for him in the back of the tour bus.

"It'll be nice." I shrugged. Outside, the sun was setting, throwing orange streamers of light over the comfortable residential street. Houses flew past us in suburban uniformity, wearing matching outfits of lush green grass, terracotta brick, and brown-tiled roof.

"Nice is going back to the city and getting you laid." Benny smirked, and I threw my hand out and hit him on the arm. "Hey!"

"It's creepy that you find me 'picking up' nice, man." I

shook my head. "Seriously, dude. I know you get paid to watch me, but you don't get paid to watch me, know what I mean?"

Benny chuckled despite himself, and I pressed my lips into a smile. In all honesty, Benny had a point, a damn fine one. When Kate's mother, Deborah, had sent the band a message on Facebook asking if we wanted to come over for tea a week after I'd seen her in the city, I'd been a little surprised. What the hell was I doing here, out the front of the house of this chick I'd met twice, maybe three times before, ready for dinner with her family?

Sure, when I'd met her at the gig six months ago, I'd been intrigued. She was beautiful, but not in the usual way I saw every damn day. There was nothing fake about her. She was just … real.

Still, that wasn't the main reason I was here. Family. That was why. Because if there was one thing I was good at, it was being a family guy.

That was how I paid my debt.

We pulled up outside one of the identical houses, our black Chrysler rolling into the driveway with ease. "This it?" Sam, the driver, asked. He jerked his head toward the brick two-storey house with timber beams decorating the porch.

"If that's what the GPS says …" It was Benny's turn to be a smart ass.

"Shit! You actually know about that? My bad. I thought you still thought there was an actual woman on the other end of that box." Sam laughed.

"I didn't know Siri was a thing, okay? Lay off. That joke's getting old." Benny rolled his eyes, referring to the time when we had managed to effectively convince him Siri was a real chick.

"Okay, I'm gonna head in now. You gonna wait in the car, or want to check the place for ninja spies first?" I asked Benny. He gave me a sardonic look, all eyebrows and lips raised to one side.

"I'll come to the door with you," Benny grunted.

"Oh! A true gentleman." Sam held his hand up for me to

slap.

I rolled my eyes and gave him a gentle tap. "I'll be an hour, maybe two. Go grab yourself a bite to eat if you're bored, but maybe don't go too far into town. This car isn't exactly subtle."

I pushed open the door and swung my jean-clad legs out onto the sidewalk. Immediately, a wave of heat hit me, and I tilted my head back into the cool air-conditioning of the Chrysler to suck in one more breath.

Seconds later, Benny was by my side, his head swivelling left and right up and down the street. Thankfully, no one had followed us. It was just one of the many reasons I had been so keen to get back to Australia for a second tour. The paparazzi were nowhere near as bad here as they were in the States. Or maybe they just weren't that smart. Either way, I wasn't complaining.

Benny and I walked up to the front door of the unassuming house, and I knocked, three sharp raps. Benny nudged me in the side, and thrust something into my hands—a silver-wrapped bouquet of flowers, yellow gerberas, I think. They were sunny as hell and screamed "friend" which was just what I need them to do. "Nice touch." I nodded my appreciation at him, and he smiled.

"I make you look good," Benny purred in an overtly sexual manner, just as the doorknob rattled and the brown wooden door in front of us swung open.

"Lee! So glad you could make it." Kate's mom launched—and I mean launched—herself at me, kissing me on the cheek. She smelt like perfume and wine, and I smiled. Maybe this wouldn't be so bad after all.

"Hey, Deborah." I nodded. "This is my security head, Benny."

"Oh! Are you here for dinner, too?" Deborah asked. "Do stay. We have enough. I always aim to try and feed an army—I can only imagine how malnourished you must be living on the road." Deborah shook her head, and I stepped back. There was something about the look in her eyes that made me think she was about to pinch my arms to try and gauge my body fat ratio.

"Oh, he's not—"

"I'd love to stay for dinner. Thank you for inviting me." Benny smiled down at Deborah, his large frame towering over her.

"Well, come in, come in. Don't just stand there in the doorway." Deborah bustled inside, and Benny shot me a pointed look above her head.

"I ain't turning down a free meal," he whispered.

I tapped his stomach gently. "I don't doubt it."

Benny slapped me on the back of the head as I followed Deborah into the house. We walked into a living room, decked out with two long suede lounges and a glass coffee table in the middle, some magazines stacked neatly in a rack to the side. On the wall was a big flat-screen television, speakers flanking it. Floral curtains bookended the window that looked out onto the street.

None of that grabbed my attention, though. What captured me straight off were the series of frames sitting on the mantel. They painted the picture of a happy family with an easy ride, and I knew that no matter what story they outwardly told, these guys had had anything but.

"Come through into the kitchen. Let me make you a cocktail." Deborah turned around and rushed us forward into the next room, a combined dining room/kitchen, with a wraparound bench. On the burner, a pot bubbled away and the smell of garlic and onion wafted toward me.

"Would you like a mimosa? Or I can make a …" Deborah paused, studying the bottles of liquor lined up on the kitchen bench. "I could try a mojito? Or just one of these spirits with juice, or soft drink? I don't know, you're probably so used to fancy—"

"Just a beer would be great, if you have one." I interrupted her speech before her face got any redder.

"Yes! Yes, of course we have beer. I'll just get—Kate!" Deborah yelled, and I flinched just a tiny bit. "Kate, come and get your guests a beer. Two beers. Get them a beer each."

Benny nudged my side, and I thrust the flowers forward. "Sorry, Deborah. These are for you."

"That is so sweet," she said. She took the flowers and bent over the cupboard below the sink, rifling around and then producing a vase.

Footsteps thudded down the stairs behind me, and I turned around. Standing at the entrance to the room was Kate. She looked different to the last time I'd seen her, and yet the same. Her brown hair was pulled back in a ponytail, and she was wearing black jeans and a large black shirt that seemed to hang off her tiny frame. Her face was pale, as if she hadn't seen the sun in too long and the look in her eyes, that of the lost.

Or, it was that of the lost, I should say. Now, it had been transformed into full-blown rage. "Mum …" There was venom in her voice, and her eyes flashed with anger. "Did you invite Lee Collins here after I specifically asked you not to?"

Ouch. Good to know I was a welcomed guest. Benny shuffled awkwardly by my side.

"Oh! Did I forget to mention that, dear?" Deborah didn't even make eye contact with her daughter, instead filling the vase with water and arranging the flowers within it. "And I'm sure he's fine with just Lee. The Collins part really isn't necessary."

I stifled a laugh. Only because I was afraid that if I let it loose, Kate might take one of the dining table chairs, break off a leg and stab me with it.

"Kate." I smiled. "Nice to see you again."

"Nice to see you too." She smiled, but it didn't reach her eyes.

"Hey, I'm Benny." Benny stepped forward, his arm outstretched, and Kate took his hand and gave a limp shake before shoving her hands back in her pockets.

"I'll just get those beers." She power-walked/ran to the sliding door and flung it open, storming through the backyard. I'm thankful I'm not a misplaced ant on that path right now.

"I must have forgotten to tell Kate you were coming. Ah, well, she's glad you could make it," Deborah said. She returned to the stove and gave the simmering pot a stir. "Dinner shouldn't be too long; make yourselves at home. Take a seat in the lounge, or here if you'd like."

"I'm going to …" I glanced at the door, then back to Benny.

"Go, man." He nodded, and I returned the gesture, then walked outside.

The path from the house to what I presumed was the garage wasn't long, ten feet at most. When I reached the open door, I looked in, past the parked Ford Ranger parked, and over to the corner …

And there she was. Leaning against the brick wall, her head tilted to the ceiling.

"Hey."

She whipped her gaze in my direction, and I couldn't read her expression. It was somewhere between anger, fear and … indifference.

And I knew all about indifference.

"You didn't have to come, you know," Kate said. "I'm sorry if I was rude, it's just … You didn't have to, and now you're here, and I'm sure there's probably some cool bar you could be at, or some girl …"

The words hung unspoken between us. I was happy to let them stay that way.

"It's cool. I wanted to see how you were doing. We had to give Michael and Stacey a lift up here anyway; I thought it'd be nice to drop in. Say hi. See how you're holding up." To my ears, the words sounded weak, but it was the honest truth. I swallowed. How truthful would her answer be?

And do I want to hear it?

"I'm okay." Kate shuffled one foot on the floor, sweeping it in an arc in front of her. "I'm actually doing good." She managed a smile.

It was fake as all hell.

"How's your dad?" I changed tack.

"He's … he's okay, too." Kate seemed to shake off whatever it was holding her in one place and walked to the fridge, retrieving three beers and handing one to me. "Everything's just … okay, you know?"

She was inches from me, and her eyes, her hazel-coloured eyes were flecked with gold. There was something about her—the fineness of her features, the fullness of her lips … I licked my own. You could cut this tension with a knife.

Or, with the dropping of a beer bottle, which was what Kate did.

"Shit, sorry." She bent down to pick it up, but I did too, and it was like a scene from a bad romantic comedy. I swear—all we'd need was to butt heads on the way back to our feet.

Come on, Lee. Take control. Do what you came here to do and be the family guy.

I straightened my body, looked her in the eyes, and spoke. "Listen, I wanted to tell you … I've spoken with the guys—the guys in the band"—Idiot, give her the details—"and we want to set up a small charity fund for you guys. I know how hard it can be, having one parent out of action, trying to get by on government help but having to work your ass off to do it, and I wanted to do something, you know?"

Since the word "charity" left my mouth, Kate had been shaking her head so sharply, I was worried she might strain a tendon. Shit, do you even have neck tendons?

"No, no. We don't need your help." She pushed past me, but I grabbed her wrist as she did, and I swear a tiny gasp escaped her mouth. I bit down on my smile.

"I'm not saying you need it," I said, pulling her closer to me. Her chest rose and fell as she breathed, and I immediately pulled my gaze away from it. I was here to help her. Not to stare at her boobs. "I'm just saying it's something we're doing. It's non-negotiable. Just something small, say two grand a month. I'll make the checks out to you guys, or we can put it in your account—whatever."

Kate threw her wrist down, and this time, there was a definite fire in those golden eyes. "You will not do any such thing! We're not a freaking … we don't need your pity, Lee Collins. We do just fine on our own."

"Don't you see?" I raised my voice to match her volume.

"I know you don't need my pity, and that's lucky, because I'm not offering it. This is me helping a friend out, because I get it. My dad …"

I trailed off as recognition flashed in her eyes. My father had Parkinson's. It wasn't identical to her unique familial disease, but it still sucked ass.

She bit her lip, and stepped back again. "I forgot," she said, and I leaned closer in case she spoke again. "I still can't take your money, though."

And with that, she spun on her heel and fled back into the house, leaving me standing there with a bottle of beer and a slight case of wandering eyes as I found myself wondering how skin-tight those jeans must be to give her ass such amazing shape.

I shook my head. I came here to try and help them, to have dinner, and to leave.

That ass was off-limits.

For more reasons than one.

THree

KATE

"SO, HOW did Michael adapt to life in a big band like yours?" Mum asked. Her eyes were wide with excitement, and it was hard not to at least giggle a little.

But then, every time I giggled, I felt guilty. The weight of oppressive sadness would wrap around my shoulders, encompassing me in its misery. Lachlan still wasn't here. And nothing, no amount of ridiculous words from Mum or flirting from a too-privileged pop star would fix that.

I shoved my plate forward, losing interest in the food. How could I eat when my stomach churned with memories? When this time only a week ago I'd been celebrating my birthday with my dead ex-boyfriend?

Mum looked at me and all but pushed the plate back to its spot, her eyes telling me to eat. I guess it was better than her eyes telling me to launch myself at Lee Collins. Not only was I missing Lachlan with a heartache that broke me in two—a crushing pain that had me losing interest in everything—but I'd had my fair dose of flirting with artistic types with Dave.

Tortured artist really wasn't my thing, especially when the torture they were inflicting was on me.

"He went really well. It's a bit different to touring here in Oz, you know?" Lee smiled easily and leaned over to grab a second helping of potatoes. I saw a flash of approval in Mum's eyes. She loved seeing people eat. She shot me a nod, and I could practically read her subtext of See? What a healthy, strong boy!

"In what … way?" Dad asked. He was seated between Lee and Benny. Who brought a security guard with them to dinner, anyway? I got it, he was famous, but I didn't see any crazy fans running around outside. Was it really necessary?

"Lots more people. Lots more shows. Lots more media." Lee nodded. He spoke a little slower for Dad's benefit, but not too slow—not the sort of slow some people did when they made him feel ridiculous. Where they made me feel ridiculous.

"So what about you, Kate? What have you been up to recently?" Lee turned his attention back to me. Thankfully, despite Mum placing my drink down next to Lee's, I'd managed to rearrange the seating so I was safely between Benny and Mum. I had a feeling that sitting that close to Lee-freaking-Collins could possibly result in me trying to punch him in the junk for insulting us with his handout offer. Heat crept up my cheeks as I thought about what so many other people had probably done with that 'junk', what they would do to be seated so close to him right now.

I shook my head. He was hot, sure, but it didn't matter. He wasn't Lachlan. No one would ever be Lachlan. And six months wasn't enough time to even begin to change that.

Guilt crept in at my conscience, the ever-present assistant to my main man, depression, who haunted my thoughts at night. I shrugged to try and shake it off, to clear my thoughts, and stared at Lee. He didn't hold a candle to Lachlan. In fact, that rich, American, dinner-attending, security-shadowed type was about as un-Lachlan as you could get. I bet he'd never done anything spontaneous in his life. He'd probably need to clear it with the FBI first.

"Kate's been doing a lot of soul searching," Mum said, smiling. Soul searching? Really?

Mum patted my hand lovingly, and I gritted my teeth. Oh, yeah. He'd asked a question. Oops.

"It's been a little hard on her, but she's getting there."

"Are you working?" Lee asked, as he twirled some pasta around his fork.

"I am now, but not for much longer." I shook my head. "The café you performed in, Sideways? Johnny's getting in a new team. He's taking a break for a while."

I studied my hands, laced underneath the table within each other. Work was this bittersweet pill I took every day. I was close to him there. I could feel his presence, see his art, smell that invigorating scent that used to lace his body—

"Oh, that's cool. Taking time off after something like what he's been through ..." Lee shocked me out of my reverie, and my focus snapped to him. "... I have no doubt he needs it."

Are you going to offer him charity money, too? I asked myself, then snapped it back. Shit, why was I being such a bitch? He was just trying to do something nice.

And there. That was the crux of it. There was no reason. Since Lachlan died, all I had become was a heap of lazy, unmotivated and depressed, with a dash of bitch thrown in on the side.

"So Kate is going to look for jobs elsewhere, aren't you, petal?" Mum asked, tapping my hand again. I swore, she was going to run a path in my skin. "She always wanted to do event management."

A light shone in Lee's eyes. "That's right. You hooked up Dave & The Glories playing with us in December."

"She did." Mum beamed.

"You know, we might have an opening coming up on the next leg of the tour." Lee spoke the words slowly, a calculated gleam in his eye. "Don't we, Benny?"

"We ... do," Benny confirmed. His lip twitched and I shook my head. Oh no. Oh, no, no, no, no, no.

"You'd just have to do hotel bookings, make sure we're

where we need to be on time … Check we have what we need, when we need it … that kinda thing," Lee said. "You'd be perfect for it."

"Kate would be. She is the most organised little soul." Mum smiled, her eyes wide, leaning so far forward over her plate with excitement so that her loose floral top drooped against the red sauce covering her pasta.

"It'd be all expenses paid, in the States."

"America," Mum repeated, eyes widening at me.

"And on top of that, we'd pay you an initial …" I waited for it. I raised my eyebrows. "Two grand a month, for the two-month leg."

There it was. Surprise! The rock star couldn't get his way with that initial charity proposal, so he was forcing it down my throat.

"That's a lot of money, hon." Mum patted my hand again, and this time I pulled it away. She bit her lip. "We'd miss you a lot—so much—but I think it's important for you to take opportunities when they come to you."

I pressed my eyes closed and ran my finger around the collar of my shirt. Even though it was only just coming on spring, it was suddenly hot in here. Too hot.

"Be … good." Dad echoed Mum's enthusiasm, and I gave him a weak smile. He'd already sent me off.

I looked back at Lee. "You don't have to give me an answer now. But I'd really like to have you with us." His eyes flashed with sincerity.

"And we could use a new member on the team," Benny said. "Someone with a feminine touch would be well appreciated, now Stacey's staying here. Keep Lottie company."

"Lottie?" I furrowed my brows.

"Our stylist." Lee flicked his hand, as if the question wasn't important. "Anyway, we fly out on Tuesday. Let us know if you want to go and we'll talk to the record company about trying to employ you through their Aussie branch, so you don't need to worry about a working visa and can hopefully swing it on just a visitor's pass."

"Great. Kate will be in touch. Now, tell me more about yourself, Benny. Do you have a girlfriend?" Mum speared a piece of potato and popped it into her mouth.

Conversation = closed.

They didn't need me here for the discussion. That was more than fine with me. For the last six months, I hadn't really wanted to be here, anyway.

I mentally checked out for the rest of dinner. It was getting easier and easier to do—closing myself off to the rest of the world, putting on a smile-and-nod show and counting down the minutes, the hours until I could be alone with my memories.

Benny and Lee left straight after dinner, Lee handing both Mum and me cards with his contact details on them. I snatched Mum's away and stashed it in my room, deep in my dresser. Left in her possession, my bags could be packed by sunrise.

When the final clang of dishes stopped downstairs and the lights in the house dimmed, I pulled on my runners, lacing them up tight. I tiptoed down the staircase, careful not to disturb Mum and Dad. It was hardly an illicit activity I was out to do, but it was one they hated all the same.

They didn't like to see me running. It wasn't good for me. I was too skinny, and running in the dark wasn't safe.

They didn't know it was the only way I could get to sleep. That until I'd exhausted myself—pushed my body to the very limits of its capacity to feel, to hurt, to embrace pain—I couldn't get there.

I started at a slow jog, past the identical houses that lined our street, then headed toward the main road. My feet slapped hard against the pavement, the cushioning in my shoes not enough to stop the jolt up my legs.

Pound, pound, pound.

Lachlan. His face, his smile, his laugh.

Pound-pound-pound.

Making coffee, skinny-dipping, watching movies on the couch.

Poundpoundpound.

His lips, pressed to mine, his hands running over me, in the car, careening down the freeway.

POUND.

I doubled over, gulping in shallow breaths of air that were too thick to penetrate my lungs. The ache in my chest stabbed at me as if I'd been knifed, but the stitch was nothing to the ache in my heart.

When I got home, I collapsed in bed, covered in sweat despite the early spring temperature. My hair was plastered to my forehead, my heart thudding at top speed.

And still, I dreamed of Lachlan. It seemed nothing would make that stop.

That wasn't the worst part, though.

The worst part was waking up.

"So, let me get this straight. The lead singer of the Grammy-award winning Coal asked you to go on tour with them, and pay you a stupid amount of money to do so, and you said no. Capiche?" Stacey threw a tennis ball at the ceiling and then caught it with a snap against her chest.

"Something like that," I mumbled, slurping the dregs of my milkshake and then sliding it across the red Formica tabletop. I looked around, taking in the 50s-style diner set-up, the black and white tiles … the coffee machine …

Lachlan, grinding the beans. The smell of coffee as he ran it through the machine. His chocolate-brown eyes, flicking up to me as I spoke.

Me.

Him seeing me.

Him touching me.

"Kate."

I blinked, and I was back where I was two seconds ago, only it was Stacey's hand around my wrist. And Lachlan wasn't there.

Lachlan was never there, despite how many times I was convinced I'd seen him. He'd left me. For good.

"Sorry." I pulled my wrist back into my lap where it busied itself with my other hand, twisting and scratching and pulling. I had all this energy, all the time now—and nowhere to expel it. Lesley, my counsellor, said it was because I was feeling so much emotion but I wasn't getting it out, so it expelled itself in a physical manifestation. Mum just thought I had a massive case of the fidgets.

"Don't apologise, sweetie." Stacey gave my arm a gentle rub and then pulled back, perhaps thinking the better of it. "It's allowed to still hurt, you know?"

Tears welled in my eyes for the zillionth time in the last six months and I blinked them back. It was stupid how often I cried now. Anything could set me off, from a trip down to Sydney, to my best friend caring.

"Anyway, so no, I'm not going on tour," I said, shrugging the emotional stuff off. Sometimes, it was easier that way.

"Why?"

"Heaps of reasons. He's doing it out of charity. I'll be away from my family. And I need to stay here, for Johnny." I let my eyes roam to the counter where Johnny was just finishing up the milk on a cappuccino. He saw me looking and smiled. I grinned back at him. Both of our eyes were empty, but we got each other. And it was nice. It was nice having someone who understood.

"Charity? He's paying you to perform a job. And pretty crap money. Two grand? That's five hundred a week. After tax, and considering you'll be on call seven days, that's nothing," Stacey scoffed, leaning back in her seat, conveniently leaving the 'all expenses paid' part out of the equation. "And yes, you'll be away from your family—for the short length of two months."

"A lot can happen in two months."

"It can, Kate. But what has happened in the last two? I mean, aside from me coming back from touring with the band to find you've lost about half your body weight and now look like a microphone stand." She shook her head. "But seriously, how did you keep your boobs? I exercise, and I exercise, and they're the first things to go." She looked miserably at her chest, and pushed up her more than ample breasts. An elderly gentleman at the table next to us widened his eyes to the point where I worried they may fall out of his head. I smiled.

"Okay, so I get that it's not that long a time, and Mum can probably handle anything family, but what about Johnny?" Stacey's eyes scanned the room and I saw the moment they locked on Johnny. I saw because they got this look of depth, of sadness, of regret. Had my best friend always been so empathetic when it came to death? "He needs me."

"Kate, I have no doubt he does." She leaned forward and rested a hand on my knee. Why was everyone so touchy-feely with me lately? Did I look that needy? "But the thing is, he's stepping back from the café to be with Lesley. You told me so yourself."

I swallowed. It was true. My former boyfriend's brother was dating my former genetics counsellor, now turned regular counsellor. They were in love, and there were even talks of them going on a yoga retreat. It was twisted, to say the least. And not just in the downward-dog department.

"So … you think I should just … go?"

"I think the last thing Johnny wants is you sharing a bed with him and sexy counsellor as he tries to find her Zen-spot." Stacey raised her eyebrows. "Besides, you'll have a good time. I just got back, and I had a ball."

"With your boyfriend." I pursed my lips.

"In another country," she corrected me, and I smiled. She did have a point. "Look, if you won't do it for the fact that it's advancing your career, paying decent money and giving you an opportunity to see the world—dear God, what am I saying? Why do I even need a further argument?" She rested back in her seat and I smiled. You couldn't help it when you were around her. It was contagious. "If you won't do it for all those amazing, stellar, super fabulous reasons, do it for Lee."

I pulled my neck back. "Lee?"

"Lee-freaking-Collins." Stacey smiled, then shuffled her chair closer, lowering her voice conspiratorially. "You know, super-hot rock god, who pretty much asked you out back at the memorial for Lachlan?"

Images of Lee swelled to the forefront of my mind, his eyes—those striking, blue eyes that held me in one place. It still seemed weird to think that he had more or less asked me on a date, and I hated that a little, tiny something stirred inside me when I thought of that. Because nothing should. Because Lachlan was the one guy who was perfect for me, who understood me—who got me.

I love Lachlan.

"That was a pity ask." I shook my head, placing my hands around the bottom of my milkshake glass.

"That was a legitimate question—and this is a legitimate opportunity." Stacey paused, then her hand reached for my wrist across the table. She squeezed it. "Kate, I know you're still hurting."

"I—"

"And I know you don't want to hear this. But Lachlan … he'd want you to be happy. You can't be his girl forever, Kate."

Her words hit me, hard, like a dagger to my chest. I jerked back my hand and put it safely in my lap. I wanted forever. I wanted to be his forever so bad. "I'm not …" I shook my head. God, I didn't even know what I was anymore.

"Kate, I know this is hard for you, but …" Stacey looked up at me, sincerity bleeding from her eyes. "It could be really good for you to have a change of scenery, too. Stuck here in this café, your house, those places that remind you of him? It can't be good for you to be so—"

"I like my life," I snapped. "I need to be here, Stacey." And if I go, I can't visit the grave anymore. Can't close my eyes and pretend, just for one moment, that he could come back.

"I'm just saying, go into it with an open mind, okay? I spent five-odd months on tour with them in the States. Lee is a good guy—he's not Dave, Kate. And you need someone good."

She smiled reassuringly, and I offered her a weak version in return. "And if all that—all that—isn't enough, do it for me."

"Because …?"

"Because my boyfriend is going on another international tour, only this time, he'll be without me."

"Are you worried?" I tilted my head to the side. "I'm sure he wouldn't—"

"Hell no, I'm not worried. I just want to make sure he's not having too much fun while I'm slaving away over my TAFE books. I need someone to make his life miserable, you know? And I think you'd be perfect for the job."

This time, I grinned. It seemed the only thing to do.

"Plus, you'll get to meet Lottie. I hung out with her during the last few weeks while the boys were doing band stuff when I went with them," Stacey said. "She's great; you'll love her."

I let my mind explore the idea, the possibility. The concept didn't hurt as much as it used to. When it came down to it, it would be good for our family, too. My income, combined with Mum's, had allowed us to keep Dad in the best of care, ensuring he got good treatment when he needed it. But now that I wasn't going to work at Sideways anymore … well, there'd be a definite gap in our financial plan. One that last night I'd tried to ignore, but that today, with this all-too-real information in front of me, I knew I'd have to handle.

Still, that didn't mean I needed to fly halfway around the world. I should just get a job here, somewhere close by, to be with them.

But will you find something you like, that pays you that much money that actually advances your career?

"So, I guess there's only one question left," Stacey said. She stood, picking up my milkshake glass to take it to the counter.

"And that is …?"

"How many fabulous pairs of shoes are you going to take?"

Four

LEE

Five years ago ...

I WAS NEVER a sucker for heartache and excess emotional turmoil. I knew I'd find true love one day—hell, my parents had made me believe it existed, and it was real as sin. I just didn't know it would be so easy.

I didn't know that falling in love would be like diving into a deep pool of silk. I didn't know it would it wrap around you, caress you as its curves moulded to your body, and then push you up as you surfaced. Consuming. Easy.

"Five," I muttered as I ran my hand through my hair and stared up at the sky above me: blue marred by fluffy clouds of white, scudding along in the breeze. Today they moved so fast, whereas other times, you could barely see them move. Was that what time would be like in this deal? Sometimes it would move so fast, and other times it would stand still?

I turned my attention to the patchy green grass and kept walking. The sky couldn't help me with this one. Answers rarely dropped out of it and fell into your lap, no matter how strong your desire.

I pulled the piece of paper from my pocket again. The piece of paper I thought I had been waiting all my life to receive. So why the hell was it making me so damn nervous?

Dear Mr Collins,

We are delighted to inform you that we are in a position to offer you and your band, Coal, a five-album contract, to be produced over a five-year period.

Please find following our terms and conditions regarding royalty payments, splits, and details of distribution for your $500,000 advance and recoupment.

As discussed in our meeting today, this deal is based upon you remaining as front man of the band, and all band members' ability to steer clear of negative media attention.

There will be a one-week period during which you can discuss the following contract with your legal team. After that, we will need you to sign or return all legal documentation, and we can discuss our next steps together.

Congratulations once again, and welcome to the Spinner team.

Kind regards,
Tony Osmond

I creased the paper again and shoved it back into my pocket, shaking my head. For three guys just out of high school, that advance was a lot of money. It wouldn't last us five years, but it sure would get us somewhere.

It was everything else that I was worried about.

We'd only been together for twelve months; what if we couldn't produce the material for an album a year for the next five? So far, we only had five songs, for fuck's sake. Would we have to pay back our advance if we couldn't make it?

And then there was the fact that they mentioned in the cover letter that media shit again. They'd brought it up with us when we'd first met—something to do with them getting burnt by the last band who signed with them. One month after their first album release, the lead singer was in jail for sexual abuse, the bass player had punched the quarterback of the local football team and the drummer had had an affair, cheating on his wife. With a dude. "Altogether a very unpleasant business," Tony had said, shaking his head as he did so. "So we need to be careful, you understand, that you boys are squeaky clean."

The idea of a squeaky-clean rock 'n' roll band seemed at odds with the job to me, but what could you do?

I sucked in a deep breath of clean air, enjoying the quiet of the park. No one came down here during the middle of the day, but I knew that in a few hours time, it would be filled with moms, dads, kids, and dogs as they got their after-school/work exercise.

"Um, excuse me?"

I blinked. I thought no one came …

I turned my head left to right, trying to identify the speaker.

"Up here."

This time, the voice was a tiny squeak.

I leaned my neck back and looked up … and there, in the branches of a tree above me, was the most beautiful girl I had ever seen.

She had short blonde hair that flapped in the wind, toned bronzed arms that were currently wrapped around a branch and her eyes—her eyes were the most spellbinding things I'd ever seen. They were deep green, like the sea, flecked with these shards of emerald that just glittered in the afternoon light, capturing me, drowning me in their depths.

"Any chance you could, say, lend me a hand?" She clutched the tree branch tighter as it swayed dangerously in the wind.

"Yes, sure." I jogged to the base of the old tree and looked for any footholds. "How'd you get up there?"

"I kind of … shimmied, I guess?" She bit her pink, plump lip.

I threw my arms around the trunk and tried to wiggle up as she'd suggested, but it didn't work. It was unsurprising; I wasn't exactly known for shimmying skills. Maybe if I could just find a ledge, or a low branch to hold on to, or …

"What are you doing up there, anyway?" I asked while my eyes scanned the area for a different approach. I circled the trunk twice and finally saw the tiniest knob sticking out just above my head. If I could use that for leverage …

"Promise you wont laugh?"

I looked over. She was biting that damn lip again. "Promise."

"Well, I was trying to save a cat, and—"

"You climbed a tree to save a cat?" I snorted. I couldn't decide if it was the craziest or the most humanitarian thing I'd ever heard.

"Hey! It was mewling and being all sad, and I couldn't just leave it up there."

I took a short run-up and jumped, grabbing onto a tiny knob sticking out from the tree and pulling like crazy until I could swing up and grab onto the lowest proper branch with my other hand. I huffed out a breath. "Aren't you supposed to call a fireman if that shit happens?"

"Well, yes, but—are you okay? You're making some funny noises."

I grunted as I tried to fling my other hand from the knob to the branch. Looked like I was making a stellar first impression. "Fine," I said.

"Anyway, so my father is in the local fire department, and he would be pretty pissed if I called him out for this."

"Heartless," I managed to choke out.

"Right? The poor little thing," she said. "So, I climbed up here, only the kitty got scared and climbed down … and I got …"

"Stuck?" I swung like a monkey from the branch before something ran over my hand. Something with many tiny, little legs. It took everything I had to keep my hold. I didn't give a shit if it was manly or not. I was absolutely petrified at the very thought of spiders and their little legs and their fucking creepy-as-shit eight eyes. What the hell did they need to see so bad? Or was it just so they could take extra aim with those little stingy fans?

I dropped myself to the ground, shaking my hands to rid myself of the invisible assailant.

"Yes."

I stuck my head around the side of the trunk. She really was a long way up; at least eighteen feet, I'd guess. The problem was that even if I did manage to get onto that branch I'd been so close to before, all the branches between her and me were kind of puny-looking. And while I may not have been a steroid-using gym junkie, I did work out, and I wasn't light.

It seemed she had the thought at the same time as I did, as she spoke. "Maybe you could stay there and … talk to me? Give me, um, directions?"

It was then that I twigged.

She was afraid of falling. She needed someone to guide her; I got that, all right.

"Of course, sure. So shuffle backward … that's the way, good." She moved her body along the branch, her ass wiggling in these dangerously short denim cut-offs. "So, um, what's your name?"

"Carly." Her voice was breathless as she backed right into the trunk. "What now?"

"Lower your left leg slowly—slowly—and the branch is maybe just a little longer than your"—ridiculously toned, amazing-looking—"leg."

"Ah!" She gave a girly squeal as her leg flailed about, her grip on the branch tightening. I pursed my lips, but she quickly gained purchase on the branch and I breathed again. "Maybe … Oh God, I don't know if I can do this!"

"It's okay, Carly, it's cool. You got this. Just slowly move your other leg, your arms to the trunk …"

She extended her other leg and moved her arms so they were wrapped around the tree trunk as she lowered herself onto the branch below.

I quickly ran around to the other side of the tree, positioning myself underneath her. I would catch her if she fell. I could do that.

"So, distract me. What are you doing here?" Her voice was riddled with tremors.

"I …" And for some reason, I told her the truth. "I'm in a band, and we just got sent out contracts for a record deal."

"That's"—she shimmied her arms around the tree trunk—"good."

"Yeah … there's just … there are a few things that make me nervous about it, you know?" I moved around the tree a little as she attempted to lower herself onto a branch on the other side. "The advance … I mean, what if we don't sell and we can't make it back? What if I can't write any more songs?" I chewed on my lip. "Plus there's this whole—whoa!" I braced my arms in a cup shape as she scrambled for footing on a particularly thin branch.

"Shit!" she cursed, then righted herself again and continued her descent.

"So yeah. There's this clause, right, that says we can't have any negative media attention. I mean, how the hell do I control what someone else prints about us?"

She finally put her hands on the bottom branch and lowered her body, her legs swinging beneath her. I wrapped my arms around her knees, and she let me take her weight, dropping from the branch and jerking her arms to my shoulders.

I slowly lowered her down my body. Hers was warm against me, her flat stomach, her boobs … God, they were close to my face. I scrunched my eyes shut. Don't be the creepy guy in the park who licks a stranger's cleavage.

"Why are your eyes shut?" she asked, and I blinked my lids open. Her face was inches from mine, her green gaze penetrating me with its intensity.

"I …" I paused. Her breath was warm, and it smelt like fairy floss.

"Did you just sniff me?" Her lips twisted up in a smirk, and I felt my cheeks heat as I let my arms drop to my sides.

"Oh my gosh, you're blushing!" She moved her hand to hold the back of it against my cheek. Her fingers were cool as they touched me. Her other arm stayed wrapped around my neck. "That is the cutest thing."

Another wave of fire attacked my face. This girl, the things she was doing to me …

Carly licked that luscious bottom lip of hers. Her gaze turned from mischievous to serious all in a second.

It happened before I realised. One moment she was looking at me, studying me, the next her lips were pressed against my cheek, dangerously close to the corner of my mouth, soft, warm and sweet. My arms worked their way back around her, pressing her curvy body against mine. This kiss went on a little longer than it should have, her lips murmuring against my cheek, and even though it was such a minor thing, it was better than any kiss I'd ever had. It was fresh. It was cool.

It was different.

I liked different.

"Sorry." She jerked away from me and pulled her arms back, retreating into a Carly bubble that I had no place entering.

"It's fine, it's—"

"No, it's not okay." She shook her head and ran her hand through her cropped, blonde hair. "I shouldn't have—I'm sorry."

Her eyes turned a dark green, the light in them

extinguished. She turned around and started walking away. I stood there, my arms still extended, as if at any moment she might morph back into my embrace.

"Thanks for saving me," she called over her shoulder. A smile had returned to her face.

"No worries." My voice was empty, hollow.

I studied her as she darted around trees, walking back in the direction of the main road. Of life. Of the opposite to this alternate universe we'd just shared.

"Oh, and Lee? It is Lee from Coal, right?" My mouth parted. How did she know my name? "Take the damn deal. You guys are an incredible band."

My eyes widened. She'd heard of us? We'd only played a few gigs, nothing major.

"Trust yourself. I sure do."

She didn't look back again.

She was all I could look at.

It was in that moment I knew. We had a connection. She'd made me laugh, made me smile, made me really think. She made me believe.

Carly and I were meant to be together.

Present day

"ALL PACKED?" I asked Kate. She pulled a large, grey suitcase through her narrow front doorway, and I smirked. Rookie error. Once she was on the road, she'd realise how cumbersome luggage of that size can be.

"Yep." She smiled back. Her hair was piled high on her head in a topknot, and she was wearing denim shorts and an oversized soccer T-shirt. I stared at the insignia, trying to work out what team she supported.

"What?" She folded her arms across her chest and my eyes snapped back up to her face. Shit. What if she thought I was staring at her boobs? "I like to wear comfy clothes when I travel, okay?"

"It's cool." I shrugged. Her golden eyes gleamed at me. There was something captivating about them, something that made me so utterly incapable of looking away. They made me feel naked. Isolated. "Was just … forget it."

"I'll take that." Benny stepped forward and grabbed her suitcase, turning and pulling it toward the car. Thank God someone was being a gentleman around here.

Kate's parents hovered in the doorway. How had I missed them before? I hoped they hadn't seen me staring at their daughter's rack. Way to instil confidence pre-overseas trip, dickhead.

"My baby girl!" Deborah pressed her lips together. There was a glossy sheen of tears in her eyes.

"Mum." Kate wrapped her arms around her mother's waist, resting her head on top of her shoulder. Deborah's auburn hair splayed on top of Kate's brown locks. It was sweet. Touching.

I couldn't think of the last time I hugged my own mother like that. It had been too long. And I wasn't entirely sure which of us to blame.

"You … take carrrrre of … my girl." Paul, Kate's father, staggered forward, extending an arm to me. I took his hand and shook it, a firm gesture. I wanted to impart as much solidity toward this man as I could.

I always used to think that with my dad. If I could just be steady and still enough around him, it would help him somehow get a grip on his own shaky problem.

Turned out, it often just made it worse.

"I will." I nodded, smiling. "I'll bring her home to you safe."

He gave me a grin, then turned to Kate, arms outstretched. "C'mere," he growled.

Kate launched into his embrace and closed her eyes, her eyelashes resting on her cheeks, a hug so tight I could see his shirt puffing out around her fingers on his back. Once again it hit me. She was such an amazing girl. Such a supportive daughter.

She has such sexy eyelashes …

I dug my finger into the pressure point on my palm. Do not think sexy thoughts about Kate.

I was doing this to help her. To help her family. And I couldn't hit on her, no matter how much I wanted to.

She was way too real for me to risk.

"I'll email you ... all the time," Kate whispered in her dad's ear.

I shuffled forward, scraping my shoes against the concrete footpath. Moments like that felt too private for me to overhear. After all, this was a very tight family.

Family. It was something I worked hard to protect.

Because I had to atone for ruining not one, not two, but three.

FIVE

KATE

Things I Have Learnt About Coal:

They are the least organised group of individuals I've ever met

This is despite them having a cast of thousands to help keep them in line

"Lee! Lee, I love you!"

"Can I get your autograph?"

"Come to New York!"

"Overwhelming, right?" Lee flashed me a grin, and I looked up at him and tried for a smile.

"Overwhelming would be one word for it." I pulled my shoulder bag around so it rested closer against my body as one particularly confident fan reached out and touched it over the airport barricade. "Noisy would be my first pick though."

"Ha! You get used to it." Lee raised his hand, as if he was about to give my shoulder a rub, then jerked it back and scratched his head instead, as if he'd realised the error of his ways. Cameras flashed in the crowd, and I nodded. He was a smart guy. I'd no doubt that a picture of him with his hand on my shoulder would quickly go from Lee being a nice guy and comforting his new employee, to Lee Brings Home Aussie Souvenir on the front page of whatever gossip rag bid the highest for it.

"This way please, Mr Collins." A big guy in a black suit opened a door that took us away from the screaming hordes in the airport terminal and over to a giant bus. The back of it was open, and guys in tanks and shorts were loading equipment in by the eerie white glow of several temporary floodlights. I spotted my suitcase being thrown in the back, and I breathed a sigh of relief. I'd been wondering how on earth we'd get our luggage from the baggage claim area and avoid getting mobbed at the same time.

The bus door was open and Lee half-walked, half-galloped up to it. He climbed the stairs and turned and waved to a few fans, who were craning their necks over a fence to see us.

"Bit of a joke, right?" A shoulder nudged mine, and I looked up at Xander, the drummer. His dark eyes flashed to the crowd in the distance and then landed back on me. He wasn't smiling. His lips were thin.

"It is what it is." I shrugged. "I mean, I guess you kind of have to play up to it, right?"

He looked at me, really looked at me, so penetratingly it felt as if he were seeing me naked. Or, as if he wanted to, anyhow. "I'll protect you, you know. If you need it."

"I'm … I'm sure I'll be fine." I studied my feet and kept walking toward the bus.

"That's what they all say …" Xander put his hand under my chin and raised it so my gaze met his. "… at the start."

He stalked off to the bus, and I tried to ignore the sinking feeling in my stomach. Between Mr Show Biz and Mr Sleazy, I didn't exactly feel at ease.

"Don't worry 'bout him, Kate." Michael threw an arm around my shoulder.

"I'm not." I forced a smile.

"That's not what your face says." He winked and squeezed

me tighter against him. "He can be a bit of a douche," he whispered, "but he's all right once you get to know him."

We walked to the bus together, and I ignored the flash that illuminated the air behind us. At least if a photo of Michael and me hugging appeared on the front page of a paper back home, Stacey wouldn't be concerned. She knew just how much he adored her—and it wasn't hard to understand why. Stacey was every guy's wet dream—beautiful, fun and sweet. If she weren't such a good friend, I'd hate her.

Inside the bus was not as I expected. There were normal seats, plus an area down the back with a bed and a little door that led to what looked like a bathroom. Some of the seats had curtains that could be drawn around groups of two, allowing for a little privacy. Xander stalked to one near the back and immediately shoved the curtain around him. Michael laughed.

"Where should I …?" I looked at the seats and shrugged.

"Anywhere, Kate." Lee nodded, standing in front of me. "Let me just do a few quick introductions."

I'm about to ask 'to who?' when a small figure came running around Lee's legs and toward at me at full-speed. Tiny arms wrapped around my leg and when I looked down, a cheeky little smile beamed up at me.

"Catch me." The boy giggled. His eyes were a deep blue, and the way they twinkled just churned my heart. It was impossible not to smile in return.

"Not now, Jay." A gorgeous blonde with long, plaited hair stood up from a seat where she must have been slumped, her hands on her hips. "What do you do when you meet new people?"

Jay's eyes went wide. "No candy."

This time, it was my turn to giggle. "And …?" The woman pressed, but I could see she was fighting a smile. Jay's little face frowned, and he shoved his hand in his mouth. Suddenly, his eyes widened and he wiped his knuckle on his shirt.

"Pweased to meet you." He shoved his hand out to my waist, and I smiled and shook it. His fingers were slimy, but it was so freaking cute I didn't care.

"Hi, Jay. I'm Kate," I said.

He furrowed his brow. "Your voice is funny."

"Jay …" The woman skipped down the aisle and hoisted him up in the air, pulling him close to her. "Manners." He buried his face in her shoulder.

"He means your accent," Lee offered. He swung his bag into the overhead compartment and slouched down on a seat across from the one I'd seen the woman and Jay come from.

"C'mere, little buddy." Lee stretched out his arms. Jay gave him a look—the kind of look that only kids can. The one that means 'please don't make me, strange man.' Lottie smiled and placed her hands on Jay's shoulders, leaning down to whisper something in his ear. Seconds later, Jay wiggled out of his mother's embrace, throwing himself over the seat for a hug with Lee. I smirked. A rock-star image it was not.

The woman turned her attention to me, and with the mega-watt smile that graced her face, there was no doubt in my mind that Jay was her son. Their grins were identical. "Hey, I'm Lottie."

"Hey. I've heard so much about you," I said. Just wasn't told you had a kid, that's all. I silently berated Stacey for not mentioning that useful piece of information. Although I guess she only had known her for a month.

"All good, I hope." She raised her eyebrows. "Come on, you can sit near me. That is, if you don't mind the occasional child snores. He's not a quiet sleeper."

"Sure." I walked over and placed my bag on the seat in front of hers.

Thirty minutes later, the bus was packed. Security, the band, Lottie—who I had now found out was the stylist—the driver, five dancers, the techs—three of them, because no one should have to tune their own guitar—two sound guys, one label rep—who wouldn't be with us all the time, apparently—and four women, who sat up the front and didn't seem to talk to anyone. They were dressed to impress, showcasing their long, golden-brown legs and exposing a fair bit of cleavage.

"Meet the girls," Lottie whispered in my ear. I looked back

at her, then returned my gaze to the women. Or, the teenagers. Because seriously, I doubted any of them were over eighteen.

"Who are they?" I asked, but the sinking feeling in my stomach told me I already know the answer.

"Well, at a guess, I'd say they're Xander's, but there's a chance one of them might be Lee's. They usually don't decide till we get to the hotel." Lottie smirked, and my eyes widened until they felt dry. What the hell?

"Where do they come from?"

"Everywhere." She shrugged. "The front row at gigs … these ones they probably picked on the plane, and got Benny to go ask them if they wanted to come back with us for a while. Lee doesn't usually indulge in that kind of thing," Lottie said. She shot him a furtive look. Jay was sleeping against his chest. "But they come anyway."

I blinked. This concept seemed so far removed from the Lee Collins who'd shown up at my doorstep with flowers for my mum, the Lee Collins who'd shown such concern when Lachlan …

Lachlan.

The pain stabbed me in the chest and I nestled back in my seat, clutching at my stomach. Gosh, it was … every time it was a new wave, fresh, powerful and raw.

Lachlan, racing me in the moonlit lake.

Lachlan, telling me his secrets.

Lachlan, his body against mine.

His body against mine …

"Kate." Lee's hand was on my arm, giving it a gentle shake. I gasped for air, clutching at my heart, which was pounding at a million miles per minute. He put his other hand on my shoulder, staring at me with his steady blue gaze. "Breathe, Kate. Breathe."

In-out-in-out-in-out.

In, out.

In, out.

Finally, the air got thinner, easier to suck in. My heart returned to its normal plodding pace. Everything was going to be okay. Everything.

"S ... sorry," I stuttered.

"It's fine." Lee dropped one hand but the other stayed on my arm, rubbing tiny circles. They made me feel warm. Safe. "You just started shaking, and I was saying your name but you wouldn't answer."

I shook my head. I didn't remember any of it.

How can I help with the tour if I blank out like this?

"You okay, sweets?" The smell of pink bubble gum invaded my nostrils, and I turned and saw Lottie's head poke over the top of my chair. She tucked a strand of hair behind my ear. "Stacey told me you've gone through some ... rough times. I'm here for you, if you need it."

I swallowed and pressed my eyes shut. Please don't make me talk about it.

"I was just saying, come sit by me for a bit. We'll go over your role and responsibilities," Lee said, but at Lottie's glare, countered with, "when you're ready. You guys ... you guys stay here and talk it out. Whatever you need."

He nodded and stood up, backing away to his own seat where Jay was sleeping peacefully.

"Sometimes it's good to have a little girl time." Lottie smiled and stroked my hair again. It was a lovely gesture, but coming from someone I'd met only seconds ago, it offered little comfort. "I'm here for you, if you need it."

"I think I'll go talk to L ... Lee." Shit. Almost slipped. "You know, get my mind off things."

Lottie nodded, but something flashed in her eyes. I wondered if I'd hurt her feelings. "No worries, lovely." She gave me another brilliant smile. "When you come back we can talk some."

I pushed over my chairs and walked toward Lee, whose attention was fixed firmly on his phone. As I sat next to him, he shoved it in his pocket, way too quickly in my opinion.

"So, let's talk about what you'll be doing for the next few months." Lee grabbed a manila folder from the pocket at the rear of the chair in front of him. He had to stretch forward to do it; this was no ordinary cramped bus. Each seat looked as if it could move to a full recline before it came close to touching the one in front or behind it. "Now, I've made a list of all the stops on the tour in here. This will become your bible. The only thing you'll need more than this on your trip here, is this."

At that, he rifled around in the seat pocket again and pulled out a shiny black cell phone. "Obviously, your phone won't work here, so we got you this. Keep it with you at all times. Seriously, take it with you when you pee."

"Guys, can you keep it down?" Michael groaned from somewhere behind us. "Some of us are trying to get some sleep."

"Suck it up, Aussie," Lottie yelled with a smile, but she pronounced it "Ossie" and I stifled a giggle.

"Hey! I just came off twenty hours on a plane, Yankee," Michael grumbled. "Have some goddamn sympathy."

Lee stood up, taking the phone and the folder with him. "Come on." He stepped one long leg between mine, and just for a second, he looked down at me. Something burned in his eyes, and for a moment I felt it burning in mine too, then lower down. I stared at the part where my thighs encased it. He was warm, and the heat ran up my legs, pooling in my apex. I pressed my lips together. I could reach out and touch—

Then everything seemed to snap back into normal time and he stepped his other leg forward and removed the offending limb from its treacherous position. I clamped my knees shut, and swallowed. Shit.

"Come on." Lee jerked his head toward the bed at the back of the bus. "We'll work in there. We can close the door, so we don't disturb the kids."

"Good," Michael grunted, and I couldn't help but wonder if Stacey put him up to this in the hope Lee would suggest such a solution. I wouldn't put it past my best friend to try and get me in bed with a rock star the first day on the job.

Lee extended his hand to me and I took it. His hand was cool to the touch, and I swear it trembled just a little as he wrapped my fingers in his hold. His grip was firm, comforting

… but it was too big. It wasn't Lachlan's hand. Lachlan's fingers, that fit perfectly to mine …

No. Focus on the now. As much as I wanted to think about Lachlan until every breath of his was relived in my mind, I couldn't do it. Not at this moment. Instead, I stood and the bus swerved, sending me flying forward into Lee's chest. It was hard, rock solid, and I looked up to see those fierce blue eyes staring back at me again.

His hand wasn't cool now.

It was scorching hot.

"Don't forget to tell her about the media commitments, Lee."

Xander's words snapped me out of my reverie, and I looked to his closed curtain and smiled. I stole my hand into my jeans pocket. God, what was I doing? I'd just gotten off a plane after a twenty-hour trip. I probably stank, and looked like fresh hell. His hand was probably heating with repulsion at this sweaty girl in front of him.

"Of course," Lee said. He started to walk down the bus, giving Lottie's shoulder a small squeeze as he passed her. "I would never forget."

Heat flamed my cheeks. Turned out he wasn't even close to hitting on me. Lee Collins just happened to be the world's most touchy-feely guy.

As if to prove my point, as we walked down the bus aisle Lee squeezed Jay's shoulder, bro-punched Michael through his curtain and even somehow managed to coerce Xander into sticking out his hand for a high-five. Yep. The guy liked skin-on-skin contact.

I shook my head, trying to delete all thoughts of less-than-appropriate skin-on-skin contact that just flashed their way in my mind.

Lee shut the door behind me and gestured to the bed. I sat on the edge, almost afraid to ruin the crisp grey quilt.

Clearly, Lee had no such concerns, and he slid across the top of the mattress, stretching his body along it. Holy hell, this guy was long. I knew he was tall, but something about the way he stretched out, graceful but kind of dangerous at the same time … His T-shirt bunched up, and I caught a glimpse of tanned abs staring back at me. I licked my lips. One word—wow.

"Here." Lee had his phone in his hand. He pressed a few buttons and then handed it over to me.

I looked down. The screen was lit up with a photo of him and the rest of the band—sans Michael, old bass player in place—on the cover of Rolling Stone magazine. Lee was at the forefront, shirtless, his black denim jeans slung low, designer underwear on display. Ink rippled up his arms and down his sides, over those washboard abs I'd gotten a preview of just a moment earlier, and—

Wait.

I looked up. Lee was smirking at me, a devilish twist of his lips. "Instead of saying you could take a picture, I thought I'd show you one instead."

Heat rushed to my cheeks and I opened and shut my mouth in my best goldfish impersonation. I'd clearly been caught checking him out. Well, this is awkward.

"It's okay. Half the people in the country have probably seen that pic." Lee shrugged, taking the phone back from my hand, his fingers grazing mine, and placing it facedown on the bed. "Plus, it gets hot when we play. I take my shirt off a lot."

"And people stare?" As the words came out of my mouth, I started kicking myself. Idiot, idiot, idiot.

"Some." Lee shrugged. "Just maybe not as obviously as you."

The fire in my cheeks continued to rage. I shouldn't have checked him out. I wasn't interested in him.

The last guy I'd seen shirtless was Lachlan, lying in my bed, rolling under the covers with me. His skin, so soft, his hair curled in my fists as we made out, our bodies alive against each other.

The morning before he died.

The last day I was truly happy.

I angled away from Lee and straightened my spine,

pushing down the agonising pain, compacting it. When was it going to get easier?

For what felt like the millionth time that day, I rolled my shoulders, trying to push away the hurt and focus on the now. I was here to do a job and help Mum pay for our bills. That was what mattered. Lachlan I could let crush me later. "Let's get down to business, shall we?"

Lee sat up. "Is everything okay?" His eyes bled concern and his hand rested on my shoulder again. Once more, tingles shot down my body at his touch.

I shook it off. I didn't need that right now.

"It's fine. I just want to make sure I nail this, you know?"

Lee's eyes met mine, and the depth in those icy-blue orbs struck me to the core. "I know you're gonna be great at it."

"You don't even know me." I shook my head.

He paused. "Wanna know a secret?"

I nodded. "Go on."

Lee glanced around, as if he were afraid that at any moment someone could come bursting out from behind the bus window curtain. "I'm not really a true musician."

His words were so quiet I had to think them over before their meaning registered in my brain. "What? You didn't take singing lessons as a kid?" I raised my eyebrows.

"When I first started, I was tone deaf." His eyes flashed sincerity at me.

"Bull," I countered.

"True story."

"You can't fix that though, can you?" I scrunched up my nose, and he leant forward and gave it a light tap.

"If you practise enough at anything, you can make it work. And I was lucky enough that my parents supported me, helped me have about a million lessons to learn to hear the notes with ease."

It was a weird confession to say the least, but it did ease the tension. "I don't think that necessarily makes you an untrue musician."

"I think it takes away some of the legitimacy, though. But

that's why I know you're gonna be good at this." Lee flashed me a grin. "Because practise will make perfect. Now it's your turn. You need to share a secret with me."

I racked my brain, trying to think of something, anything. Anything that didn't hurt.

"Well, I …" Come on, brain think of something. "I really, really, really like to run."

"That's not a secret."

"It is, though!" I protested. "Because I never used to do it. Ever. But a few months ago, I started getting up early and just chasing shadows around the block. It helps … helps clear my head, y'know? Focus on the day in front of me." It helps me try and escape my thoughts. To wear my body down. "But Mum and Dad don't really know I do it, and neither do my friends, so I guess that's a secret for you." I nodded triumphantly, arms folded under my chest.

"Is it because you still think about him?" Lee's eyes drilled into me. It would be so easy to fall apart in front of those eyes, to fall under their spell.

But I couldn't.

I wouldn't.

"Can we just get back to work, please?" I said, softening the words with what I hoped was a convincing smile.

Lee paused for a moment, silent, then something flashed in his gaze and he broke into an easy smile again. "Of course."

He grabbed the papers from behind him once more. "Your main job will be to make sure we are where we need to be on time, and to make sure everyone is ready for us. In here is a list of gigs, hotels, and drivers. Before we are supposed to be anywhere—anywhere—it's important you call ahead and let them know our ETA."

"So they have security ready?"

"Exactly." Lee nodded. "It's also important that probably a few hours before we are supposed to be anywhere, you check in and make sure all band members are present and accounted for."

"Where else would you be?" I frowned.

Lee licked his lips. His eyes darted to the pillows on the bed. "Sometimes things get ..."

I decided to just come out with it. "You guys sleep around?"

"No!" It was his turn to blush, and I couldn't help but smile. Something about this guy, one of the most famous lead singers in the world, and he was ... blushing at the idea of me thinking he had sex with strangers. I'd seen him linked to a few people in the tabloids, but nothing like what I'd seen some other musicians get up to. He was pretty tame, actually.

"I mean, sometimes Xander does, and I ..."

"You ...?" I pushed.

"I do, and I date, occasionally."

"Like Inga." I nodded, remembering the bimbo that Dave had brought to dinner that time. She'd been ridiculously good-looking, legs that went till forever and a gorgeous body. Swiss, of course.

That night, that long night ... I'd run home, desperate to escape from it all.

Lachlan had kissed me.

Lachlan had kissed me.

My chest heaved as the memory of his lips on mine raced through my brain, and I fought, fought with every cell in my body to keep those tears from flowing from my eyes, those sobs from escaping my lips. Why was this so hard? It was always bad, but this? It wasn't fair.

But then again, nothing ever is.

"I forgot you'd met her." Lee picked at a non-existent thread coming loose on the bedspread. "She wasn't anything—"

"You don't need to explain it." I shook my head. Hurt was still rushing through me, reminding me of all I'd lost. "I know you said ... you know, you kind of asked me out back at the ... the ..."

Funeral? Wake? Celebration of Lachlan's life? None of the words felt adequate. None of them were close to it.

"At Sideways." Lee supplied the words for me, and I flashed him a grateful smile.

"Yes." I nodded. "And I just wanted to say, I know you

were just, you know, being polite. I don't think you're holding a candle or anything for me." I rushed it out all in one breath. I was rambling, and I couldn't stop the words from escaping, but I wanted him, needed him to know I wasn't here because I thought he liked me, despite Mum's obvious suggestions. "I mean, you don't know me, and even if you did, I probably wouldn't be your type, and—"

"Yes."

I blinked. "Yes, what?"

Lee leant in close, so close I could smell the piney, woody scent that it was so unfair for a guy who had just spent close to twenty hours on a plane to have lingering on his body. God knew what I smelt like …

"You are." I glanced down at his lips. He gently placed his hand on my exposed thigh, and the shockwaves from his touch rippled through my body. The tension between us was strung tight like a rope. "You are my type."

I swallowed. I'm Lee Collins's type? Was Stacey right about all of this after all?

"But obviously, you're also my employee, and I wouldn't cross that line." Lee cut his gaze back to the paperwork on his lap, and I acted like I wasn't about to pass out from overexertion. My body had gone through devastated, to turned on, to rocked to its very core, all in the space of ten minutes. Note to self: do not try to have a business meeting with Lee-freaking-Collins on his bed in the bus after a twenty- hour flight.

Then, a devastating thought hit me. What if Lee was using me as material? Dave had sung a horrid song about me once; what if I was just some colossal joke to Lee?

I looked at the guy lying across from me. Surely he wouldn't … would he?

There was one easy way to deal with it. To not be a joke. To not give him the opportunity to make me a laughing stock. To not let him fluster me again.

"Okay, so let's talk about your requests at the shows." I clasped my hands over my knee and pointed to one of the sheets in front of him with the word "rider" on the top of it.

"We don't need one thousand thread-count sheets, or only blue M&M's or anything like that," Lee said, oblivious to my inner turmoil. He used his hand to emphasise what he was saying, making wild gestures to illustrate his point. "We just have some basics, mostly booze, and some snacks that won't make me wanna hurl on stage."

"Hurl." I giggled. "You're so freaking American."

"Freaking." He smiled, and shifted his body that little bit closer to mine again. "You're so innocent."

This time, there was no mistaking the danger flashing in his eyes. "You're travelling with a band." He swallowed, and his Adam's apple bobbed up and down. "We say fuck."

I'd never been one for swearing, but that word, the way he let it fall from his lips had layers of sex loaded in it. Parts of my body tingled that I swear never tingled before, and I pressed my lips together. His breath was hot, so near to my lips, and someone must have turned the heat up in the bus because I was suddenly super aware of the line of my T-shirt against my neck, the heat in my cheeks, over my chest, up my legs.

That was when I looked down and saw it.

His hand was still on my thigh.

He caught my gaze and looked down, too, jerking his arm back and running his fingers through his thick, brown hair.

"Sorry." He shook his head and collapsed back on the bed, staring at the ceiling.

"It's fine." I turned my head from side to side, and it was. I am in love with Lachlan. Nothing could change that. I felt it in my bones, pulsing through my blood, and in my heart.

"Let's talk about loading in and loading out."

And just like that, the moment passed.

Lee talked about music.

I thought about Lachlan.

And I was certain we did not think about each other.

Three days later, as I was doing my morning tour rounds that basically consisted of me knocking on the guys' doors, then yelling, and sometimes getting a key from reception and waking them up myself, I found a letter. It was sticking out from under Lee's door, and it had my name on it.

I ripped the envelope open, anxious to read what was inside.

Dear Kate,

I know you're going through a lot, and I know you're probably pissed at this whole work situation. I get that you were kind of railroaded into it; really, I do. For what it's worth, I'm sorry, but I don't want you to doubt yourself, okay? YOU hooked that tour up, back when Dave & The Glories joined us on the road. YOU organised all their bookings and YOU made it work.

On the bus, you seemed a little nervous, as if maybe you thought you weren't good enough for this job.

Well, let me share another secret of mine with you: If I'd thought you were gonna be more trouble than you were worth, I never would have hired you.

Don't ever forget that.

Lee

SIX

LEE
Four years, nine months ago ...

STRUMMED THE notes, sang the words and gave the crowd all I had in the most I-don't-give-a-fuck way I could. Because really, right now? I didn't give a fuck. It was no longer just a smart business decision for me to act too-cool-for-school on stage without actually engaging in any scandal. Yes, that was right. After long talks with Tony, our label rep, about not getting into any media trouble, it became clear that while he didn't want actual sandal, he also wasn't a fan of us being the grown-up equivalent of a boy band, either. He wanted us to act bad-ass, without actually breaking the law. Easy, right?

Apparently not. My mind flashed back to the email I'd received earlier today, stating Tony wanted us to hire a stylist. Because we didn't look rock 'n' roll enough.

"Thank you so mu ..." I started, then paused, as screams of appreciation rang through the two-thousand-strong venue. It was packed, and the high-pitched squeals, the deep yells that rolled through the room right now ... I gave a wide smile. It had only been three months since we'd signed professionally, and I could barely believe it.

"Thank you ..." I started again, and once more fans drowned my voice out. A bra landed on stage, right in front of my feet. Ollie, the bass player, walked over, giving me a nudge with his elbow.

"Dude ... you gonna get that?" He nodded his head toward the piece of lingerie and I smirked.

"If you want it ..."

Ollie wasted no time in stepping forward, picking up the piece of lacy material and pressing it to his face, sniffing it then waving it above his head, all to more screams of enthusiasm. I shook my head. I guess we were that band now. The band people throw underwear at.

We all smiled and waved, and Xander threw his drumsticks out into the crowd as we walked off-stage. Or, Xander and I walked. Ollie kind of strutted. He was the only guy I knew who dug wearing leather pants. Hopefully when we hired a stylist, she would change that ...

"Well done, boys." Hamish, the sound guy, clapped me on the back as I walked past, and I nodded my appreciation. My shirt stuck to my arms, and right now I could think of nothing better than a cold shower, washed down with about eighty beers.

"So, after party?" Xander asked, a smile playing on his lips.

"Sounds good, man. Tony organised a meet-and-greet for a few fans at the Bowler's Inn. You know it?" I asked. I didn't know why I had to remind him of things like this, but I guessed it was just my place. It was my name that was underlined on the contract. And if I was honest, that contract was the only way I could afford to fund Dad's treatment.

Speaking of ...

"Great show." Mom and Dad stood together, arms linked, beaming at me like I was the second-born Jesus. I walked over to them and smiled, letting Mom put her arm around me. God knew what Tony would say about the rock 'n' roll-ness of that.

"Thanks." I nodded. "You guys heading now, or ...?"

"Actually ..." Darkness flashed across Mom's face, and I

didn't miss it. Not for a second. "… we thought we'd see what you're doing after."

Her voice was so quiet I had to lean in to hear her, and as she swallowed, I saw her throat bob, saw the hold she had on Dad's arm tighten.

Something was wrong.

Something was seriously fucking wrong.

"We have a fan thing. Can it wait till—"

"Oh, it can wait." Mom's eyebrows relaxed, and she loosened her hold. "We'll tell you another time, we—"

Something about her readiness to push this subject off bothered me, and I interrupted. "Actually, let's go to my hotel room now. We can chat there before I head out."

It was as if Mom were a jack-in-the-box, and someone had tightened the coils again. "Fine," she choked out. "Do you … want a lift?"

I shook my head. "I have Sam and Benny."

Ten minutes later and the boys and I were in the car speeding toward the hotel, located a short three blocks from the club we just played. We pulled up at the back entrance, and after checking for camped-out fans, Benny escorted us to the service elevators that took us all the way up to our floor.

"You gonna help us shower, too?" Ollie snorted as Benny did a quick check of our rooms before we walked in. I couldn't help but smile. It was a little ridiculous to think the label was going to all this trouble, just for us.

"All clear." Benny, the nicest of the security guards we'd had to date, nodded and gestured that we could in fact enter our rooms.

"Thanks." I gave him my appreciation and walked in.

I jumped in the shower and had just walked back into my room, towel hung around my hips when the door knocked and Benny bellowed, "Your parents are here, Mr Collins."

"Send 'em in," I called back.

The door opened and Mom and Dad walked in, Mom still with her arm linked in Dad's. She guided him to a chair and sat him down, and then perched on the armrest next to him, smoothing down her soft pink skirt.

They both looked out the window, their eyes focused on the twinkling lights of New York City thirty-one floors below. We'd never done stuff like this when I was living with them. Hell, I doubted most middle-class families from the 'burbs did stuff like flying across the country for a gig, and staying in a five-star hotel. This was a new band thing, and it was one I loved.

I also loved that Dad could see a specialist while he was here. Dr Houswell was one of the best speech therapists in the country, and I was so proud I could get Dad treatment with him, even if it was a little sporadic. It was one request that management could usually find the funds for.

"So … what did you wanna talk about?"

Two heads spun to face me.

"W … well, we ha … ha …"

Mum placed her hand on Dad's arm. "We have something important to tell you, dear."

"Should I put some pants on?" I looked down to my towel and laughed.

No one else did. Two faces were blank masks.

I walked to the couch opposite them and sat down, leaning forward, my hands clasped over my knees. "Let's talk."

"We've … there's something about our past that we haven't told you. Something that you should know, especially now …" Mum swallowed.

"Now?" I sat back.

"Now that you're becoming a public figure." She pressed her lips until they were a thin line. My stomach lurched, and a sense of foreboding clawed at my insides. All my life, my parents had been honest with me. We were a close family, way closer than most of my friends were with their folks— probably because there are only three of us in the whole wide world. Mom's parents passed away when I was three, and Dad's died when he was a kid. Both of them were only children. Yep. Christmas was always cheap in the Collins family.

"Whatever it is, just tell me. You can tell me anything." I

shook my head. "I know my contract said no scandal, but shit, guys. You're pretty clean-cut."

Silence coated the room. Down below, a car horn honked. A siren wailed. More lights stopped and started, caught in the humdrum of big-city traffic.

"Your father and I … we met at a very early age," Mom started.

"We fell in love," Dad blurted out, and he looked up at her with that look again.

"We did." Mom studied her hand, linked with Dad's. "We met at fifteen, and we just … it was like the stories say. When you find the one, you know. You just know."

"And you guys did." I grinned. I'd heard this story before, and it had shaped my views on romance. My folks were the kind of parents who held hands at my school concerts, who made a big deal about going on date nights as soon as I was old enough to be left alone. The kind who would stay together forever. "The perfect romance."

"We … there might have b … been some things we haven't told you, s … son," Dad stuttered. His hands worked circles over my mother's stockinged knee, and my shoulders tensed. If he was getting worked up about it, this must be serious.

"We met when we were fifteen. It was at a church barbeque at your grandma's friend's house." Mom's blue eyes glassed over. "Your father was there, a friend of one of the other families, and I still remember to this day the moment I laid eyes on him." She looked down at Dad and I saw their hands squeeze together. "His eyes met mine across the yard. I was playing tennis, and straight away he drew my attention. He was the handsomest boy I'd ever seen …"

She got a faraway expression on her face and I raised a corner of my lips in a grin. My phone beeped, but I didn't check it. It was probably just the boys, hurrying me along.

"He mouthed the words 'You're beautiful' to me, just as I served the ball … and hit him straight in the head with it." At this both Mom and Dad giggled, and I managed a laugh. "I knocked your father out cold. He came to with me pressing a bag of frozen peas to his forehead …"

I shook my head and laughed, imagining my usually quite proper mother's awkwardness. "But you hit it off, right? Then you dated, got married, and had me?"

At this, Mom paused. "Not exactly." She swallowed. "We've always encouraged you to follow your own beliefs and dreams, do your own thing, right?"

"Yes," I said slowly, angling my head to the side.

"And you know that I grew up in a very religious household, right?" This time I just nodded, and made a movement signal with my hands. Get on with the story. "Well, the first time we had sex was not actually on our wedding night."

"Mom!" I frowned and leaned back. I did not need to hear about this.

"Lee, just hear me out. It was there, at that party, that day. The first time I met your father."

My eyes widened. Now that was weird. My up-until-that-point virgin, religious mother lost it to my dad instead of waiting for marriage?

"Wow," I muttered. "I mean, that's fine, but I really thought you would have waited. With your upbringing, and all."

From the way she bit her lip, I could tell this was no random sex confession. In my head, I was doing the math. Is this the story I think it is? That instead of being nineteen, I was actually twenty-four, and they'd lied to me about my birthdate to hide the truth from Mom's zealously religious family?

"We didn't. And much to our surprise, we fell pregnant."

I nodded. I couldn't believe it. I mean, I guess I'd always been taller, a little broader in the chest than a heap of guys my age in school, but—

"We had a baby. A little boy." I nodded. What a mind-fuck. "And then we put him up for adoption."

What?

I stared at my parents, the same mother and father I'd always known, with fresh eyes. It was only a few minutes in that I registered my mom's mouth was still moving. She was telling me more.

"My parents, they didn't support me. Didn't support us, and I couldn't really blame them." A single tear fell down her cheek, and I'd almost have thought it was poetic if it were anyone but her. Dad reached over and gave her a hug. His hand shook so badly, it was as if there were an earthquake inside his body. "They sent me away, and I had the baby … and then let it go." A full-blown sob escaped her mouth, and I walked over and put my hand on her shoulder.

My folks were the kind you saw holding hands in the street. Sharing kisses in the snow. They were good people, the kind who went out of their way to help others, who always look out for their family.

They were not the type of people who made mistakes. They were not the kind of people who had secrets.

Not child-sized secrets that could rip you apart.

I couldn't imagine that; so alone in the world, a kid at fifteen, and with a baby to a guy you'd just met, who you'd presumably—

"You guys did still lose your virginity to each other though, right?" I asked through narrowed eyes.

"Yes!"

"Of course!" Mom and Dad replied at the same time, and air whooshed through my lips. I mean, nothing wrong with having sex with a few people in your life. But probably not when you were fifteen and younger, was all. Or specifically, if you were my parents. Because, ew.

"So I have a …"

"A brother." Mom nodded, and she smiled. I gave a small shake of my head. This? This was a lot to take in. But it wasn't the end of the world. I mean, it was hardly the scandal they'd made it out to be.

"It's …" I nodded. "… a lot to take in. But, you know, cool." I gave a weak smile. It was a heap of news, and I was overwhelmed, but I really had to get to this party. I stood up, checking my towel was still secure, and turned to head to the bedroom in the suite.

"Wait," Dad called.

There was something there, in his voice. Urgency, maybe. No. It was desperation.

"We got an email from him this week." Mom's voice was trembling now. "When we gave him up, we left our details in the system in case he ever wanted to get in touch."

"And he ... did?" Thu-thump. My heart pounded, loudly.

"Yes." Mom nodded. "He still has no interest in meeting us. But he wants to speak to you."

Present day ...

IT WAS waiting for me on my seat when I sat down on the bus. A small white envelope. My name scrawled in black pen on the front.

"What's that?" Lottie asked, leaning over.

I shoved the letter under my arm. "Nothing."

"Nothing, huh?" She raised her brows, and I smiled. At least she was being nice.

I scanned my gaze past her to the small boy sitting by her side, his eyes glued to the window. "How's he doing?"

"He's good." Lottie gazed adoringly at her son. "I mean, touring's a lot to get used to, but he's getting there."

Silence washed over us, but she didn't look away. Did she want something from me? "If you need to go grab anything at the next stop, you know I'd be happy to look after—"

"Thanks." She pressed her lips together, a smile curling them up at the sides. "That would be good, Lee."

I settled back in to my seat and she settled back into hers. When I was certain Lottie's eyes were back on Jay, I turned my focus back to the letter. I ripped it open, eager to read the contents.

Dear Lee,

Thanks so much for your letter. It was really nice of you to write, and you didn't have to do that. You know, I kinda thought you might have been some jerky rock star who, say, likes to take his top off to make young employees feel flustered, but maybe I got the wrong impression of you after all.

I stopped my reading and looked over at Kate, but she was asleep, her head resting against the windowpane opposite me.

Still, you need to know that you don't have to do this. If you need me to leave, or if I'm not pulling my weight, let me know. Just don't jerk me around.

It's strange—I've never met anyone who has family problems similar to my own. I feel like we maybe ... maybe have this connection, or something? Like I can trust you.

Don't be one of those dumb tortured artists who looks for an opportunity to make everyone else feel inferior. Who uses people for lyrical material. I know you apologised when Dave wrote that song about me, and somehow I don't think you would ever do anything like it, but it still ... well, it still stings.

Trust is a big deal. Please don't let me

down, Lee My heart has already experienced more than it can take.

Kate

I crumpled the letter up. The fact that she even thought for a moment I'd do something like that ... it made me so damn angry. My muscles tensed, and my fists clenched.

I was not that guy.

I wasn't the guy who hurt people.

Not anymore.

seven

KATE

W HEN I'D sent Lee the letter, asking him not to use me for material, I'd felt a little like an idiot. But I just couldn't really see why he'd wanted me on the road, why he was being so damn nice when I was just a kid from Australia.

All I could think of was the parent connection. It made sense. And I so desperately wanted to believe it was that, rather than the horrid alternative.

Still, when I found my next letter, this time sticking under my hotel room door a few days later, apprehension stirred in my veins, pumping my blood at double-speed through my body.

Dear Kate,

It's taken me a few days to reply because your letter made me so damn mad. I would never do something like that dickhead ex of yours did. I would never treat a woman, an employee, and especially not a lover the way he did you, so don't for one second think that I would. I know it seems strange that I hired you ... let's just say I have a debt to pay to society. And if I can help you, help your family ... that's gonna mean a lot to me.

Anyway, enough of the heavy shit! You're doing a real good job on tour at the moment, but I just thought I'd let you know that this morning, you'll probably need to go in and wake Xander up. I think he took sleeping tablets last night.

Lee

Dear Lee,

It's taken me a few days to reply because I AM SO MAD AT YOU! You knew, didn't you? When I opened Xander's door and saw him with that woman—oh my God! Thank goodness I heard him first, so I was able to close my eyes before the image of him banging some random was burned into my retinas I was just grateful that even though I lost my ability to form a coherent sentence, I was still able to yell 'no' when he asked if I wanted to join in.
You know, this is kind of sexual harassment ...

Kate

I shook my head, staring at my letter before I left it on Lee's seat in the bus. It hadn't really been all that bad. I'd seen no naked body parts, unless you count Xander's back—to be honest, it was a really fine back, too.

I hadn't known how to respond, but after a few days I'd decided to have a little fun with it. After all, the guy was clearly asking for it.

That was why I tucked a condom that I'd dosed in milk a

few times and then let dry into the envelope. It mightn't have look one hundred per cent believable, but it was close enough.

Dear Kate,

You are sexually harassing me. Did you seriously just send me a used condom? And dear God, please tell me it wasn't one of Xander's. No wait; I don't think I want it to be one that you've used, either. Seriously, when I got that I pissed myself laughing. And then rapidly tried to hide the "balloon" from Jay, who wanted to blow it up. Lottie was not impressed.

You know, most employees we've had in the past just smile and say "Yes, Lee". They don't bite back when I put them to the test. You're different, Kate.

By the way, how's your dad? Heard from him since you got here?

Lee

P.S. I like different.

Dear Lee,

First up, let's get one thing straight:
if most of your past employees let
you play practical jokes on them,
they were idiots I'm nothing special,
Lee I'm just not gonna let you
walk all over me. Gosh, have you met
any Australians before? We don't
take crap!
On a more serious note, though, I am
sorry about Jay and Lottie. That's
actually seriously not cool of me, and
I didn't even think about it. I
should have popped the note under
your hotel door instead. Or maybe
just taken a Polaroid of Xander
doing the deed and left that for
you to enjoy more discreetly ...
Dad's okay. Mum sent me an email
the other day letting me know how
he was I just ... I haven't been
able to write back yet, you know? I

don't know what to say ...
Do you ever find that with your parents?

Kate

Dear Kate,

Do. Not. EVER send me a photo of Xander in any form of compromising position. The only naked photo you're allowed to send me ...
You can probably still read that, but interpret it as you will.
I actually do know what you mean. It's—I've never been able to kinda say it to anyone else, you know? My folks are separated, and when I go to email Dad it can be kinda hard. How do you say things about your life when you know in comparison, theirs isn't that great? And then I worry that

he'll get frustrated typing back. That the shakes will become too much, that he'll feel this obligation when really, I just want him to be happy. I know that in the past, things I've done have upset him, and I have no doubt they made his condition worse. Now, I would give anything to make him healthy,

Kate.

Anything.

Lee

I read the letter one more time, then folded it up into a neat little square and stored it in the side compartment of my bag. Somehow, during my first week on the road, Lee-freaking-Collins and I had developed this friendship, this strange bond.

It didn't take away my pain.

It didn't help me sleep when thoughts of Lachlan danced in my mind, taunting me with their ever-growing elusiveness.

But it did make me feel less lonely, and that made a difference.

It was that little bit of something that made me have faith.

EIGHT

LEE

RECOGNISED THE pain in her eyes. She wore it every day, a new mask trying to cover the grief that lurked underneath.

The sort of grief that churned in your body.

The sort of grief you couldn't forget.

That was why, after the first few weeks on the road, I'd decided to make it my personal mission to make this girl smile. I knew it was dangerous; knew I shouldn't spend too much time with her.

But sometimes, you don't always do what's right for you.

And you don't always do what's right for other people.

The problem was, the more I saw of her the more I was finding it hard to keep it professional. I felt this connection to her, for some reason. She was different to the usual team of women I saw, who were all too eager to give in to my requests. She fought back. Not only that, but I'd started to share parts of myself with her in those letters, parts I didn't share with anyone. And given my current circumstance, that wasn't good at all.

I glanced across the aisle of the bus to her. She was resting her head against the window, her pale skin lit by the setting sun in the distance. We were on our way back to LA again after a stint up the coast in San Francisco.

"Stop looking at me."

I frowned. "Your eyes are closed. How can you even see?"

Kate's lids blinked open, and she raised her brows. "You have this kind of penetrating stare thing going on. I can feel it."

I raised one side of my lips in a smile. Kate was not afraid of me. It was … weird.

"You can penetrate me anytime." One of the dancers, America, I think her name was, giggled, and I quickly checked the bus to make sure Jay was still down the back with Lottie and hadn't heard. Sometimes those girls had no thought for others. Still, their attitude was what I was used to. Blatant flirting. Innuendo. Not … indifference. Not like I was getting from Kate.

I stood up and crossed the aisle, setting myself down into the seat next to her. She gave me a lazy smile, but it didn't reach her eyes.

Silence.

And then …

"Sometimes, until I was about fifteen, Dad would come into my room at night and just stare at me." Her eyes stay fixed out the window at the passing traffic. "It used to really annoy me—sneaking out was that much harder when your father checked in so often."

"Is that creepy?" I furrowed my brow.

"No." Kate's word wasn't angry or shocked. It was surprisingly calm. "It was just … it was his thing, you know? And when I asked him why he did it, he'd say it was because sometimes he just couldn't believe I was real. That he and Mom made me. And that he needed to keep me safe."

Safety. Family. I shuddered. They were on my mind a lot lately.

"Of course, he doesn't do that anymore." Kate gave me a quick glance, and I saw the pain flash in her eyes. "But I can usually tell when people are staring at me, even if my eyes are closed, all the same."

"Do you miss that side of him?"

"Yes. No. Everything." She sighed, her head turning to face the window again. Cars sped past, the ocean a glimmer of turquoise in the background. It really was a pretty trip. "He's still protective, and he still loves me. Sometimes it can just be hard to remember, when you have to protect him."

I nodded. "Yeah. Not even ... not even against physical things. But sometimes protect him against things people say, or do." I'd sure had a lot of defending my dad from stranger's looks since Parkinson's had tightened its ugly hold around my father's neck.

"Exactly." Kate smiled again. She rested her head against the windowpane and closed her eyes. "Do you miss things your dad used to do?"

"Sure." As I spoke the word, a pang hit me in my chest. "I miss talking on the phone, having a really decent conversation, you know?"

Her eyes fluttered open, and she leaned forward. "Yes! And you feel bad, for not being able to fill in the blanks ..."

"Or understand each word." I finished, and we shared a knowing look. I'd never really spoken about Dad like this with anyone. Sharing it with Kate ... it just felt so right. "And then you feel bad for feeling bad. Because you know that they would hate to be felt sorry for, that they shouldn't be a responsibility, someone you feel you have to fill silences in for, but someone you should enjoy silence with."

Kate puffed out a long breath, and looked at me up from under her eyelashes. "You know, for a rock star, you're a pretty wise man, Lee Collins."

This time, my chest didn't ache. My heart did instead. It burned.

"You can just call me Lee," I said in a voice so soft, I wasn't sure if she heard me. She slowly let her eyes drift shut again, and I stood up and walked back to my seat, turning my head to look at the mountains flying past as we cruised along.

Seconds later, my cell phone beeped. I picked it up, seeing Kate's name on the screen, and turned to look at her. She was smiling, her cell tucked tightly under arm.

Kate: Your silence is safe with me, Lee.

I knew exactly what she meant, and we spent the rest of the trip quiet, occasionally opening our eyes, occasionally smiling. For the first time in I had no idea how long, I felt as if someone truly understood.

"Lee, open up!" Kate banged on the hotel room door. I smirked, and ruffled Jay's hair. He gave me a small, shy smile. We'd been running around my suite playing wrestling while Lottie went and got the band some new clothes for a photo shoot we had lined up later that afternoon. It was the first time I'd ever been alone with him, and we'd kind of been having fun, much to my surprise. I was stoked.

Kate probably wasn't, though. This wasn't the first time she had knocked.

In fact—I gave a quick glance at my watch—she'd almost been at it for three minutes now. I looked down and shrugged. I wasn't wearing a shirt, but since seeing her blush that first day, I'd almost made a point of trying to find ways to go shirtless around Kate. Watching her blush was just too much fun.

Punctuating each step with a light pant—seriously, for a small kid, Jay could really run—I walked over to the entranceway. I wrenched open the door and she stood there, clipboard pressed against her chest, looking fresh as a goddamn daisy, as per usual. She looked me up and down, and I wiped my sweaty palms against my jeans before using one to usher her in.

"I don't need to …"

"Sure, come in." I closed the door behind her and walked

over to a lounge, sitting down and throwing my hands over my head. "I'm screwed," I moaned, my eyes shut.

Silence.

I squinted one eye open, then the other, to find Kate looking at me, eyes wide, jaw practically on the floor. Or, I say looking at me. Really, she was looking at my bare, sweaty chest. I couldn't help but grin.

"I meant from chasing Jay around, you perv." I picked up a cushion and threw it at her, catching her smack on the arm. She pushed it aside and her face scrunched up till it got really cute and angry looking, and it was hard to stifle a laugh.

"I don't see any—"

"RAWR!" Jay jumped out from behind the other couch and Kate jumped about a foot in the air, dropping her clipboard and grasping her chest.

"Shit!"

Jay's eyes widened. "Kate said a bad word."

"Now you've done it." I laughed, watching as Kate alternated between looking horrified and searching for words to try and rectify the situation.

"Jay, I didn't mean it." Kate finally found her voice, squatting down to his eye level. "But sometimes, when a grown-up gets very, very scared, they're allowed to have one bad word."

"One." Jay frowned.

"Just one." Kate agreed.

"Then how come Lee says bad words when him and Mommy—"

"That's enough, Jay." I jumped off my seat and jogged the three steps over to them. For a small kid, he sure seemed smart. "Maybe you should go find your new shoes. We're gonna head out soon."

Jay shrugged and skipped down the hallway to the bedroom where I knew Lottie had laid out all his belongings. Jay liked to choose his own clothes. With a fashion-lover for a mother, it was bound to happen.

"You are right. We are going soon, and I wanted to check

you're um …" Kate's gaze swept my body again. I puffed out my chest, just a little. "Ready."

"Do you think I look ready?" I smirked.

"No. Not really." She shook her head, as if snapping from a trance. "Not at all. You should wear some clothes."

I gave a light laugh and picked up my shirt from where I'd thrown it on the couch, shrugging it over my shoulders and pulling it down my chest. "Better?"

"Much." She pursed her lips. "Now, do you need me to run over your list of commitments for today?"

I agreed, and she started running through the list of media activities that Tony and the team at Spinner had planned out. While she talked, I stared at her. The way her mouth moved, forming the words. The way her voice was calm, in control, even though I knew I'd flustered the hell out of her only moments before. There was something about her I liked— something about her that just seemed so … real.

"Do you like working for me? For us, I mean?" I interrupted.

Kate snapped her jaw closed and looked at the clipboard in front of her. "Yes."

"Just yes? That's it?"

"Yes, I like working here. I like organising things, and making sure people are where they're supposed to be when they say they will. I like music, and I like learning more about this whole process while being on the road with you." Kate stammered, and I smiled. Learning. It had been a long time since I'd met a girl who liked to learn. Not since …

"The only thing I don't like are lead singers who think it's funny to take their shirts off every time they're near me." Kate gave me a pointed look.

"Even if they're really good-looking?" I tried.

"I wouldn't know what that's like," she replied. Score one to Kate.

She ran through the rest of the schedule and I made my mind focus on the words coming out of her mouth. There was something about her that was different to all the other women

I had around me. They were 'yes' people. Kate was … it had taken her a few weeks of being on the road, but now a little hint of fire was shining through. A wicked sense of humour. A strong sense of fun.

Kate was going to be a problem.

A dangerous one.

NINE

KATE

ONE OF the good things about my new job was the down time. Sure, I had to work weird hours, and check on things at odd times of the day and night, but I did often have ample time free in the middle of the day. And that meant shopping. Or at the very least, coffee drinking.

I'd struggled to find good coffee in the States so far, and was currently returning empty-handed from my mission to find such a thing when I spied Lee, Lottie, and Jay standing just inside our hotel.

"Hey." I waved as I walked past, but Lottie grabbed my arm.

"Kate, good. Lee needs a hand minding Jay this afternoon. Can you …" She nodded her head toward the two of them, and both Lee and Jay gave me their best cheesy grins.

"I guess, I—"

"Thank you so much! It'll only be for an hour, maybe two. I just have to go check on the clothes for tomorrow's photo shoot. The damn courier didn't show up." Lottie glanced at her phone and then looked back at the two of us expectantly. "Are you guys … good with this?"

"Fine." I nodded.

"Seriously?" Lee raised his eyebrows. "We'll be fine. And I don't really need a babysitter." He gave me a pointed look.

"Lee, I meant that I want him to be looked after without you getting mobbed or taking him to do something I disapprove of." Lottie's eyes darkened. "Besides, sometimes I just think a woman … you look like you'd be good with kids. He's still only new to all this," Lottie said, looking at me, a sardonic smile twisting her lips. "Okay, Jay. Love you."

She held out her arms and her little man came flying into them for a big bear hug. Something in my heart twinged. I wanted unconditional love like that.

"Thanks, guys." Lottie gave us both a wave, then waited till I was holding Jay's hand and mouthed no monster trucks to me and left. Lee tugged the hat on Jay's head down and we followed after her, leaving the safety of the hotel for the driveway.

We had barely been outside alone for three seconds when it happened.

"Lee? Lee Collins!"

"Lee! Lee, take a picture with me!"

"Lee!"

The screaming continued, and Lee smiled, waved, posed for a few pictures and then led me toward the waiting car with a gentle hand on my back, Jay's fingers linked firmly in between mine.

When we were safely inside, I turned to him. "Wow," I breathed. Fans lined the street, and some of them had even found a spot in traffic to cross and were encroaching upon the car. "Is it always this bad?"

Lee shrugged. "Sometimes worse."

Huh. It seemed too crazy to be true.

"By the way, Kate, meet Sam, our driver. Sam, meet Kate, our new tour organiser." Lee made the introductions and Sam, a middle-aged guy with twinkly eyes and a dubious moustache, smiled.

We drove through the city streets in silence. Even Jay was quiet, as he looked nervously from Lee to me until we pulled up at a water park, Raging Waters in San Dimas.

"What are we doing here?" I frowned. Surely the place would be closed. It was autumn; who wanted to waterslide then?

"Going for a swim," Lee said.

"Cool!" Jay enthused. "I haven't been swimming in soooo long, Lee. Not since I was three."

"Wow." Lee's eyes widened. "That was a long time ago. Are you sure you're ready?"

Jay acted as if he was considering it, then nodded, agreeing. "I'm ready."

"Great. Let's do it."

The three of us walked to the entrance desk where a bored looking teenager had her day made by meeting Lee-freaking-Collins and agreeing to shut the water park for him, if we paid entrance fees for the capacity. Thankfully, we were the only ones stupid enough to be here in this cool weather, so we didn't have to kick anyone out.

"Let's do it," Lee yelled and Jay roared after him as they dashed to the biggest slide, a three-storey number that looked seriously dangerous.

"I'll mind your clothes," I called out, but I needn't have bothered. Apparently, the current strategy was drop them where you feel.

Seconds later the boys flew down the slide, Lee in a pair of board shorts, which he must have been wearing earlier, Jay in his underwear. They looked cute together, as if they were having a heap of fun, and Lee never lost patience with the little guy, even when he wanted to do the same ride multiple times.

At some point, the ticketing assistant came over to watch, and I saw her get out her phone. I glanced over at the boys. Jay's hat was still firmly on, and it was no longer just sunburn I was worried about protecting him from. It was a different danger entirely.

"Excuse me," I said.

"Yeah?"

"Can I please ask you not to take photos?" I scrunched up my nose. "He'll do a selfie with you when he's off the slides; hell, I'm sure he'd even kiss your cheek in it. But this is private stuff." I didn't know how Lottie felt about having her son in the media, but since I'd never seen photos of Jay in the magazines, I doubted it was something she was keen on.

"Sure." The girl nodded and put her phone in her pocket after deleting the pictures she'd taken. Really, what was stopping her from taking more when my back was turned? I guess all you could do was hope.

Lee came jogging up, his wet hair flicking everywhere, Jay talking a million miles per hour at his side.

"Coming in?" Lee asked me.

"It's freezing!" I protested.

"Warmer in than out. I promise." Lee spoke the words, but I didn't really hear them. It was hard to concentrate with all the visual noise his chest was making. It was so shiny, and well-defined, and sexy, the edges of a tattoo wrapping around his lower ribcage.

"Kate?"

"Huh?" I jerked my gaze back to the present. Oops!

"I said, you could wear your underwear. It covers just as much," Lee suggested, and I had to agree with him here. It did cover just as much as a bikini would. It was the way it covered it that was a problem.

"Somehow, I don't think lace mesh bikinis will ever be in-fashion swimming items," I said sarcastically, and Lee laughed.

"You could try it and see?" he husked. That line, and the combination of sexy, half-naked lead singer made my cheeks heat, and I became a little too lost in the moment again.

But that wouldn't do. I was here to work. It had only just been a fortnight; I wasn't here to swoon over Lee-freaking-Collins.

I pressed my hand to my temple and closed my eyes for a moment, willing Lachlan's face to disappear from my mind, then clawing it back desperately. Flashes of our happy times together, working at Sideways, running in the rain, holding hands …

I shivered. Seven months wasn't enough time to heal a broken heart. I still needed him like I needed to breathe.

"You guys make a really cute family," Selife Taker said, snapping some more shots of us on her camera phone.

"Oh, we're not—"

"Thank you." Lee gave her a megawatt smile and she all but melted under its intensity.

"Delete those ones too, please." I gave an asinine smile, and was greeted with a pout but compliance nonetheless. She slowly retreated back to the front desk.

Lee and Jay ran around the water fountain, Jay's hat flying off behind him as they chased some invisible assailant.

"No pictures, thanks," I reminded the girl, in case she chose this moment to take another.

Lee stopped running. He froze. He picked up Jay's hat, placed it firmly on his head, and then he took five steps closer to me. Five long steps, during which I analysed how his chest glinted in the sun with each movement. How his legs were just coiled muscle, ready to spring. How good he was with Jay.

"You can take a picture," he said, his breath hot in my ear. He was so close to me that tingles bolted up and down my spine like lightning.

"I …" I started. Guilt rolled over me, but for just one moment I focused on the firm lines of chest, his pecs at my eye level. I couldn't finish the sentence. Not when he was so close. When he was so naked.

Heat rushed to my cheeks again.

"Why are your cheeks red, Kate?" Jay asked, his tiny, slightly chubby arms folded across his chest.

"Yeah, why are they, Kate?" Lee asked, a mischievous twinkle in his eye.

"No reason," I mumbled, my arms now folded across my chest. There was no way I was getting into a situation like this again.

I stared at the blinking cursor in front of me and rapidly typed out the rest of an email to Dad. It was hard, trying to explain to him what this was like—sometimes the words just got stuck in my head. Still, I tried my best.

Dear Dad,

> Life's pretty good out on the road. There are a whole heap of us driving 'round in this big bus that has all the mod-cons There's even a coffee machine Funny, right? How are things back home?

That was where I got stuck. I stared at the blinking cursor for ages, willing more words to fill the space, but I couldn't make them form and the computer sure as hell didn't seem to be willing to aid my cause.

Why was writing to Lee so much easier? I smiled, thinking of the note I'd left under his hotel room door a few hours ago, while he and the boys were out partying at some product launch thing.

Dear Lee,

> Thank you for hard copy of the Rolling Stone magazine featuring your naked torso on the cover. I truly appreciated finding it under my door when we got back from swimming. Then again on my seat

in the bus when we went to sound check this afternoon. And once more from Benny in the hotel lobby when I came back. I sincerely appreciate it.

Thing is, I saw your naked chest all morning already at the water park, and I kinda have to say— do they do a lot of Photoshop work on those covers? I don't know ... Comparatively speaking, it doesn't quite look the same.

Kate

I was looking forward to seeing what he came back with. Still, the whole situation frustrated me. How come with Dad, the words stuck in my head? I hit save on the draft and did something a whole heap easier instead. I opened up Skype and called Stacey.

She answered on the third ring, her bright-eyed face filling the screen. "How do you look so awake?" I yawned, covering my mouth with my hand.

"It's only, like, five p.m. here, sweetie. Time zone. Remember?" Stacey rolled her eyes. Of course it was only five there, even if it was after ten at night here. What was wrong with my brain?

"How's things?" Stacey asked. She snapped closed a book and placed it on the bed beside her. "I needed a study break, anyway."

"Things are ..." I took a deep breath. "Things are confusing. The job is good—full on, but good."

"Did you meet Lottie?" Stacey asked, her eyes lit up. "She's such a sweetheart. She only came on tour right at the end, when there was only a week or two to go. And little Jay ..."

"Yeah. They're both pretty awesome," I agreed. "Do you know where his dad is?"

"Not really." Stacey grabbed some of her hair and twisted it around her finger. "I asked one day, and Lottie told me he wasn't around anymore. Guess it's one of those sad stories."

"Wow. I couldn't imagine falling pregnant single, raising a kid on your own. She couldn't be that much older than twenty-five, right? And yet she's still so glamorous and stylish. How does she do it?"

Something strange flashed over Stacey's gaze, and I opened my mouth to ask about it further but she changed the topic. "How's Mr Sexy Lead Singer?"

"A jerk." I rolled my eyes. "Well, not exactly a jerk, but you know what I mean."

"I don't, actually." Stacey's lips twisted into a smirk. "To be honest, he never really paid that much attention to me, but when he did he was always nice."

"He's just ... he keeps trying to embarrass me." I pulled at the hem of my shirt, twisting it round in my fingers. I didn't want to tell Stacey about the letters. They seemed like a little secret, between Lee and I.

"Embarrass? How?" Stacey crawled closer to the screen, her face dancing with excitement.

"Stace, it can't be coincidence that I've seen him without a shirt six times in two weeks."

"Oh!" she squealed, and clapped her hands. "He totally likes you."

"Likes making me blush."

"Likes the idea of getting naked with you."

I grabbed my clipboard and waved it around in front of the screen. "He likes that I do this. Make sure he's where he needs to be, when he needs to be there. And he likes to make me embarrassed, I think ... but it's some kind of weird control thing, I'm sure. He'd never hit on me. In fact, when I get all red and hot—"

"I bet you do."

I levelled her with a steely glare. "Can it, Allison."

"Sorry."

"When I get flustered, he teases me even more."

Stacey chewed on her lip in thought for a while, then tilted her head to the side. "I don't think ... can you ever remember seeing him have a girlfriend?"

I chewed my lip and thought, clippings of the band in gossip and music magazines over the years flitting through my brain. The more I thought about it, the more blanks I drew. "The only girl I've seen him linked to more than once was that chick Dave was seeing."

"Me too." Stacey pursed her lips. "I wonder why that is ..."

"Maybe he isn't looking for love."

"Maybe he was waiting for you." My insides gave a little churn when she spoke.

I hated it. I hated that my body was betraying me like that.

"From what I saw of him on tour, Kate, I just ..." Stacey chewed her lip. "I think he could be good for you."

So do I.

That was the freaking problem.

I couldn't risk forgetting the past. If I let go of that, then what was the point? Did it mean Lachlan wasn't what I'd thought he was in the first place?

I pushed myself up to a sitting position, then pointed my finger at the screen. "That's enough from you, missy. Now tell me: how am I going to get him to stop making fun of me?"

A wicked grin flashed across Stacey's face as she wiggled her eyebrows. "Easy," she said. "You're going to make him feel uncomfortable, too."

TEN

LEE

Four years, eight months ago …

IT STARTED with some emails, back and forth between each other. He asked me about my favourite rugby team. I asked him about his taste in music. We danced around the serious and stuck securely to the light, to the easy, to the surface-level stuff, a deliberate choice on my behalf after Tony warned me to be careful. "Everyone always finds a long-lost relative when they hit the big-time, kid." He'd clapped me on the shoulder, his wise, grey eyes all-knowing. I shook my head at the thought of it. I sure as shit hoped not.

And so it was that I pulled up outside of a bar just out of town in the middle of the afternoon on a Tuesday, nerves racing through me like firecrackers. I was going to meet my brother. Today, I was going to meet my goddamn brother!

I opened the car door and walked to the front of the building. A few people, jackets buttoned up against the cold, winter air, gave me a second look, but no one spoke to me or called my name. I guess that was the difference between checking into a bar with a mostly male versus mostly female patronage.

"I'll just check—"

"Wait here." I put my hand out to stop Benny from entering the bar first. While it hadn't been officially announced, I was fairly sure his job description was to make me look like I was a pussy who couldn't protect himself.

Benny narrowed his eyes at me, but let me enter the bar by myself, like the grown-up I was. Well, despite being of not legal drinking age, of course. Small mercies …

The stench of stale beer hit me and my feet stuck slightly to the carpet as I trod my way over to the stained mahogany bar. Again, a few people looked at me, but not many. The place was mainly patronised by guys in the uniform of the unemployed—checked shirts loosely framing their tanks, a three-day-old stubble gracing their jaws.

I pulled at a bar stool and tucked myself in, glancing at my watch. 1:29 p.m. I was thirty minutes early.

"What can I get you?" a feminine voice asked, and I looked up, straight into the eyes of the woman from six months ago. Carly.

We were meant to be together, Carly.

A smile flushed my face, and I could tell she remembered too, as her cheeks turned this bright red colour as she glanced down.

"Not saving kittens today?" I smiled. My eyes travelled over her shirt, her smooth décolletage, the buttons opened a little too low to her golden nametag pinned firmly over her round breast. Carly.

"No." Carly gave a small shrug. "I learned my lesson last time." When she looked back up, I saw mischief in her eyes. "Although if I knew you were always going to be there to catch me …"

"I bet you say that to all the guys who crawl into your fine establishment here." I looked around the room again. From the corner, I heard a series of belches. Looked like there was a burping contest underway.

"You'd be surprised." She raised her eyebrows and flashed

me another smile, and my insides shrivelled up into nothing. She was … she was a tall glass of water, refreshing, cool and clear, and I was a parched man.

"Can I grab a bourbon and Coke, please?" I asked, almost because I just wanted to speak to her again and was rapidly running out of clever things to say. Carly had that effect on me.

"Sure." She nodded, and I let out a tiny breath of relief. I never usually had problems ordering booze in bars. Not since we got to number one. And even though most people would have been able to guess I was only nineteen, no one ever questioned my fake ID. That was one of the perks of being a rock star—you could afford the best in counterfeit.

Carly turned to the shelf behind her and stretched up high, so high that her black shirt rose, exposing an inch of gloriously tanned skin and cute little dimples that rested right over her—

"Single or double?" She looked back over her shoulder and winked. "Like what you see there, rock star?"

"Single." I met her gaze dead-on. "One from you will be more than enough for me."

She bit her lip and tension spiralled between us, thick as a forest, as she grabbed a bottle from the top shelf then walked over to me, placing the bottle on the counter and pulling a glass stacked with a block of ice out from under the counter.

After unscrewing the lid, she tilted the bottle upside-down, free pouring the amber liquid into my glass. It cascaded over the ice cube, a small drop spilling over the side and crawling down to the spotless counter beneath it. "Oops." She extended a finger and swiped the drop up, then slowly took her finger to her mouth and sucked on it, her lips taking it down her throat and then slowly sliding back up again, her tongue swirling over the tip.

My dick twitched in my pants, and damn, it didn't matter if I was there to meet my brother or the goddamn Pope, I would have left in a heartbeat if this chick asked me to.

I swallowed, and pulled at the collar of my shirt before she burst out laughing, a gay, joyous sound that had me smirking along with her. "What's so funny?"

"You," she breathed, mirth written all over her face. "Acting all sleazy, and then your face when I just went down on my finger." She cracked up laughing again, and at first I frowned, then I couldn't help but smile. She was right. What was I, a kid?

"Okay, you got me." I nodded my defeat.

"Twice." She grinned. "You just bought my most expensive bourbon."

I laughed, because what else could I do? And it seemed the better option than saying I could afford it, which I now could thanks to the record deal. I glanced at the label, trying to make out the name. Macallan. At least, I hoped I could.

"So what brings you to Oak Lake?" Carly asked, topping my drink up with a small portion of Coke and then sliding it across the counter to me.

I wrapped my fingers around it, the condensation already dampening my skin. "Meeting someone."

"Oh! Blind date?" She wiggled her eyebrows with a wicked grin, and I caught myself smiling—a-fucking-gain. It was as if I couldn't help it around her. Her sense of fun was contagious.

"Kinda," I agreed, because it seemed the easiest thing to do. "But I'm early."

Carly narrowed her eyes at me. "How early?"

I looked at my watch again. "Now? Twenty-five minutes."

Carly looked around the bar, and waved her hand in the air toward a guy standing in the back of the venue who was leaning against a chair and talking to a patron. "Aaron, I'm leaving. You good?"

He nodded and waved her off. I turned back to her, a quizzical expression on my face. "You just …"

"My shift finished at half past one, silly. I'm not walking out, if that's what you think. Now let's go." She took a tea towel from her back pocket and draped it over a railing, typed in a few buttons on the register and then came around to the front of the bar to meet me. "Come on." She grabbed my hand, linking her fingers through mine. "This will be fun."

My brain told me to stay where I was, but I couldn't hear it over my rapidly thumping heart, which wasn't sure if it was about to get laid or fall in love. Either way, it wanted in, and my dick was more than keen to come to the party.

Carly led me through a few smaller rooms then one larger area set up for dining, until we pushed through a glass door out the back and reached a grassy knoll, overlooking a muddy, fast-flowing river. She dropped my hand and flopped down onto the grass, staring up at the sky, patting a spot of dirt next to her enticingly. Hell, it was a spot of dirt. The fact that she could even get away with making that look enticing? The woman was an angel.

I lowered myself to the ground and sat next to her, my legs bent at the middle. "So, what are we doing, exactly?"

"We are going on a practise blind date." Carly nodded sagely. "To set you up for your real one."

"Oh yeah?" I challenged. "And what makes you the dating expert?"

As soon as I posed the question, I tensed. Why had I asked that?

"I have been dating since I was fourteen." Carly placed her hands together in a praying fashion. "You should worship at my temple of seven years of dating knowledge."

There was a whole heap of things I wanted to worship about her, and whatever she was calling it was fine with me. I opened my mouth to try and gain her sage dating advice, but Carly chose that moment to lean up on her elbows, offering me a view straight down her shirt and over her pink, lacy bra. Her thin, pink, lacy bra.

"Something wrong?" She pouted.

"Nothing." I clamped my jaw shut. She moved, and I could see the faintest hint of darker pink where her nipple would be. Nothing wrong at all.

"Okay, so … hi. I'm Carly." She extended her hand. Now that she was speaking again, and with direction, I could stop trying to check her out like some sick pervert. She was single.

I've got this. Be cool, Lee, be cool.

"Hi. I'm Lee." I took her hand in mine and gave it a gentle shake. Her skin was cold to the touch, and smooth, like silk.

"No, you need to be more assertive with your shake." Carly shook her head, still not letting go of my hand. "Like this." She gave a firm pump and a squeeze.

"That wouldn't make a girl feel intimidated?" I tilted my head to the side.

"Some of us like to be dominated, Lee." There was darkness in her eyes, and I stared at the clouds again, trying to imagine her in a variety of unattractive positions. The problem was, even covered in dog shit I think it'd be difficult to find this woman anything less than sexy. I mean, I could always make her take a shower, right?

I swallowed. Images of her wet and soapy were not helping with my focus.

"So, Lee." Carly broke my thoughts, and I snapped my attention back to her. "Tell me something that not many people know about you."

I racked my brain for a suitable answer, something cool, something that would impress this incredibly attractive woman who was lying outstretched next to me. "I ... my dad has Parkinson's disease." It was the first thing that came to mind, and from the clouds that shadowed Carly's eyes, I knew it wasn't the right answer.

"For a blind date? Probably go with something a little more light-hearted." She bit her lip, but she reached out her hand and took mine again, stroking her fingers over my knuckles. It was the best and the worst feeling I'd ever had. Somehow, my lust had turned into sorrow.

We talked for hours on the lawn, laughing, smiling and just generally being alive. She made it easy to breathe. She made my stress about meeting my brother melt away.

My brother never showed up that day. But my love for Carly did.

Present day ...

"LEE-FREAKING-COLLINS, IF you don't get your ass back-stage in five minutes, so help me God, I'm gonna come in there and piggy-back you out." Kate's voice came through the door, accompanied by her pounding fist. She'd only been on tour with us for three weeks, but already she had the whole 'nagging tour girl' routine down pat.

I flung the door open fast, so fast that her fist, which was coming down for a further knocking, instead pounded my naked chest, causing her cheeks to turn this damn cute shade of red that had me stifling a grin.

"I ... um ..." She looked down, to the left, to the right—anywhere but at my face, or more appropriately, my chest.

"You okay?" I asked, and this time I couldn't stop my smirk. She was so freaking cute. She was driving me crazy. There was something about her—the way she went red at anything, the littlest of things ... it was nice. When you had girls throw their underwear at you, if they bothered wearing any, seeing someone who got a little shy at touching your naked chest wasn't just a rarity—it was something to be treasured.

Kate's lips formed a thin line and she somehow managed to look around my chest before meeting my gaze head on. I shook my head; she should be used to it by now. Since she'd joined the tour, she'd seen me without a shirt on or with my shirt undone or raised no fewer than six times. And yes, I had orchestrated each of those appearances.

"You. In." She pointed to the room behind me, and I glanced over my shoulder.

"In there?" I smirked again, but her cheeks didn't get any redder, to my astonishment. "Is now really the time?"

She pushed against my chest, her steely eyes fixed on my face the whole time, then slammed the door behind us with her foot.

"If you wanted some private time together, you just had to say so," I joked, leaning back against the chair that was positioned in front of the mirror in my dressing room.

"You think this is funny?" Kate asked, her head tilted to the side.

"Actually … yeah." I nodded and smiled again, not unkindly.

Kate looked down, and for one God-awful moment I thought she was going to cry.

Then, she did something better than crying. Holy mother of crap sticks, was this better than crying.

She raised her hands to the top of her black button-up shirt—and she undid the top button. Creamy, white skin was exposed, defined collarbones, teasing my eyes down to—

She undid another button. Holy fuck, what was Kate doing? Her cleavage heaved in front of me, and I got a hint, just a hint of her black lacy bra.

"It cannot be a coincidence that one man is shirtless in front of me seven times in three weeks."

I grinned. She'd counted.

That totally means she's into it.

Then she did something that completely surprised me. Hell, it shocked the living daylight out of me. In one fluid movement, she grabbed the sides of her shirt and pulled, press studs popping open her entire top, and then she shrugged it over her shoulders so she stood there in the world's hottest black, lacy bra, skin-tight black denim jeans and these shoes—how the hell did I not notice them before?—that were red, high, and sexy as sin.

I swallowed.

This girl was trouble.

Come on, Lee. Get your act together. I tried giving myself a pep talk. I saw naked women on a regular basis.

But for some reason, seeing sweet, innocent, shy Kate standing there like that? It was doing things to me. Things that my body should not have been doing in response to my employee who had gone through enough emotional trauma to last a goddamn lifetime. Who I couldn't be with anyway. Not now.

And besides, the last thing she needed was a quick screw,

someone like me using her up, too.

"So … this is a revenge …" swallow "… strip?"

"This is me trying to get you to pay attention and listen when I ask you to do something." Kate's voice was honey as it melted into me.

I raised my hand to the back of my neck and rubbed at the muscles there that had suddenly become tight with tension. "Oh, I'm paying attention, all right." I widened my eyes. There was absolutely no doubt about that right now.

"Get back-stage, Lee. Seriously. This is your last warning."

I swallowed again, and the clamminess of perspiration beaded against my brow. Was it hot in here? It sure felt hot.

She stepped closer to me, till her chest was almost touching my chest. Shit, she smelt like soap and hairspray and … apples. How the hell did she smell like apples when Sam told me she'd been helping the sound guys lug some of our gear into the venue, despite me telling her not to? By all accounts, she should smell like ass.

But no. Apples.

"I …" My gaze flicked to her lips, and I wondered if it would really be that bad if I kissed her. After all, that was hardly promising her marriage, and no one had to know. Just one taste. And her lips—they were so red, and plump, and— oh God, she just licked them with that sweet-as-hell little tongue, and—

The palm of her hand made contact with my face before I even registered her arm moving. Five elegant fingers stung my cheek and I jerked backward, cupping my jaw in pain. "What the hell?"

Kate walked over to where her shirt lay on the floor and picked it up, casually shrugging it on. She had the biggest shit-eating grin on her face, and I couldn't help but give a little smile myself. I'd not seen her look so animated since she first boarded the bus.

"I told you it was your final warning," she said, doing up her buttons, then turned to the door, wrenched it open and made a sweeping gesture with her arm, allowing me passage through. "Now, Mr Collins, if you please."

I turned my head so I could see my cheek more clearly in the mirror. The side she'd hit was definitely pinker than the other. I shook my head. I guess I should be thankful she wasn't wearing rings.

"Thanks," I mumbled, walking past her and out into the corridor. I passed Xander's door, and a thought flashed through my mind. What if she stripped for all the guys to get them on stage? I couldn't have her just—

"Lee?" The voice halted me in my tracks. I spun to face her.

She threw my black shirt at me, the one I'd had hanging over the chair by the mirror. "Put some clothes on."

I shrugged the shirt over my head, but as I walked out on stage to the thousands of screaming fans, my mind wasn't on the notes I was about to play, the lyrics I was about to sing.

My mind was fixed firmly on Kate. Who stood up to me like that?

There was something about that girl …

We played a one-hour set, and it was another successful gig. At the end, the crowd was on its feet, cheering. It seemed even the dancing girls that I was once so unsure of were actually worth their weight in gold, as we left to the shouts of "one more song" and the chicks ran back out to shake what their mamma gave them one last time. It was a 50/50 split crowd of guys to women, and having the girls with us seemed to get the blokes on side, especially during some of the slower numbers. They'd dance and sway their hips seductively in a manner that would have made my parents blush. Luckily, my folks they didn't come to shows anymore.

Huh. That was the first time I'd ever thought of that as a good thing.

The girls spun and gyrated in a variety of barely-there

outfits, black and red lace numbers that left very little to the imagination.

I wonder what Kate would look like in an outfit like that …

"Not bad for a bunch of ex-strippers," Xander said, slapping me on the back as he saw my eyes still focused on stage. He didn't know that I wasn't seeing a second of what was going on there. All I was seeing was Kate's body, which I had committed to memory, and wondering what sizes we had spare in those lingerie sets.

"Leave them be," I managed to spit out. Still, he was telling the truth. When Tony told us we needed to get some dancers to help "flesh out our act" a bit—with real flesh, mind—I'd suggested we hire strippers, to try and give them a new life. Well, for those who wanted out of the game, anyway. And much to my surprise, the concept was sexy enough without being too risqué for Tony to agree.

There was a fine line between being a sexy rock star and downright scandalous. A line that we seemed to tread far too often.

"Ah, good ol' Lee." Michael came up and ruffled my hair. "He's trying to save the world, one loose woman at a time."

"Knock it off." I pushed him away, but there was a smile on my face. It was true; I'd thought we could help get a few reluctant strippers out of that life, not because I wanted a private show in my room post-gig. Although that hadn't stopped them offering the first few times, mind.

We walked back down the corridor together to our separate rooms. It wasn't always like this; sometimes we had to share, but having our own space before we went on stage was nice. It gave me time to focus, and to warm up, something the other guys loved to give me shit about. It wasn't like I was singing opera, after all, but I still thought it important to keep my voice in good shape, and I was still always worried I'd stop hearing the music. Six years of lessons as a teenager … I shuddered, thinking what could happen if it all went away. Thank God I had my tone deafness under control.

As I reached my door, I couldn't help but think back to Kate before the show, how she came and … motivated me to go on stage. "Hey, Xan?"

Xander stopped with his hand on his door. I glanced up the corridor. A few security guards were loitering, and I could hear the thuds and grunts of our road crew as they loaded our gear off-stage. "Yeah?"

"When Kate came to get you to go on stage … did she …" The words stuck in my throat. I didn't want to embarrass her, if that was special treatment just for me.

Or maybe I'm afraid to tell him in case she doesn't do it again.

"What, bro?" Xander asked, a flicker of amusement in his eyes.

"Did she … do anything different?" My brows drew closer together as the words escaped my lips.

"No, man." Xander shook his head. "Oh, wait; maybe, yeah."

"Yeah?" My pulse thudded in my wrist. I swear to God, if she was stripping for my boys, I was going to kick her ass from here to next Tuesday. I'd call her folks, I'd turn her over my knee and spank her so hard I—

Images of an entirely different sort infiltrated my mind, and I huffed out a breath. What was wrong with me?

"She was a little more tetchy than usual." Xander nodded. "Wouldn't stick around for a drink or anything."

Air deflated from my lungs and my shoulders lowered. Thank fuck.

"You okay, man?" Xander walked over to me, his big hand wrapping around my shoulder. "You look like you're losing it."

"It's nothing." Nothing that I could pinpoint, anyway. Why was I so weird about this chick? Was it because I knew I couldn't have her?

Because she challenges you?

I ignored the voice in my brain. Having someone who you connected with, who made you think, with whom you had stuff in common, and who didn't just throw themselves at your feet didn't mean shit.

Carly had shown me that.

"You need to get laid, man." Xander shook his head and walked into his room, and as I turned to face my own door, I couldn't help but agree.

But I knew that I wouldn't.

Not while she was watching.

eleven

KATE

Dear Lee,

I do hope my little impromptu strip show was outrageous enough to help keep you clothed around me more often, but not so outrageous that it means I'm going to lose my job. After all, this is quite a fun and non-taxing position. And as much as I hate to admit it, one of the perks of being employed by a guy who rarely wears his shirts is that at least I don't have to worry about you going out on stage with mustard, or some tramp's red lipstick all over your clothes—not that you'd be fraternising with tramps, of course. I also thought you should know that I didn't take my top off for any of the other band members tonight. So if you could please keep that little strip private, it'd be great. I don't get half-naked for just anybody.

Kate

After the show the boys showered and changed, and I monitored the road crew bumping all the gear out, my clipboard pressed tightly to my chest. Or at least, that's what I appeared to be doing. What I was really doing was alternating between freaking out that Lee Collins was going to fire me for inappropriate shirt-removing behaviour, or that worse—he was going to ask me to do it again.

And that if he did, I might like it.

I shook the thought away. I honestly didn't know what had come over me in that moment, but I knew I had to do something to stop him constantly teasing me, and Stacey's advice had certainly shut him up. I couldn't help it if my stupid cheeks went red at the slightest thing.

"That's the last of it, Miss." One of the crew, a guy I referred to as Gropey due to his perpetually wandering hands, gave me the nod as he loaded the final guitar into the bus. It was something I'd learnt the hard way on my first day; guitars go in last as they're lightest, not first as they're most expensive. And Gropey had been physical in his demonstration of this order: apparently that required some tits-and-ass contact.

"Great. You can knock off now." I nodded and ticked the item off my clipboard run sheet. It was ridiculous that I carried it, really. I knew like the back of my hand the things that needed to be done pre- and post-gig. It had only been three weeks, but when your list of responsibilities was quite short, it wasn't too hard to figure out what to do. Sometimes, I thought I just carried the piece of plastic to make sure no one confused me for one of the dancing girls. Even if earlier today I had acted like one.

"Katie!" I turned with a smile and was wrapped in Lottie's embrace. "How are you, baby doll?"

"Good." I nodded. "Tired."

"Again?" she screeched, and I gave a small laugh. Every night post-show, Lottie came up to me and asked me to join her for some drinks back at her room while Jay slept. And every night, I refused.

I was here to work. I wasn't here to have fun, to go out and enjoy life.

Not when others couldn't.

It hit me once again, a bowling ball to the stomach, and I pressed my thumb into the pressure point on my hand to make it stop, to try and give myself a physical pain to hold onto. Anything to stop the pang of missing, the pang of loneliness washing over me.

"Well, I have some bad news. This time I'm not taking no for an answer." Lottie grabbed my wrist and pulled it away from my hand with a small shake of her head. "I've finally convinced Benny to sit Jay for me, so I am child-free—and you owe me at least one drink."

I couldn't help but smile. Lottie had this positive energy buzzing about her, and I had to admit—I kind of missed some girl talk. Bossing around the boys was kinda getting tiring.

And that was how I found myself walking into a bar about an hour later. I followed Lottie's lead as she waltzed up to the security guard out front and whispered something in his ear. He gave a curt nod and unclipped the rope, letting us through, much to the chagrin of the other people waiting in line.

"Did you tell him we were with the band?" I yelled in Lottie's ear to be heard over the grinding rock beat of the music.

"Nope." Lottie gave me a wicked grin. "I told him I'd show him my boobs later if he'd let us through."

I laughed, even though I had no idea if she was kidding or not. From what I'd seen, despite being a dedicated mother, Lottie was a bit of a wild child. It could be either way.

We pushed our way through the heaving throng of people to the bar. Well, I pushed. Lottie seemed to stare and they effortlessly parted before her, closing back in when I needed to muscle my way through. She was tall, a waif-like figure, with this impish smile and a dancer's body—it was no wonder people moved out of the way for her. She had a presence that simply could not be ignored.

We got to the bar and she ordered shots. We downed three Wet Pussies each in the space of five minutes, then each took a beer and wandered through the club, searching out the boys. Finally, after ten minutes we spotted a roped-off VIP balcony, and after more bouncer negotiation—this time I heard her, and she definitely did not offer a strip show—we were able to move out of the sweaty masses and into the spacious upstairs area.

"Get ready to party." Lottie gave me a wink. I looked around. The area was quite large, much bigger than it had looked from the floor. Tables and bar stools were lined up the back, with decadent leather lounges lining the balcony railing, so you could recline in comfort while spying on the people below.

There were about thirty people up here; six guys from the crew, Sam, the driver—who nodded politely at me—about five of the strippers, three random dudes who I guessed were mates with someone important, and no less than twelve other scantily-clad females, whose sole purpose here seemed to be gyrating. Every single one of them was gyrating on a piece of furniture, on a band member, or even on each other.

"What's the point in having a private area if you're just

going to invite all these randoms in?" I asked, looking at the dozens of people to the three staff manning the bar and the two security detail standing to attention.

"I guess to stop mobbing." Lottie shrugged, then turned to me. She pulled the sides of my dress down, to the point where I knew I had out more cleavage than I usually would display—although I was the girl who took off her top today. Apparently, I wasn't the usual me anymore. "Better." She nodded, proud of her handiwork. My hands itched to pull my dress back up before I remembered that she was a stylist. Who was I to argue with that?

"The party has arrived!" Lottie threw her hands up in the air, sending a splash of beer over some unfortunate gyrater to our left.

"Kate." Michael's face was bright red, and I couldn't help but smile. There was a girl grinding her hips against the arm of the couch next to him, but he looked as if he were trying to meld his body into the other arm of the chair. It was obvious he didn't want to be here.

"So you've finally decided to live it up." Xander stuck his head to the side so I could meet his gaze around the girl who was sitting on his lap. He pushed a lock of her strawberry-blonde hair over her shoulder. "Sweetheart, get my girl here a drink, please."

I threw my hands to my hips, my jaw dropping to the floor. Sure, my job was to fetch things, but for the band and for the purpose of shows! I was not his freaking servant, and I sure wasn't being employed to line up drinks for whatever skank he took home that night. There was no way in hell I was—

"Okay." Strawberry-Blonde slid off Xander's leg and headed to the bar.

Overreacting. I was overreacting.

He'd asked her to get a drink for me.

Xander chuckled and scooted over in his seat, patting the space next to him. "Come sit with Uncle Xan, Kate. I'll look after you."

"Like hell you will, man."

I searched for the man behind those words and found him on the seat a few inches away from Xander's, even though I knew who had spoken. Lee-freaking-Collins.

"Kate's-our ... 'sistant. She isn't here to ... sex." Lee slurred, and I couldn't help but giggle.

"Glad you're around to protect my virtue." I walked over and sat in the seat next to Xander. Lee nodded in an over-pronounced fashion and I patted his hand, being careful not to touch any exposed skin on the blonde woman who was currently gyrating her crotch against Lee's chest.

"I will." Lee leaned forward, shouldering Blondie in the chest and grabbed my hand from where it rested on top of his, pulling it to his mouth for a kiss. "I'll look after you."

Something warm stirred inside my body and I had to pull my hand away. *He's drunk, Kate. He's really drunk.*

"Hope a strawberry martini is okay." Strawberry-Blonde handed me a wide, sugar-rimmed glass and I smiled. I was a little surprised; she seemed to actually be ... nice. Weren't all band sluts supposed to be bitches?

"Thanks." I nodded.

"So, how are you liking the job so far?" Xander asked as Strawberry-Blonde resumed her gyrating.

"It's pretty good." I thought back over the last three weeks. It had been busy, sure, but I loved the challenge of thinking on the fly, of making sure everything worked out. "And you guys aren't nearly as bad-arse as I was expecting."

"I'm ... baaaaad." Lee's head dropped as his tone did on the final word, causing his gyrater, who had regained her perch on his lap, to end up with a drunken man in her more than ample cleavage. Not that she seemed to mind.

Or at least, I presumed he was drunk. "He's not on ..."

"No! Hell no." Xander shook his head vehemently. "Doesn't touch the stuff. The guy barely takes ibuprofen, for Christ's sake. 'Fraid he'll end up like his old man."

I took a sip of my martini. At least that was one thing I didn't have to stress about, anymore.

Still, it reminded me that I hadn't sent that email to Dad,

and I made a mental note to finish it before I went to bed, or first thing when I woke up.

"There you are." Lottie came dancing over and perched herself on my knee, wrapping an arm around my neck. She was light as a feather; I barely felt her weight.

"Partying hard tonight, Lotts?" Xander asked. There was something lurking in his eyes. I couldn't tell if it was danger or desire.

"Sure am." Lottie gave an infectious laugh, then turned her head to the side. "But not as hard as Lee."

She leaned closer to him and wedged a finger between his chin and Gyrater's boobs, lifting his head up. His eyes flickered open and he met her gaze, smiling. "Wasn't doing anything."

Lottie laughed and let his head flop back down. "Come dance." She held out a hand for me and I took it, but as we moved together next to the railing, looking over it to check for guys on the floor, I couldn't help but keep flicking my gaze back to Lee. He was really drunk; ridiculously drunk, and that girl was all but licking his face. And despite them not kissing, he was letting her! I hadn't seen any reports in the tabloids about him being a crazy drinker, or engaging in public sex acts, or anything. Does he always get like this?

Suddenly, my lack of partying seemed like a blessing in disguise. I think I preferred the sober singer.

"Do they always go this big?" I yelled to Lottie. She pulled me closer, dirty dancing with me, and I moved back just a little as her hands ran up my sides.

"Not always," she yelled, her breath hot against my ear. "This is the biggest we've had this leg of the tour."

When a guy I didn't recognise wrapped his arms around Lottie's waist and she leaned back appreciatively, I took my opportunity to leave. Now Lee was sitting with just his gyrating friend, Xander having disappeared to who knows where, no doubt with his lady friend.

I let myself fall into the comfy leather couch and turned just in time to see Lee's friend sucking hard on his neck, one hand wrapped up in his hair, the other working its way into his pants. I widened my eyes. Was she for real? She was going to do this in public?

Then I saw her pull his dick from his jeans.

Oh my God, she is going to do this in public.

I had to stop it. And I hated that it was for more than just the obvious reason.

"Lee." I leaned over and gave his shoulder a shake, keeping my eyes firmly above crotch level. "Lee!" I shook again, but his head just lolled about. I didn't even know if he could hear me.

It would be so easy to just leave them there right now, but I couldn't do that. He'd hired me to look after him. And really, if I was being completely honest with myself?

I didn't want anyone else to touch him.

The admission shocked even me. Lee Collins was arrogant, liked to tease me, and was way out of my league.

I pressed my eyes shut and thought of Lachlan again. Lachlan, the man who had saved me, pulled me deep from a depression I hadn't been sure I'd recover from. He took me from rain to sunshine. That was how liking someone was supposed to feel.

Then why did Lee make me feel … squishy? Like there was something gooey and gelatinous inside my stomach, like my knees were having problems with that whole standing-up thing I'd been getting them to do?

I shook myself out of my reverie and focused on the one person I could easily remove from the situation. "Um, excuse me, lady, can you stop?"

I still refused to look down, but her arm was moving in a way that implied …

Sucking in a breath, I reached over to the table and grabbed what was left of my abandoned strawberry martini, then emptied it over her head. The gyrater looked at me, her bottom lip pouting, her brown eyes fiery.

"Bitch!" she shrieked, wiping the sticky liquid from her arms.

"Please leave." I smiled sweetly, and even though the look she gave me was pure murder, she stormed off. I furrowed my brows. Who knew it would be that easy?

I looked left and right, but I couldn't see Michael, couldn't see anyone I knew. Spotting Sam at the bar, I yelled out and he came to my side, concern marring his forehead. "Everything okay?"

"Will you help me take him home?" I jerked my head in Lee's direction, and chanced a quick glance. Now his head was resting against the couch behind him, his eyes still closed. I took the shortest of short looks down and saw his open pants, his briefs and—nope, not looking, back up to Sam's face. This cannot be the third time I see a real penis. Seriously.

Sam nodded and walked to the other side of the couch. He looked down briefly before gazing back up at me, and I could tell he'd seen it, too. "Are you going to …?"

"Can't you?" I asked, biting my lip. It was bad enough that this was the third time I'd ever seen one; this couldn't be the third time I touched one, too.

Sam shook his head, and it appeared we were at an impasse until I thought of the one person who I knew wouldn't be uncomfortable dealing with this. I scanned the room, and saw just the person I was looking for coming back from the ladies room, her arm linked with one of the dancers. "Lottie!"

She slowly looked over, a smile in her eyes, and skipped to my side.

"Can you …?" I jerked my head in the direction of Lee's pelvis. Lottie shrugged and leant forward, fiddling with … his bits. "Sorry to bother you, I just—well, it's not my place, you know?" I played with the hem of my dress, the brand new black one Stacey had gotten me as a going away present. "And I figure if anyone would be comfortable with tucking his bits away, it would be you. You know, being a stylist and all. Hell, I'm probably sure you do it all the time, and—"

"Kate." Lottie fixed her gaze on mine. Her lips were in a thin line now, as if she were unimpressed with the whole situation. "It's done. Are you gonna make sure he gets home with Sam?"

I swallowed. Was my nervousness that obvious? "Yes," I

squeaked.

"Good. I'll see you in the morning then." She raised her eyebrows and swayed her hips as she strolled back to the girl I'd called her away from. She gave me a tiny wave, and I waved back then returned my attention to the problem man at hand.

Sam and I lifted Lee up and walked to the back of the club's service entrance. I saw two cameras flash as we did, but they were just idiots with their iPhones, and Sam let Lee rest against my shoulder, his head lulling from side to side, while he went and talked to a guy behind the bar. Just before the doors closed I saw one of the venue security team members walk over and demand the pictures were deleted. I smiled. I guess that was why you went to all the trouble of having a private area.

We got to the car with only two paparazzo seeing us, but Sam just opened the car door and ushered us in. I didn't see any flashes of light, but I held my hand up to my face to protect myself, just in case. Then Sam drove off, whizzing through the quiet late-night streets, and we headed to our hotel.

My eyes were fixed on the lights of the city as we sped past. It was a different country, and yet it felt like home; something about the familiar takeaway joints, the high- and low-rise buildings, the giant intersections … it all screamed of familiarity.

Stacey had said it would be like this. She'd said I'd feel at home. It just surprised me how easy that feeling would be to come by, especially when by being in this new place I was abandoning people I loved; people I held dear.

A new wave of guilt washed over me, this time not for Lachlan, but for Johhny. I'd left him to cope with his grief alone, and hadn't even sent him a text, not once in three weeks.

I grabbed my cell and typed out a quick message.

Me: Hey Johnny, how you doing? Hope everything is going good, and you're happy, and life is just … good! How's Leslie? And …

My mind flashed blank. Before Lachlan's death, Johnny and I had always had an easy friendship. It was a no-brainer; the kind you didn't have to think about.

Now, things were tricky.

Now, words had extra meaning.

> **Me: Anyway, I'm going okay. On tour in America with Lee, the guy who played at the—you know who Lee is.**
> **Anyway, just wanted to say I'm thinking of you.**

I didn't type out 'and Lachlan.' Sometimes, words were better left unsaid.

We pulled up to the hotel a few short minutes later and Sam helped me rouse Lee, who had once again dozed off after jerking his head up at the traffic lights, his neck at a rather uncomfortable-looking side angle, his jaw hanging open.

We stood in the lift, both of us with one of Lee's arms over our shoulder, and now I had an extended knowledge of exactly how important it was that the hotels we stayed at had service entrances and exits. There was no way behaviour like this would get by unnoticed in a regular lift. It had public scandal and gossip magazine written all over it.

When the doors finally pinged open and we hit the top floor, Sam helped me take Lee to his door and then, using the spare key I already had from reception—to make sure I could get the boys up if need be, after the banging-on-door-waiting-five-minutes incident of the week prior—we entered his suite, depositing Lee on the couch.

"Wow." Sam gave a low whistle under his breath. He wasn't wrong. This room screamed opulence, from its floor-to-ceiling windows that offered a stunning view of the city at night, to the plush white carpet, to the elegantly tasteful white lounges, all done in a firm leather with gold trim. I had never been somewhere with so much money attached in my entire life.

"I'll be going then." Sam dipped his head at me and walked

for the door.

"Yes." I nodded, checking my handbag was still laced over my shoulder. "Me too."

"I thought you were going to stay." Sam furrowed his brow at me. The breath escaped from my throat, and I was certain my skin turned pale. My heart thudded in my chest and all of a sudden I was overcome with excuses, desperate to get them out before Sam thought this was all a part of an evil plan by me to seduce the lead singer of Coal.

"I don't even like him like that. I … I think he's cute, but this was about me making sure he was okay, not trying to get him into—"

"Kate." Sam held out his palm in a stop signal. "I meant to make sure he's all right. You know, in case he chokes on his own vomit or something."

That feeling, how bad it was when I'd thought Sam thought I was seducing Lee?

That. Only a thousand times worse.

"Yeah …" My voice was so quiet, Sam leaned in to hear it. "That's what I meant, too."

I saw him out and shut the door behind him, resting my head against it as I berated myself for what an idiot I'd been. Seriously. Dumb.

After a few minutes, I sucked in a deep breath. Get it together, Kate. Do your job.

I walked down the hall of the suite into the master bedroom and opened the closet doors, searching for a blanket. I couldn't find one, except for a small thing that looked as if it would cover less skin than a robe, so instead I tugged the white, airy linen from the king-sized bed, trailing it over my shoulder and back into the living room. I draped it over Lee's body, my hand lingering a little over his sweaty bicep before I tucked the edge of the blanket into the couch.

Next, I walked into the kitchen and poured a giant glass of water from the tap and grabbed some ibuprofen from my purse, then, just before I headed back to Lee, I grabbed a large-sized bowl from under the sink. As much as I wanted to believe that rock stars, like Santa Claus, didn't spew, I'd rather be safe than sorry.

"Lee." I extended a hesitant finger and poked him in the shoulder. "Wake up."

"Ugghrhnmmm." He rolled to his back and promptly started snoring. Fabulous. Way to kill the dream, buddy.

"Lee." My voice was louder, a little more insistent. Seriously, if he didn't drink this water he was going to feel even more like shit in the morning than he probably did right now.

Finally he opened one eye, and it locked on mine. Even though he was drunk, even though he smelt kind of as if he'd gone for a swim in a vat of bourbon, his eye was still a bright, bright blue, the kind of searing colour that is forever etched in your brain.

"Kate." He managed the word, and a lazy arm extended from his body, reaching up to brush down my cheek. "You're looking after me."

"Sure am." I pressed the glass of water to his lips. "Drink, please."

He pushed himself up onto one elbow and took four huge gulps, then collapsed back onto the couch as if the effort had exhausted him.

"Do you want some ibuprofen?" I took the glass away and placed it on the coffee table beside me, then sat cross-legged on the floor, my gaze in line with Lee's.

"No." His voice was surprisingly coherent, but I didn't really buy it. You don't go from passed out to sober in a second.

"Okay." We sat in silence for a while, and I wondered if I should go back to my room. We were staying at the same hotel; I was just a short ten floors down, and not in a suite so much as a single room. In fact, if Lee's room were a grand piano, mine would be an accordion. A broken one.

I pushed to my feet, and just as I took a step forward a hand gripped around my wrist. I looked down to Lee's wide-open eyes.

"Stay."

My head wanted me to leave. My heart was torn in two.

But I was starting to feel things for this man, things I couldn't ignore, and in that moment he was just a normal guy who'd had too much to drink, and I was a normal girl with a tiny crush on a guy. He wasn't a rock star, and I wasn't broken-hearted.

We were just … us.

I sat back down and rested my back against the couch. Lee stroked my hair, and his fingers traced soft patterns against my head, soothing me, comforting me, and I tried to pretend like it wasn't the best and the worst thing I'd felt in a long time as my guilt warred with my affections. "Tell me something that not many people know about you."

"Haven't we already played this game?" I asked.

"Again. These are … the best games."

I licked my lips and stared at the flat-screen TV in front of me. The thing was big, but not obscene, and I could see our reflection in it. "Um … well, I'm a virgin." I went for the obvious, the one I was fairly sure Lee already knew, thanks to my dickhead ex-boyfriend. Seconds later, I wanted to give myself a giant slap to the forehead. What was I thinking? He didn't know what I had or hadn't done with Lachlan. Idiot, idiot, idiot …

"A virgin, huh?" Lee's hands didn't miss a beat as they traced over my skull. "I didn't know there were any of those left."

I snorted, and shook my head. He was clearly still drunk. "What about you?"

"I …" His hands paused in their journey, then resumed again seconds later. "I have a secret love for television series. Not cool ones, like Sons of Anarchy or anything. Embarrassing, daggy ones. Like Hart of Dixie."

"What? With that chick from—"

"The OC, which I also loved." We both laughed, and Lee's hand trailed down my neck and started its pattern play against my throat. There was something about the way it lingered there, so sensual and delicate … I shivered.

"Your turn." Lee's voice startled me out of my thoughts and

I gave a small shake of my head, trying to regain my senses.

"Okay, um …" I racked my brain for something, anything, but I was pretty much an open book. I didn't have secrets; they weren't something I'd ever been a merchant of.

All I traded in was misery.

"There must be something …" Lee's fingers traced over my jaw, and God, did I want to tilt my head down and take one into my mouth, lick, suck and run my lips along it and—

Kate. Focus.

"Isn't there something you haven't told anyone?" Lee pressed again, and this time it struck a nerve. There was one thing. One big thing that I didn't talk about at all.

Ever.

"I … I don't know what happens when we die." My voice was small, and Lee's hand stilled.

"Whaddya mean?" His voice was a tiny bit slurred, and I knew sleep was near. Hell, he probably wouldn't remember this in the morning anyway.

"When we die … where do we go?" I chewed my lip, trying to find the right words. "You know, I was brought up Christian, and I believed in Heaven, and Hell, and everything like that, but really? How can that be a thing? How can there be a god who just lets people die when they're not"—a sob choked its way up my throat—"ready?"

"Hey, it's okay." Lee pulled me close, and I smelt the bourbon on his breath as his lips neared my ear. "It's okay."

For some reason, his words had the opposite effect to their intention. I pushed away and spun to face him, tears freely flowing down my cheeks. "You know what it is? It's not even that. I could believe that whole 'everything happens for a reason' crap, but then what about—what about evolution? What about fucking dinosaurs, Lee? Were they in the garden before Adam and Eve?" I was shouting now, screaming so loud my throat felt raw. My chest shook with the sobs that tore through me, and the pain, the pain that haunted me, that still wouldn't freaking leave me alone was there, and it was real, and it was stabbing me in the gut.

Pain's a vicious bitch like that.

"I just—I can't deal with it, you know? But it scares me. It fucking—it fucking scares me till I want to curl up in a ball and die, because after this, there's nothing, Lee. Nothing. And so what's the damn point." It wasn't a question.

It was what had happened to Lachlan.

Where he was right now.

I heaved my chest over my knees and curled up into a little ball, the tears no longer coming but my body still aching. Aching, aching so badly. "And now I've just had a mini meltdown in front of my boss, who will no doubt fire me when he's sober enough to remember this."

I didn't know how long I stayed curled up, but when I finally lifted my head, Lee Collins was looking at me with a pensive expression on his face. He extended his arm and I took it, then he pulled me up toward him so I lay beside him on the couch, careful to leave a small space between us in case he thought this was me taking advantage of a drunk guy. Because I wasn't.

Right now, I just really needed his arms.

We lay there in silence for so long my lids heavy, my breath slowing, and I started to wonder if falling asleep here would really be so bad. Lee's arm was draped around my middle, heavy as a sandbag, pinning me to the spot, and it was nice to have some kind of security holding me in place.

That was all I really wanted; something to hold me together. Someone to hold me together.

"Kate, for you? I know there's something else." He shifted his body so one leg rested slightly over mine, resulting in me becoming the bottom layer of a Lee toastie. "You've been through a lot; you're a tough chick. I know that you're going someplace after this, someplace good, real good."

I shook my head. "But how do you know?" It was a nice sentiment, but seriously, how could he have faith in that?

"I know, because I'm going to Hell."

I furrowed my brow, thinking of all the bad-arse things I'd heard or known Lee Collins to do. "What? That's ridiculous.

You might have taken advantage of a few groupies, gotten drunk a few times, but you're a good person, Lee. You're a really good guy. Why would you think you'd be going there?"

I turned to see emotions warring on Lee's face. He fought this demon inside him, then pressed his eyes shut so tight I could see the tension creasing their corners, popping the vein on his forehead. Then, seconds passed with nothing, and his face returned to a calm, even state, his breathing long and drawn-out as he drifted toward sleep. I let myself relax against him, the lulling rise and fall of his chest compelling mine to fall in synch. I could just fall asleep here … we weren't naked or anything. Being wrapped in these arms might make sleep come easier. It wasn't like I was really crossing any boundaries or anything … was I?

"Because I killed my brother."

TWELVE

LEE

Four years, seven months ago ...

I'LL NEVER forget the day I finally met my brother. It was the third time we'd arranged to meet, and this time, I was far less nervous than I had been. Maybe it was because I wasn't sure if he'd show this time, either. How was I to know?

Instead of walking into the bar, nerves jangling in my stomach, my senses on high alert, I casually meandered in, checking my phone for a message from Carly. She didn't know quite what I was doing today—telling people I had a secret brother wasn't high on my to-do list—but she knew I was in town.

> **Carly: Can't wait to see you guys perform again tonight! Looking forward to seeing you :)**

Carly ... I thought of her luscious lips, her bewitching eyes and her amazing body and the breath just floated away from my chest. But more than that, it was her mind. The way she asked me things that no one else did. The way she spoke to me, listened, and really understood. She was so interested in everything to do with the band in a way that didn't seem superficial. It felt real.

"One Bud, thanks." A man walked up and placed his order, pulling a cardboard coaster close to his chest and then angling his body to face me. "Lee."

I turned to look at him, and my first thought was shit. I guess, in the back of my mind, I'd hoped that maybe Mom and Dad were wrong; maybe I didn't have a long-hidden sibling. It seemed stupid now. I'd wanted a brother for years, but I guess when you're a kid, wanting a sibling is filling a void, offering you a playmate. Now, I looked at this guy who could almost be my twin, if I were somehow rougher, edgier, and I couldn't help but wonder if he'd screw with Tony's scandal clause. He'd sure as hell better not.

"Hi." My voice cracked a little on the word. His dark hair was longer than mine, pulled back in a ponytail, and he had a two-day stubble marring his chin and cheeks. He was skinnier than me, too; I could see his shoulder bones, and the thin lines of his arms as they snaked out of his top. My teeth clamped down on my lip. Was he … what sort of an upbringing had he had? Did he have money? Was he a good person?

"Here you go." The bartender slid my brother's beer across the counter to him and picked up the notes he had left, placing them in his register.

"Wanna go …?" My brother jerked his head toward a booth, and I nodded, grabbing the drink I'd had sitting there since earlier.

He led the way, scooted along the leather and I followed and sat down a respectable distance away from him.

"You're Lee Collins, huh?" He took a swig from his beer, then slammed it back down onto a coaster. "Ryan. Ryan Abrahams."

I leant over to shake his hand, but he didn't take mine, and after leaving it hanging there awkwardly for a few moments, I pulled it back to my side, resisting the urge to swipe it through my hair and play it cool, as if I were just taking the long way round.

"So … you're my brother, huh?" The words left my mouth and I gave myself one helluva kick up the ass. What the hell was I saying? Couldn't I string a damn sentence together?

"Looks that way." Ryan nodded, then pointed his finger from his face to mine and back again. "You don't see the similarity?"

I gave a half-hearted chuckle. "Well, yeah."

"Yeah," Ryan said. He twirled his beer in his grip. "When I first saw you on TV, I thought we looked alike. So did my girl. That's what prompted me to look up my parents, y'know? Never had any great desire to get in touch—since they fucking abandoned me." You couldn't miss the bitterness that laced his last phrase. It dripped like honey off the edges of a spoon, seeping to my consciousness below.

His words were everything I was afraid of come to life. He didn't want to be my brother, or to meet the fucking family. He wanted to make a quick buck out of my newfound fame, to get a free ride from his rich younger 'brother'. Tony was gonna kick my ass over this one.

I looked up and Ryan was staring at me, expectation in his eyes. "I mean, they were only kids." I tried to make excuses, but it only fuelled his anger. His fingers wrapped around the glass in front of him, his knuckles turning white as he exerted his strength.

"So was I." Something dark flashed in his eyes.

Sometimes in life, people got hurt. And that pain, it ran so deep that it tore into their very being, ate away at their soul. I could see that hurt in him.

And I wished he hadn't had to go through that.

I took a deep breath and tried to compose myself. I had to give the guy a chance. How would I feel if our situations had been reversed?

"So … what do you … uh … do?" I turned my beer in my hands and took another sip, more for the desire to do something with my hands than anything else.

"I'm a carpenter." Ryan nodded. "Just finished my apprenticeship ... I'm travelling a bit now, trying to get a contract."

"Oh." I smiled. "That's cool."

We sat in awkward silence for a few minutes, and I noted that he didn't ask what I did for a living. Once again, the difference in our lives was blatantly obvious, from my designer jeans to his cut-price skate shoes.

I looked around the room. This was a much more upmarket joint than the place where Carly worked, where Ryan and I had first agreed to meet. This place had wide, open windows and a long marble bar, high-end liquor decorating the shelves behind it.

"This is a big thing, huh?" I nodded, gesturing between the two of us. "Insta-brothers."

"Yeah." One corner of Ryan's lips raised in a smile.

"Do you mind if I ask why you didn't come those first two times?"

"Nerves, I guess." Ryan studied me, his gaze shrewd as he took a pull of his beer, then set it back down on the coaster in front of him. "Do you think I'm after your money?"

"No." A little.

"I ... there aren't a lot of people in life I'm close to." Ryan spoke the words slowly, as if he were carefully choosing out each one. "Honestly? I kinda ... I kinda thought that maybe having a brother would be nice. But I've had a lot of disappointment in my life—a heap." His eyes flashed with something dark. "And the other two times, I ... I wanted to come, both times, and the second I even drove to meet you but I couldn't get out of the car. What if you were some dickhead who thought he was God's gift just because you're on MTV, or whatever?" He spun the beer bottle in his hands, twisting it around. "I don't think I coulda handled more family screw-ups."

A pang of guilt washed over me. He'd had a rough life. "Do you ... are you close with your ... parents?" I almost threw the word 'other' in there, but thank hell I pulled it back at the last minute.

Ryan slammed his drink on the table and eyeballed me, seeing into my very core. "Shit, no. He's a dick and she's a drug-fucked whore." There was anger in his gaze, and his pupils danced around the room, leading me to wonder if perhaps he hadn't dabbled in the art of drugs himself. "I have a girl, though," he conceded.

"Oh? How long you been together?" I prompted him. It seemed to be the only thing he'd mentioned so far that didn't come served with a side of hate.

Ryan's face lit up, and he got this faraway look in his eyes. "Since high school. Almost eight years, but I've had to travel a bit to try and get work recently, so we haven't really been seeing each other these last few months. She's ... she's damn well perfect, y'know?" He let out a long breath, then shook his head. "She has these eyes ... they're like the ocean. She's funny, too, and so easy-going. And her mouth is this, just this plump, juicy thing, and ... damn. She's just ... she's everything."

In that second, that very moment, I knew what he was talking about. Those who say love at first sight doesn't exist are blind. I knew from the very moment she fell out of that tree that Carly was something special, that we were meant to be together. And I was so glad that despite his shitty upbringing, my brother had a love like that, too.

Everyone deserves a love like that.

Present day ...

TRIED TO open my eyes, but dear God, someone had super-glued them together. What fresh hell was this?

I gave it a second shot only to find that there was a spotlight positioned directly in my line of vision, screaming its harsh, white beam right onto my face. I scrunched up my eyes, nose and mouth, and anything else I could to ward off the evil. What the—

Where am I?

I tentatively opened my eyes to a small slit and surveyed

my surroundings. I was in my hotel suite, but for some reason, I was on the couch, and not in my bedroom. The black-out curtains were sure as hell not drawn—amateur move, Collins—and a standard white hotel quilt covered me, imprisoning me in a tomb of my own sweat and hangover juice. Ugh.

"Rise and shine, Mr Collins." The voice sang, way too loudly and way too close to my head. I tilted my neck up and saw Kate walking closer to me, a white mug in her hands containing something that smelled like sex, like candy, like everything good in this world, moving closer to me. "You brought me coffee," my voice croaked, and my hand shook as I reached for it.

She smiled kindly and I shuffled myself up into a half-seated position, wrapping my fingers around the outside of the mug. I took another glance up. She looked amazing this morning, in her skin-tight jeans and tight black tank, a pair of killer heels on display. I moved my lips to my mug and tilted my head back, thinking about seeing her half-naked yesterday and grinning. Would it really be so bad if …

"What the fuck?" I spat the hot liquid out, little brown droplets covering my white quilt, the glass coffee table, the white carpet. My stomach roiled and curdled, the bitter taste of coffee competing with the strong taste of something like tequila or maybe even vodka for position of top dog in my body. I slammed the cup down on the floor, ignoring the coffee that sloshed over the sides and seeped into the carpet. Yep, I was a bad-ass like that.

Or I was when someone fucked with my morning coffee. "What the hell did you do to it?"

A few seconds later, Kate appeared back in my line of vision with the cloth from the suite's sink and started mopping up the coffee table, eyeing the stained floor wistfully. After a few minutes, she went back to the kitchen and reappeared with a bottle of vinegar. I don't even know where she woulda gotten it from …

"I just thought that some extra booze could make your hangover less painful." Kate shrugged as she scrubbed at the carpet. "And since you slept on the couch, I figured you wouldn't be feeling one hundred per cent."

Now that she'd mentioned it, I did feel distinctly less than chipper. My ribs had this soft but urgent ache every time I moved, and my neck felt as if someone had stabbed it with a carving knife, right up against a really important vein.

I forced myself all the way upright, eyeing my boozed-up coffee as if it could still somehow cause me grief from the floor, and tried to focus. Shit, everything was kind of swaying. I grabbed the couch cushions and steadied myself. Nope. It was me. I was swaying.

"What did you even put in it?" I screwed up my face.

"Whatever I found in the mini bar." Kate shrugged, as if this was the logical answer.

"Whatever you found in the—"

"You know, vodka, gin, bourbon, tequila—"

"You mixed all those things?" I frowned.

"Mm-hmm." Kate nodded, the picture of innocence, all wide eyes and open face. "Why? Do they not go? I'm not really a big drinker …" She bit her lip in an oops gesture that I somehow found hot, even though I should be pissed that she just basically tried to kill me.

"Sorry for yelling." I bit the side of my cheek. "I guess you didn't know." I shook my head and leaned back against the couch. I couldn't be mad at her. Not at someone who was so freaking sweet, nice enough to try and make me feel better when I'd clearly hit rock-bottom and—

My reverie was disrupted. I looked at her, leaning up against the doorframe, one hand over her mouth … laughing.

The bitch was laughing!

"What's so freaking funny?"

"You," she spat out, mirth making her shoulders shake, her hand risen to her mouth.

"Why?" I folded my arms across my chest. As far as I could tell, there was nothing damn funny about this whole thing.

"As if I didn't know that that cocktail of booze would taste horrible!" Kate laughed, doubling over now. "I may not be super experienced, but I'm not dumb. Give me a break."

Oh.

It took a few seconds, but I started laughing too. She went into the bathroom then came back with a wet washcloth, which she handed to me. I rubbed it over my face, relishing in the sensation of the fresh, clean scent that made the stench of booze slowly fade away. Amazing. "Thanks."

"You're welcome." She sat down on the couch opposite me, hands clasped over one knee as she leaned forward. "So you're awake now?" She quizzed me.

"Yes." I nodded. I liked playful Kate. It was one of my favourite kinds.

"And you don't feel quite as horrid as you did when you first woke up?" She tilted her head to one side, a big smile turning her lips, and I knew couldn't argue.

"Yes." Strangely, her stupid coffee cocktail did the trick.

Something washed over her face, and it turned into the picture-perfect poker player's expression. She was Switzerland. "So, let's talk about you killing your brother."

The words were like kryptonite to me, and I panicked. My throat swelled till it was so thick, I didn't see how I could possibly get any words out, and my breathing came short and sharp, as if each gasp couldn't get deep enough.

My brother? How does she know about my brother?

It was as if she read my mind, for seconds later she started to talk again. "You told me, last night. You said you killed him."

Something that was in between a bowling ball and one of those giant round things used to knock buildings down swung like a pendulum in the pit of my stomach, dread building at a rapid rate. I'd been drunk before; hell, over the past five years, I'd been drunk a lot. But never enough to tell someone about him.

I must trust her more than I'd thought. She'd penetrated my walls.

Shit.

"I … I didn't kill my brother." Only it was about two hours too late for me to try this line as a comeback, and the look in her eyes said it—the look in my eyes no doubt confirmed it. "Did I really tell ... tell you that?"

She nodded, and looked down at her hands. They were delicate, active, and currently her fingers were threading themselves through each other. If her hands had a career occupation, they would be dancers.

"You told me you killed him. It was late last night ... I was telling you about how I feel ... you know, spiritually. What happens next, and all." She studied her hands as she said this and they picked up speed, dancing to her new allegro tempo.

Her words rang a bell, and I vaguely recalled talking about life after death with her. Her confusion, and uncertainty. My reassurance that she would be okay.

It was as if last night we'd travelled from LA to New York. I could see how we'd started (at the club); I could see where we ended (apparently, I'd told her I killed him); I just couldn't figure out quite how I'd gotten from A to B. Or why the hell I'd even gotten to B in the first place, when I was trying to hit up Vegas.

I fisted my hair in my hands as I tried to piece it all together. I'd gotten drunk, so drunk; I'd needed to forget. I couldn't handle the way she'd stripped, and in my effort to forget her, to erase her from my brain, I'd somehow taken her home with me and spilled my biggest secret. Great work, Collins.

My brain worked at a million miles per hour as I tried to think of the most logical thing I could say to get this idea out of her brain, to make her stop thinking I was a family-killing maniac, but without the coffee, and with the hangover, it was all too much. Why the hell had I said that? I knew I felt comfortable around Kate, but how comfortable was too comfortable? Where had my usual self-protective guard been and why the hell hadn't it been in play?

It was in that moment I made a choice. A choice that wasn't nice; it was cruel, down to the bone.

But sometimes you had to save yourself. No one else would do it for you.

"Look, I don't know what you think you heard, but it

was clearly wrong." I shook my head and forced a smile. "Maybe you've gone a little …" I cringed, one more second of deliberation, "… crazy."

The silence in the room was deafening. It was an orchestra. It was a car cruising around the block with double-bass speakers and the sound turned to max. It was the loudest, meanest silence I've ever heard.

I expected her to crumple. I expected her to fold her body in two and run, because I knew that when I was her, when my father was at the peak of his illness, when I'd lost someone I loved, that was exactly what I would have done. Grief wasn't easy, and sometimes, you got so caught up in mourning the dead, you could forget to mourn the living. Forget to mourn the very real quality-of-life deterioration happening right in front of you.

But Kate surprised me.

She's really fucking good at that.

Instead, she straightened—yes, straightened—her shoulders, puffed out her chest, and smiled, a cold, cruel smile. "I know your secret, Lee Collins."

She stood and walked to the kitchen, a seductive sway to her hips that I was unable to ignore. She grabbed her clutch from the bench and walked back to the apartment door. "I'll keep it, but I'm going to need answers."

The door slammed behind her. Four and a half years. Five and a half years I had kept this fucking secret, and now I'd blown it. And for what? Some chick who'd made me feel like an idiot for teasing her.

No.

Some chick who'd made me feel.

Not only that, but I was fairly sure Lottie had been there last night. That meant she would have seen me drunk as a teenager with his first bottle of bourbon.

Shit.

I picked up my coffee cup from where it was sitting on the floor and threw it at the wall. It slammed, shattering upon impact and raining little chips of white porcelain all over the white carpet floor, mixed in with the brown liquid floating there.

Tony was going to kill me.

THIRTEEN

KATE

Relief overwhelmed me as I walked down the hallway, my hands shaking. It had taken so much energy to keep it together, to not fall apart again in front of Lee after my little breakdown last night.

When I'd returned to my room at something close to one, I'd been enveloped in hurt. In pain. In sadness. Because sometimes, the questions about the when, and the why, and the after? They consume you. And without my running routine, sleep had been an elusive fiend I just hadn't been able to come by.

You could close your eyes to the darkness, try forget the pain, but in the end, she'd find you. She always did.

When I'd opened my eyes again, I'd splashed water on my face, pasting on a smile and what I hoped was a damn good concealer to try and mask the lack of sleep that had bruised under my eyes. Because even if I didn't have Lachlan, I still had my family. And I had to do this, put on a show, for them.

Some show it had been. What I'd shrugged off as nonsense

last night, a throwaway line of Lee's as he fell asleep, had now been locked in my brain. Because when I went back to his hotel room earlier this morning, determined to find out if he'd been talking crap or not, I'd seen it in his eyes. He'd said no; he'd shaken his head. And I would have walked away, believing I'd made a mistake, hell, even believing that maybe I had made the whole thing up—until he'd called me crazy.

Lee Collins didn't call people crazy. He was as sensitive about the word as I was.

That was when I knew. Lee Collins had killed a man.

I pressed the button for the lift and tapped my foot, that emotional energy tearing at my insides again.

The sound of glass or porcelain smashing in the distance made me flinch. I flicked my head around, no doubt in my mind that it had come from his room. Shit. I'd never been scared of Lee before, but could that be ... could he be a killer?

I shook my head. The idea was ridiculous. He couldn't be. I processed the facts as I rode the lift to my floor. Aside from the sound of whatever that just was smashing, I'd never seen him lose control. He was a calm guy; funny, collected, smart ... I practically rolled my eyes at myself. Yes, Kate, we get it. You like Lee Collins. The maybe murderer.

Swiping my card over the scanner outside my room, I pushed the handle open and go in and pour myself a huge glass of water. My hands shook as I brought the cup to my mouth, from tiredness or emotional drive I wasn't sure.

"Get yourself together, Kate." The glass trembled against my lips, and I placed it down with force on the coffee table. I was going to cut myself, if I wasn't careful.

I picked up my wallet, opened it to the photo of Lachlan I had there. I traced my finger over his face, his chocolate hair, his deep, brown eyes ...

My throat clogged with a lump and I sucked in breath after breath, but they were harder and harder to do, and not enough to fill my lungs. My heart raced, thundering down a track, and I felt those attempted deep breaths becoming short, sharp gasps.

One.

Breathe. Hold. Release.

Two.

Breathe. Hold. Release.

Three.

Breathe. Hold. Release.

The panic attacks weren't getting any less frequent, but I was becoming more adept at bringing myself back from the brink. I had to think about something else. Something that wasn't Lachlan. Something to consume my mind.

Lee. It was a surprisingly easy progression, easy enough to make me feel guilty. It was a plague, and it was rapidly infecting my body.

No, Kate. Focus.

Did he really kill his brother? I had to think. Think carefully, logically. I didn't really believe he'd taken to him with a knife, or anything like that. Maybe a car accident? Still, I had to do some research.

I had to Google.

I grabbed my laptop from my bag and booted it up, quickly double-checking the day's itinerary before typing in: Lee Collins murder.

Immediately, a page of site suggestions came up. The first five all detailed plots to assassinate Lee, and I bit my lip. Morbid curiosity got the better of me and I clicked through to one, then quickly headed back to the main search results page. Some people were just sick.

The rest of the suggestions were all relating to the attempted murder and stabbing of a solder in the UK, a David Lee Collins, and then disintegrated into a heap of other gruesome news stories featuring people with fragments of that name. Not once did anything about my Lee Collins's act of murder come up.

My Lee Collins? I shook my head. He wasn't mine to have. Even if it had felt nice, being cherished in his arms.

Even if for the first time in a long time, I'd felt safe.

Guilty.

I shut out my head, and focused on the task in front of me. Since the search turned up no results, I decided to try a different angle, and searched Lee Collins brother. This time I got a bunch of hits, but the first six pages were all focused on one of the earlier songs of the band, 'O Brother'. I shook my head. I was never going to find anything at this rate.

I flopped back against the bed and stared up at the ceiling. Who knew Lee, knew him well enough to work out if he had any scandal in his life? I could ask Michael, but then, would he be close enough to know the truth there?

I closed my eyes, letting the exhaustion that had so artfully escaped my grasp last night wash over me. My shoulders slumped and my breathing became steady as I drifted off into another time, another place, where everything was okay. Where deep brown eyes bored into mine. The scent of coffee, infiltrating my nose …

Seconds later my cell alarm went off, and I threw my hand over my face. Looked like it was time to hit the road once more.

"Are you in love with Mona yet?" Xander asked. One of his arms was wrapped around the strawberry-blonde chicky from last night, and he was leading her onto the tour bus.

"Hold it right there, buddy." I pretended to study my clipboard. "Nope. Nowhere here does it say anything about you bringing a plus-one on the bus this morning."

"Kate, don't be a drag." Xander pulled his sunnies down his nose so I could get the full effect of him rolling his eyes.

"Mona, I'm sorry, honey—"

"She's not Mona," Xander said. "The bus is named Mona, Kate. The bus." His expression was aghast, as if I'd just told him Santa wasn't real. "How can you seriously be entering almost your fourth week of tour and not even know the name of Sam's wheels?"

I looked up at the driver who was grinning back down at

me, his eyes crinkling in the corners. Xander nudged me in the shoulder, and I moved to face him, taking in his slightly devious expression. "Go on. Ask."

I let out a sigh, but did as requested and turned my attention back to Sam. "Why do you call her Mona?" I asked.

"Because when we go long-haul, all I hear is moaning." Sam gave a grin, then mouthed the word sorry at me as Xander burst into laughter, his little friend giggling as she clasped at his chest.

"We know how to make 'em moan," Xander managed between snorts.

"I feel like moaning right now," I muttered dryly. "Anyway, do you have to bring … her?" I looked at the girl. Big aviators covered her eyes, and she was wearing the same super short shorts and tiny tank she was in last night. Seriously, the girl was so thin I could make out individual ribs on her chest. Maybe I should let her on the bus. It wasn't like she'd affect our overall vehicle weight.

"Thanks, Kate, you're a champ." Xander took my question as permission and clapped me on the back as he walked up the stairs, dragging his toy along behind him. "We'll be in the bedroom if you need us."

"Didn't need to be said," I yelled back, looking down at my list. The bus was fully loaded, and we were ready to go. We were only missing one person. One kind of super-important person.

I clambered up the stairs back into the bus and started walking toward the end room.

"Can you believe him?" Lottie rolled her eyes in Xander's direction as I passed her. I shook my head and shrugged. It seemed an odd thing to be upset about, given the circumstances. I mean, he wasn't the one late on the bus. She didn't have a thing for Xander … did she?

Reaching the room, I covered my eyes and pulled open the door. "I do not want to see any nudity, but Xander, I need you for a sex."

Oh, shit. Did I really just …

"Sec! I meant a sec!"

Hips were thrust against mine, and the distinct scent of too-much-beer-and-cigarettes wafted up my nose. "Xander!" I pushed at him with my clipboard, still leaving one arm firmly covering my eyes.

"All you had to do was ask, baby." He laughed, and I humphed and stormed out of there.

"Meet me out the front of the bus ASAP," I yelled over my shoulder. "Dressed!"

I walked up the bus, past the sound guys who are all sharing a bit of a laugh at my expense.

"I didn't pick him as your type."

"Shut up, Michael." I cuffed him over the head as I walked past. At least the strippers weren't laughing at me. I guess that was a plus.

Xander met me out the front just seconds later, having left Strawberry-Blonde inside. "So, you wanna discuss the terms of our arrangement?" He flung a sweaty arm over my shoulder and I pushed him off again. There was a big grin on his face, and I knew he was gonna milk this for as long as he possibly could.

"Xander, have you seen Lee?" I folded my arms, pulling my clipboard close against my chest.

"Sure have. Tall guy, blue eyes the ladies go gaga over—" He used spirit fingers to emphasise his point, and I cut him off with my glare. "Seriously? Nah. Sam said you guys took him back to the room last night."

"We did." I looked up at Sam, but he was tapping away on his phone, oblivious to our conversation. "But I haven't … heard from him since."

I didn't want to tell Xander about our conversation this morning. If anyone knew the real story about Lee's apparent step over to the dark side, it was going to be Xander.

"Have you tried calling him?" Xan asked, and I shook my head.

"Not yet. I was planning on giving him another five, I just thought I'd check with you first."

"Oh. Well, what you worried about? He's probably just a bit hung-over, moving more slowly than usual." Xander shrugged and turned to hop back on the bus, but I grabbed his arm. He has these amazing, firm biceps, and I dropped my grip in surprise. It did make sense, I guessed. He was the drummer.

"Xan, do you think Lee would have ..." I paused, wondering how best to phrase it. "Done anything ... bad?"

"Bad?" Xan stepped closer to me, looking over his shoulder at the bus. No one watched when he continued. "What do you mean, bad?"

"Like ... I don't know, what if the reason he's late is because he's gotten in trouble with the law, or something? Would that be something he'd do?" I screwed up my nose. It might be a long shot, but I figured it was worth a try.

"Lee?" Xander's laugh echoed across the underground parking lot, and he all but grabbed his belly in mirth. "Darlin', Lee Collins is the straightest man I know. I don't know that he even jaywalks, let alone gets in trouble with the law."

"Oh, come on ..." I hedged, shuffling my feet. "I saw him last night, getting all drunk and letting that chick practically hump him in public. Surely he lets loose every now and then."

Xander smiled, shaking his head once again. "There's a difference between breaking the law and ... indulging our fans. Lee's not really the kinda guy to be serious about a girl, you know? Although he doesn't have one every week, or anything." He narrowed his eyes, paused. "You're not thinking that maybe—"

"No! God, no!" I held my hands up in protest. "Not even interested in him like that." At all. Really.

Was I?

I tried to mentally probe my insides, but the usual hurt and physical, sharp pain was still there when I thought of Lachlan. My heart belonged to him. There was no way I was falling for Lee. I couldn't feel for both of them ... could I?

"Ah, good. Trust me, he's not the serious relationship type." Something like trouble crossed Xander's brow, but he kept on speaking. "Anyway, there's no way Lee is in trouble with the law. Has he ever told you about that document they made us sign when we joined the band?"

I shook my head, no.

"We had to sign paperwork saying we weren't going to do anything crazy scandalous, you know? Like, no getting arrested, no illegal shit, no drugs …" A wistful look washed over his face, and he ran his hand through his hair. "And that's why I think we've gone so well. Tony's a smart man; he protected us from ruining ourselves early on. Because God knows, if I thought I could have this and the kinky-arse sex, the drugs some of the other guys do …" He laughed, but there was no mirth to it.

My mind ticked over, working at a million miles per hour. So Lee had to sign an agreement saying he'd keep out of trouble with the law. Maybe that was why I couldn't find anything about him killing his brother on the Internet. Maybe whatever accident it was had happened before he was famous, and now he was straighty-one-eighty, and determined to hush it up. It was as if all the pieces of the puzzle were falling into place, bar two things: the actual killing and the brother.

"Xander, this is going to seem random, but …" Here goes nothing, "… does Lee have any siblings? A brother?"

Xander's forehead creased, then sprang back to neutral, a clean slate. "Ha! Who told you that?"

"Oh … I just was wondering …" I trailed off, unsure how to support my story without saying 'Well, Lee told me when he was drunk, but then he denied it.'

"Nah, man. Not Lee. I'm the closest thing to a brother he has." And with that, the topic was closed. "You should ring him, anyway. See where he is."

He turned and walked back toward the bus, and I was left standing there by myself, no wiser as to whether Lee had a sibling or not.

I was dialling his number when he came jogging up to the bus, backpack slung over his shoulder, sweat beaded on his forehead.

"You … okay?" I asked. His eyes were red, and he looked

tense, as if someone was holding up his shoulders and hanging him out to dry.

"Fine," he snapped, widening his eyes. He barged toward the bus, his strong hands hoisting him up the stairs and inside, and I couldn't help but to look at them. Staring. Those large, strong palms. Those long, lean fingers.

Could they be capable of murder?

I shook my head. No. They couldn't. I'd entertained the idea for a morning, but Lee-freaking-Collins just didn't seem the bad boy type. But I still knew he was hiding something.

And somehow, that hurt worse.

I banished the pain; I bottled it up. I couldn't think about Lee as being someone who hurt me. That was as good as admitting that I was moving on.

And I owed Lachlan more than that.

FOUTEEN

LEE

Four years, six months ago ...

"BROTHER." RYAN clapped me on the back, and I stood to give him one of those awkward bro-hugs.

"How you doing?" I asked. We'd caught up four or five times now, aided by Ryan's travels in his quest to find a job, and each time was better than the last. Ryan was actually a good guy. I sensed he'd had a hard life; hell, I knew he had. But he was making a serious go of things regardless, and seemed determined to focus on the future.

At least, when he wasn't dwelling on the past.

"Your shout, Lee?" Ryan grinned. "You know, being the one who got the parents and all."

I forced a grin. It wasn't the first time he'd made that joke, and it wasn't the first time I'd flinched when he had.

"Of course, buddy." I gave him a gentle slap on the back and ordered us some beers, which we then took over to a table in the corner by the window.

"How ya been?" Ryan asked as we sat across from each other.

"Good, man, good. Busy." I frowned. And I was. I'd kinda thought things would be easy once we were signed, but somehow I was working harder than I'd ever worked before. "We finish touring in a month or so, and then we'll start work on album number two."

"You should write a song about me," Ryan joked, and I laughed.

"Yeah, I'd call it 'O Brother'—a song about a guy named Ryan who never buys the beers." We both laughed, and any tension from his comment earlier on was soon forgotten.

"What about you? How's things?" I asked, when we'd settled down.

"Real good. I just got put forward as one of three potential candidates for this massive construction job. If I get it …" He shook his head. "I think this could be it, bro. This could be my ticket out."

"Awesome." I smiled. Ryan had been living in a trailer park while he got his life sorted. Having financial security would mean a lot to him. "And how's your girl?"

Ryan paused, pursed his lips. "She's good, man. Distant. She'll be better when I can offer her security, you know? Just … I'm giving her some space."

"Cool." I nodded. "Sounds like you got it all sorted."

It looked as if his whole life was taking a turn for the better. I just hoped I wasn't about to make it worse.

"There's something I gotta tell you." I looked out the window. Across the street, there was a coffee shop. Tables and chairs spilled onto the sidewalk, and littered it with caffeine-loving patrons.

"Go on." Ryan quirked an eyebrow suspiciously.

"The choice is entirely yours, but …" Here goes nothing. "See that café over there?"

Ryan craned his neck and looked through the window. "Yeah."

"There's a couple, middle-aged, sitting to the left. She's in a pink sweater, and he's in jeans and a shirt?"

Ryan studied the scene for a moment and then replied.

"Yeah."

"They're … they're our parents."

Ryan jerked his head back, shook it slowly and then picked up his beer and drained it all in one go. "Shit," he breathed when he'd finished. "You don't think you coulda maybe sprung that on me a little softer?"

"Sorry," I said, still studying him anxiously. "I didn't know how to do it. I know you're not particularly keen on them, but they want to meet you. It's so important to them, and I thought this would be a good opportunity for you to at least put faces to the names, and all that."

"Oh, I wanna meet 'em all right." Ryan's face darkened and he pushed to his feet.

"Ryan, I—" But he'd already started to storm out of the bar, and I raced after him. Shit, I knew this was a bad idea. What if he tried to hurt them? Dad was still a little fragile, and—

"So you're Mr and Mrs Collins, huh?" Ryan folded his arms, towering over my parents. Mom's lower lips trembled, and Dad carefully placed his coffee cup down.

"Ryan." Mom's eyes glossed over and she gave a small smile, the smile of the heartbroken.

Something in that must have broken Ryan, broken some rage within him, because instead of launching into a tirade, which I half-expected him to do, he ran his hands through his long hair and puffed out a long breath.

"Mind if I sit down?"

It was my turn to be relieved. I didn't expect us to suddenly morph into one big happy family; these things took time, and I was more than willing to wait. But at least we were taking the steps.

They were the first baby steps Mom and Dad had ever seen Ryan make.

Present day ...

Dear Lee,

Spill it.

Kate

I was once a hopeless romantic. I believed in love at first sight, in 'the one', in true love conquering all. Now, I knew better. Now, I knew that the one for me would always be the one available right now, and it had never been clearer to me than it was this morning when Kate stood there, asking me about my brother.

Because that was what they did, you see. They tricked you, they lured you in with their looks and then you told them something you shouldn't—something nobody should know.

And instead of brushing it off, letting it go? They harboured that thought. They let it fester and grow, and waited to use it against you.

Oh, she hadn't yet. But she would. I know she would. Everybody else had.

We spent six long hours on the bus, making our way out to Vegas for a few gigs and some media commitments. The atmosphere during the trip was party, with Xander and his chick letting loose the odd giggle in the back and the sound guys convincing some of the strippers to let them do body shots. Everyone was having a blast. Except for me.

Well, not quite everyone. Kate was staring out the window, and while she hadn't wrapped a curtain around her partition, she may as well have.

I didn't know what to do, how to act. The screwed up thing was, I felt betrayed. I know; I was the dickhead who'd told her the truth. But still, she was acting weird, and I think that deep down, even though I knew it could not, would not ever work between us, perhaps I'd harboured a secret hope that I could get close to her. That I could kiss those sweet lips, make love to her bangin' body—

Fuck! Quit it with the making love already.

I mentally berated myself, and shook my head. I still couldn't believe I'd used the 'c' word on her. She deserved better than that. She was a good person. A good person who I was still weirdly attracted to. And who I needed to make up to for the harsh words I'd said this morning.

Why am I doing this?

I didn't have an answer. All I could think of was her face, the sun shining against it, as we talked about filling silent spaces. And how I wanted to not feel the pressure to fill silent moments with her.

I sent off a quick text to Benny, asking him for a favour that started with the world's most creepy question.

Me: Mate, can you do me a solid? I need to somehow find out what size shoes Kate wears.

Dear Kate,

Nothing to spill. I had too much to drink. I'm sorry I was a dick to you this morning, too. That won't happen again. What I said about my brother? It wasn't real. It was a lie. Sometimes, I feel as if my life is filled with half-

truths. I mean, they say I'm the lead singer of this hugely successful band, right? But how successful am I when my father is in a home and my mother and I haven't spoken in a year?

Sorry to burden you with this. I just feel ... I feel like you get it.

Like you get me.

Lee

Dear Lee,

Call your mum.

Kate

PS I know it's not that simple. I know that things rarely are, and I'm sure that if it was, you'd have done it already. I don't know though, from things I've heard the guys say ... I wonder if you're even trying to be happy? Or are you punishing yourself for some imaginary sin?

"Kate was asking if you had a brother." The words shouldn't have surprised me, but they did. It meant she didn't buy my brush-off, and worse—it meant she was trying to find out more.

"Yeah?" I took a swig of my beer and leaned back in the spa Xander and I were relaxing in on the balcony of my private suite. We were both wearing board shorts, I should add. There was nothing man-love about this.

"Yeah. Wanted to know if you had one." Xander took a pull of his beer, looking out and studying the strip, the lights beginning to flick on and shine against the slowly pinkening sky.

"What'd you say?" I studied Xander, my oldest friend. Fuck, probably my only friend.

"What do you think?" The look he gave me was deadpan, and loaded with weight. "But dude … you know she shouldn't be asking me that."

I nodded, way too quickly. "I know, bro." A sigh escaped my lips. "I know."

"After last night, how are things with you and—"

"Fine," I barked. "She's not heaps impressed, but things could be worse."

"At least you didn't go home with that slut—"

"Don't." My voice was fierce, and Xander cringed. I didn't blame him; I never snapped. I was on edge today. I was tired, and I was angry, and I sure as shit didn't have time to deal with his personal questions. Questions I didn't even really know the answer to myself.

"I'm getting a beer," Xander muttered, and he stood up,

water dripping from his body as he headed over to the mini bar fridge.

I leaned over and checked my phone for the tenth time today. Benny had said he'd had trouble sneaking into her room to find out her shoe size, and I needed a progress report. Luckily, this was Vegas. Even if he didn't find out till ten o'clock at night, I'd still be able to go out and get some.

The screen was blank, and I leaned back against the spa edge and sighed, trying to relax my muscles. Things were a little rough now, but they'd be fine. They'd get better. I was going to be a friend to Kate, by only doing friendly activities with her. No more shirts-off stuff. No more coming home from a club with her, even if I didn't consciously choose to do so. And then hopefully, she'd forget what I'd told her and wouldn't ask any more questions. Questions were dangerous.

Questions I couldn't afford.

"So Kate took you back to your room, huh?" Xander asked, his head in the mini bar.

"Yep."

"Anything …?"

I sighed. "No." The spa bubbled away and I adjusted my back, the pressure from the jet shooting into it and loosening my sore as shit muscles from sleeping on the goddamn couch. "And besides … you know I couldn't be with her, anyway."

"She's a pretty special girl, Lee." Xander stood and looked me in the eye. "I've seen the way you look at her. I know that—"

"Knock, knock." Kate barged into the room, despite her vocal knocking. I glanced at Xander, but he'd clamped his mouth shut, and Kate wasn't acting as if anything were amiss. She was all cheerful and businesslike again, as she usually was. No longer was she wearing that depressed-looking face she'd had on this morning.

"Kate." Xander gave her a nod. "Wanna beer?"

"I'm good, thanks." She shook her head, and Xander walked up to her and handed her a soda anyway.

"You wanna come for a swim?" He jerked his head toward the spa.

"I don't have anything to wear." Kate smiled and looked at her feet. I shook my head. She walked right into that one.

"That's okay, babe," Xander husked, placing one wet arm around her shoulders. Droplets of water stained the pale blue of Kate's top. I studied the water bubbling in front of me. "You can go naked."

"Get off." Kate shrugged Xander away from herself, dusting the drops from her shoulders, and then further made life trickier for herself by uttering those four, far-from-innocent words. "You're getting me wet."

"What can I say?" Xander gave her a lascivious wink. "I'm just that kinda guy."

Kate's face contorted in rage, and a tiny, little piece of me twisted. She was so freaking cute …

Get it together, Lee. I had to get out of there.

"And on that note, I think I'm gonna go to the bar." I stood up from the spa and grabbed the towel sitting behind me, wiping my face and chest down before I stepped out of the pool. "Leave you two lovebirds to it."

I grabbed a shirt and my phone and walked toward the door, stopping only when Kate thrust an envelope into my hands. "I actually came here to give you this."

It was plain white, A5 in size, and had my name scrawled across the front in a messy handwriting. But it wasn't her handwriting. "Who's it from?"

Kate gave a small shake of her head. "I don't know. Doesn't say."

"Thanks," I mumbled. I stepped out into the hallway, leaving Kate and Xander still in the room, only to run into Lottie. Seriously? Can this day get any better?

"How are you?" Lottie placed a concerned hand on my arm. "You had a big one."

"Yeah. I didn't … I went home with Kate. And she left me on the couch. Alone." I pressed my eyes closed. Lottie stood close to me, too close, and I freaking wished she wouldn't do that. "Look, I gotta …" I waved the envelope and started walking farther down the hall, leaving her standing there with a bewildered expression on her face.

As soon as I was a safe enough distance away, I tore at the paper and pulled out the contents. A sick feeling gnawed at the insides of my belly, ate away at me, and I knew before I read the letter that it wasn't going to be good. Letters from unidentified senders never were.

It was a photo, a big, full-colour photo of Kate and me. It must have been taken the night before at the club, because I didn't remember seeing that nook near the lift, and I sure as shit didn't remember rubbing my face in Kate's boobs. There were three pictures all together, a sequence shot that made it very clear that it was indeed me with Kate, and each one looked more incriminating than the last. In one, it almost looked like she was holding my head there, pressing me against herself, while I knew she was in reality probably making sure I didn't spew on her perfectly formed tits, I couldn't help but give a small smile.

Then I found the note.

> This goes to the hottest gossip mags in town if you don't bring me 10 grand. Carry it with you at the press conference in three days' time. Wait for my further instruction.

Blood boiled up through my veins, its fiery tendrils licking at my soul. The air was burst from my lungs and I span, slamming my fist into the wall next to me. My knuckles cracked on impact, and chips of paint flickered down to the ground. It stung, but not enough to counterbalance the raw knife of pain slicing through me. How dare they? God, the media harassing me was one thing, but I couldn't have Kate implicated in this too.

"Fuck," I whispered, and pressed my forehead to the wall. I was hung-over, fighting an attraction to the girl I couldn't have, and now this. What the hell was I going to do?

Some moments were so low you thought they couldn't get any worse. When everything had reached its depth of depravity, or horror, of downright nasty and that the only way was up, my friends, because how could you sink any deeper than hell?

I looked up. Down the hall I saw Lottie, shaking her head at me as she walked into her room, an expression of disappointment on her face.

Then I saw Kate. Her skin was pale and there was a look of fear in her eyes that was so very real, I could almost touch it. I'd scared the living fuck out of the only person I'd told the truth to.

I'd killed my brother.

I did the only thing I could.

I punched the damn wall again.

FIFTEEN

KATE

"Here? Again?' I looked into his eyes, and they were warm and full of mirth. The sunset dappled a warm glow through the trees, lighting up his gorgeous face, highlighting those amazing dimples.

"Well, it went pretty well the first time …" Lachlan smiled, and I pressed my lips together. The first time, when we'd swum together, naked. This time, though, I hoped we'd be doing a lot more than swimming.

"So … skinny dipping?" I asked, with way too much hope in my voice.

Lachlan laughed and wrapped his arms around me, pulling me close to him. He smelt like coffee, that familiar, comforting smell, and I melted into his embrace. This was where I should be. This was where I belonged. "Whatever you want, beautiful."

I bit my lip, looking around the clearing. The trees cast long shadows behind them, and the birds sung sweet melodies of summer in the trees. The water made soft rushing sounds as it whispered against the rocks, and I knew. This was the time I was going to do it. This was the place where I'd lose my virginity.

I reached my hands behind my head and grabbed the ties of my sundress. I pulled, and suddenly my dress was billowing to my feet, and I was standing before the man I loved, absolutely naked.

There was no more mirth in Lachlan's eyes. Now there was just desire, pure, raw and wanton lust. "Kate …" He swallowed, and his Adam's apple bobbed as he took one hesitant step toward me, his feet shuffling through the rotten leaves underfoot.

Instead of feeling naked and vulnerable under his gaze, I felt free, sexy and like I could do anything, be anyone I wanted to be. I kicked off my flip-flops and skipped toward the pool, diving into the turquoise water.

The water was fresh, refreshing me, reminding me of every cell in my body as it caressed me while I swam. I surfaced, the pull of my wet hair slowing my descent, but when I turned to the shore, Lachlan was gone. Doubt gripped me only for a millisecond before he surfaced in front of me, still completely dressed. "I couldn't not follow … as soon as I could."

I laughed, tugging at his T-shirt, and he pulled up his arms, letting me lift it over his head. "So eager to be with me naked, huh?" I teased as I balled up his shirt and threw it to the shore.

Something dark and dangerous flashed in Lachlan's eyes. "Kate, I've wanted to be with you naked since the very first time we met."

My heart stopped—it stuck in my chest—then it pumped back to life, beating like a bullet train at full steam. I licked my lips and wrapped my arms around the neck of the man I loved. His skin was cool, and my hands slid over it as if he were oiled up. His eyes darted down to my chest, and I realised my movement had raised me just that little bit out of the water, the tops of my nipples dancing on the water line.

As soon as I saw him watching, they hardened, and I bit my lip and pressed myself against him, almost embarrassed that he could see just what he did to me.

He cupped my face with his hand, lifting my chin up so my gaze met his. Only what I saw in his eyes left no room for doubt about what my desire did to him. What I saw there was pure sex.

Our hungry lips met and parted, and our tongues danced together, tender, desperate, everything and nothing all at once. Lachlan's hands teased my body, skating up my back and then dancing down my sides, his fingers inching toward my breasts. I wrapped my legs around his waist and broke the kiss for one quick moment to undo his shorts, which he promptly kicked off. They might sink; they might float away. It didn't matter, because all that mattered was the here, and the now, and the slide of his bare skin moving against mine.

I locked my ankles behind his back once more and I felt him against me. Heat pooled between my legs, and I ached for him. I needed him, like no need I'd ever known. It was all consuming, leaving me gasping for air as we kissed, as our lips continued to press against each other.

Only now, it really was getting harder to breathe. His lips did consume mine, leaving me with little time to catch my breath. My lungs started with a gentle ache that soon progressed to a needy pain, pushing me to the point of breaking. If I didn't take a breath, I was going to die. I am going to die.

I had to stop.

I pushed away from Lachlan's chest and sucked in a desperate breath of air, the oxygen hurting as I forced it down into my lungs. I opened my eyes, and looked up.

There was no one there.

I looked left to right, searching for Lachlan. Maybe he'd ducked under the water again, playing, as he did before. Or maybe he was … maybe he was …

Where was he?

"Lachlan?" I spun around, treading water, my eyes

searching the shoreline for him. The sunlight wasn't dappled anymore. The trees were all about shadows, sinister, and the birds didn't chirp. It was silent.

"Lachlan!" My cry was desperate, loud—afraid.

I took one last look at the area where we'd entered the pool. Lachlan's board shorts had made their way to land and were resting upon the shore, the tide of the water pulling and releasing them with its breath.

Floating in the water, two metres from the shore, was a skull. And I knew without question that it was his.

"Ah!" I shot upright in bed, gasping, clutching at my shirt that was stuck to my chest, my sides, my arms. My pulse raced and my heart beat with such force that it hurt as I tried to slow my breathing, to calm myself down. I was … I was having a panic attack. Shit, I dreamt Lachlan was … and I … shit!

All of a sudden I was drowning, caught in a wave of my grief. Just when I was starting to breathe again …

On shaky legs, I made my way to the bathroom as fast as I could and turned the faucet on full bore, then hunched over the sink, splashing icy-cold water against my face with one hand. It didn't make the heat go away. It didn't stop the burn in my chest.

I sculled some water and it stabbed me on the way down, my big gulps too much for my oxygen-deprived body to handle. Then, with wavering knees, I sat down on the lid of the toilet. What a horrible, horrible dream. I'd dreamt he was …

That was when it hit me.

"Lachlan …" My voice trembled, and tears welled in my eyes. For all it was imagined, the dream was real. He really is dead.

Tears flowed from my eyes, and I wished for the thousandth time that things hadn't happened the way they did. I had wanted to be your forever. "It's … not … fair …" I hiccupped the words out, sobs now wrenching themselves from my chest with a sharp gasping effect.

Now, he was like he'd been in my dream. He was nothing but a skull, a pile of bones. Or maybe he was more, somewhere out there in the universe, but what hope was there of that? How do you know? How do you ever know?

The idea of him being nothing—of not existing—it was just too much for me. Just. Too. Much.

But the worst part? The bit that stung even worse?

His voice was getting harder to remember.

The edges of his face were blurry.

I was killing his memory without even meaning to.

An hour later, I dragged myself back to bed. My hair was clammy and my body still damp as I pulled the sheets up on top of me. Despite the air conditioning and winter temperatures, I was sweltering in the Vegas heat. Or maybe it was the heat of hell. Sometimes, I didn't know which would be worse.

I didn't sleep. I was too afraid to. Every time I closed my eyes, I worried that I'd see him again, and some days that thought was more than I could take. How could someone I knew for a relatively short period of time have made such an impact on my life? Such a monumental difference?

Sometime after four I forced my eyes to close, and my body to lie still. I pressed my index and middle finger to my lips, kissed them, and then pressed them against the photo in my wallet, the one I slept next to without fail. "I won't let you go."

Rapid pounding on my door woke me up, and I didn't know who the hell it was, but I did know that I wanted to murder them.

Ugh. I stomped over to the door and opened it just a little, a tiny crack, to squint my puffy eyes open and see Lee-freaking-Collins standing there, a big-arse grin on his face and a gift-wrapped box in his hand.

"Morning." Lee smiled and went to push the door open, but I held it firmly in place, all too aware of the fact I was only wearing a T-shirt. And my legs were not something he needed to see.

"We don't have to be up for another …" I checked the wall clock. Six thirty. The last time I remembered looking at the clock last night was somewhere around four, as I tossed and turned for the zillionth time. What the hell was Lee doing at my door at six thirty? "… four hours."

"We don't have to, no." Lee agreed. "But I got you a present." He wiggled the box again, and I gave a half-hearted smile. What was he playing at?

"Give me a sec." I closed the door and quickly threw on some shorts, then ran a brush through my hair. I had to hide the evidence of my grief. I couldn't handle it being on full display.

"Okay." I opened the door and Lee all but skipped into the hotel room, looking around the space. He spun, and turned to me. His eyes seemed to take in my dishevelled appearance, but as if he thought better of saying something, he shook his head and sat on the edge of my bed, patting a spot next to him for me to join him.

"Come here," he said.

"I think I'd rather stand." I frowned. I was already starting to forget Lachlan, and Lee was just too close. I didn't think adding a bed to the mix would be the best idea.

"Fine." Lee shrugged and held out the box, again wiggling it, with a twinkle in his eye. "Open it," he sang.

I stepped forward and took the box from his hand, a quizzical smile on my face. "It's not my birthday."

"I know," Lee said. "I checked your file. August twenty."

"Wow." He'd memorised my birthday? "I'm impressed."

"Open, open," he sang, giving a tiny bounce as if he were a little kid.

I ripped open the paper and let it fall to the floor, then I opened the bright orange box. Inside was a pair of Nike runners, some gorgeous, black-with-hot-pink-detailing, seriously kick-arse Nike runners.

"Lee." I held one up. It was even my size. How the hell did he know my shoe size? Was that in my employment file too? "Thank you so much! You didn't have to do that."

"Do you like them? Because, um, if you don't, I have another pair in a different colour scheme in my room. I wasn't sure which you'd prefer." He chewed his lip, and for a moment he was just a boy, and I was just a girl, and there was no Lachlan, no murder, no rock star, nothing. It was just us.

And we fit.

"These are perfect." I clutched them to my chest, then spontaneously closed the gap between us and kissed him on the cheek. His stubble brushed my lips, and he smelt like mint, and like pine. God, how did one man smell so good? "Thank you," I breathed, slowly pulling away.

Guilt immediately staked me in the heart, and I tried my best to pretend I wasn't betraying Lachlan. It was a hug. That was all.

Lee stiffened, then gave a small smile. It seemed he hadn't missed my internal punishment. "Good. So, put 'em on."

"Now?" I furrowed my brow.

"Yep. We're going running." Lee gestured down to his own outfit, and it was only then I twigged that he was wearing black trainers with some casual shorts and a T-shirt. "You said you liked to run; that it helped you through things. And after you were upset the other night, I thought maybe you could use some thinking time. You look like you could use some thinking time."

"You can't go for a run. You'll get mobbed!" I laughed.

"We're taking Benny. And besides, it's Vegas. No one exercises here, or leaves the casino. It's too damn hot."

"So why are we doing it again?" I quizzed, a smile on my face.

"Kate, I really want to help you." Lee stood up, and for a terrifying moment I thought he was going to reach for my hand, and then in a reality that was equally as terrifying as it was relieving, I realised he wasn't. "You're important to me. As a friend."

In such a short time, Lee had hugged me, confided in me, pushed me away, and then pulled me back into this weird almost formal role. Friend. It was one little word, but it held so much weight. Weight I shouldn't have let sit on my shoulders when a greater burden, the heaviness of memory, already sat there.

And I didn't know that I could keep carrying it.

Fifteen minutes later I met Lee and Benny in the casino downstairs. Benny was dressed in a basketball singlet and some shorts, shooting Lee murderous looks. "This is the worst bloody idea …"

"Come on, Benny. It's for Kate." Lee laughed.

"Hey, don't go pinning this on me," I grumbled. I still felt like death warmed up from my severe lack of sleep, but in some ways, that made me want to run more. Maybe, if I was physically tired as well as emotionally, I could finally get some rest. Maybe.

We walked out of the casino into the dry Vegas heat, and instantly I started to wonder if this was such a good idea.

"Well this was an early wake-up call," Sam said, and opened the door to a hire car.

"I thought we were going for a jog?" I quizzed Lee.

"We are." He hopped in the car and waited for me to join him. "But we're doing it somewhere pretty."

Sam steered the car out of the city, an easy feat with the minimal early-morning traffic, until we reached a sign that read Red Rock Canyon National Conservation Area. Soon after, Sam parked the car and we got out.

I looked around, breathing in the clean, fresh air, and smiled. In the distance, great red rocks poked out of the ground like oversized boulders, not too dissimilar to something you'd find in outback Australia. Long grass was scattered around the dirt walking-trail, and birds flew low overhead in the distance. It was arid, it was fierce, and it was intensely beautiful.

"Wow," I breathed, taking it all in.

"Is this a good enough place to clear your head?" Lee asked, and I smiled. It was perfect.

We set off at an easy pace, Lee checking in with me every few steps to make sure I was keeping up okay. Soon he stopped asking and we just ran, the casual breeze whipping my hair this way and that, the heat of the sun causing sweat to bead down my forehead.

Thoughts swirled in my head and I tried to pin them down, sort them out. Lachlan was still ever-present in my mind, but the specifics—the exact colour of his eyes, the specific timbre of his voice as he spoke my name … they were getting harder and harder to pinpoint in my brain. And I hated myself for it.

And then there was Lee. And I had these feelings for him. These growing, murky feelings that I didn't want to have. Feelings that churned in my stomach when he did stupid things, like showing up early in the morning to gift me a new pair of trainers.

No. Think of Lachlan. Lachlan's drawing of my lips, the streetlight shining down on them. The art, the care that had gone into sketching each little line …

Stab.

Lee. Caressing my neck, rubbing it, his skin on my skin, awakening feelings that had long lain dormant.

Lachlan. Making out on the couch, his hands exploring, caressing my body as we both innocently explored each other.

Stab.

I loved Lachlan.

But Lee was a good guy. He cared about me, about my family. He was funny, with the little pranks he'd played back when I'd first started in the job. He was deep, showing me another side of him in the letters we swapped on a regular basis. He was sweet—how did he even remember that I'd said I liked to run when it all got too much, let alone figure out my shoe size and buy me a present?

And why had it jarred when he'd called me his friend?

I studied him, jogging a few paces ahead of me. His toned, brown legs looked good pounding the red dirt beneath them, leading up to his toned, muscly—

Stop checking out his arse, Kate.

I puffed out a breath of air. Why couldn't things in life be easy?

We kept running until my shirt was drenched in sweat,

my hair sticking to my head. My breath was coming faster, in small short bursts, and I was fairly sure we'd lost Benny some way back. I was no closer to working out Lee's deep, dark secrets, but I felt like I had a solution for my feelings, for my emotions.

"Turn back?" Lee puffed, his head over his shoulder.

"Yeah," I agreed, spinning around and heading for the car.

It was simple. That was what I needed to do. I'd turn back. Focus on what was important.

Because what was important to me? What was most important? It was remembering Lachlan. Honouring his memory.

I had to do that.

Dear Kate,

I looked under my hotel door. On my seat in the bus. I even checked my guitar case, but no new letter from you. Is this thing done? Are you moving to the digital age? Should I be checking my email instead?

Seriously, I just wanted to make sure I haven't overstepped the mark with the whole 'running' thing. I know we're doing it every day, but don't for a second think this is about you. I'm

a really good-looking guy.
I need to keep my body in
shape. It's important. As
is my paleo diet, my lack
of drinking, my morning
meditation and prayer
sessions, and ...
No, seriously. I just like
spending time, thinking
of nothing and sweating.
Getting all the shit in
my head out, whether
through exertion or the
physical act of pounding
the pavement.
And I like doing that with
you.
I like being together,
alone, with you.

Lee

I was quiet. My head was spinning. It was two days later and I was sitting in yet another hotel lobby, waiting for the boys to come out of their interview while scrolling through my phone, trying to pretend that status updates like 'Nom nom nom' and 'I'm super passive-aggressively picking on you' were worth caring about.

My heart wasn't in it.

My heart was at the lake.

My heart was six-foot under.

Despite being woken daily by Lee at the door of my room, despite three mammoth runs through the national park, I still wasn't able to sleep. The hurt was just too real. It lingered in my bloodstream, eating away at my body. Not only that, but right now, my body ached from all the exercise and I needed to sit down. I figured the boys would be all right to make it from the interview room back to the lobby unsupervised, just this once. Yes, I had officially reached non-caring.

Lee, though? Lee had been nothing but caring. Every morning he'd knock, and every morning we'd run, without a word, alone but together. Separate, yet as one.

If Lachlan were alive, would I even know Lee like this at all?

I shook my head, trying to rush the morbid thought away, but it just wouldn't quit. Apparently it liked harbouring its depression within my soul; it was comfortable there. Hurt loved to hide—sneak up on you like an uninvited guest when you least expected it.

And I never sent out a damn invitation.

"Mind if I join you?" Lottie had already sat next to me before she'd finished the sentence. She scooched up close to my side on the red leather couch, placing her handbag at her designer shoe-clad feet.

"Not at all." I smiled.

"Katie!" Jay squealed, and he lifted his arms and dove across my lap, sending my phone and ever-present clipboard flying.

"Jay!" Lottie scolded, but I shook my head.

"It's fine, truly," I said, wrapping my arms around the little bundle of energy and giving him a few tickles. He squirmed under my touch, laughing with this innocence and excitement that had my stupid emotions ready to burst all over again.

"Ever since we started on tour, he sure has come out of his shell." Lottie ruffled his hair.

"How long have you been on the road for?" I furrowed my brow.

"About a month, then we had a break while the boys went

back to Oz, and then this leg now. So not that long, really." Lottie stared out the window, a troubled glaze over her eyes.

"What'd you do before this?" I tilted my head to the side as Jay wrapped his arms around my neck. "Work in styling, or more some high-end fashion stuff …?"

"Ha!" Lottie snorted. "Did Lee tell you that?"

"No."

"Well, he kinda owes me right now, so I thought …" She pursed her lips together, and looked down for a second. "Sorry. I've got to let it go. Before this, I was a dancer."

"Wow! How cool. Like, with a band, or ballet, or—"

"A stripper, Kate. I was a stripper."

Oh. My eyes widened and I felt flustered, searching for something to say. "I'm … sorry."

"Don't be." Lottie gave a short, bitter laugh. "When your parents cut you off, and you're raising a kid, you have to do whatever you can to get by."

I blinked. It really put it all in perspective. I was grieving, yes, but Lottie had struggled, struggled for years by the sound of it, just to survive.

Sometimes, you know the facts. You understand that people are doing it worse than you, way worse. They're suffering, they're bleeding, and they're dying out there.

But you still can't stop your own ache.

And that makes you feel like a selfish bitch.

"Are you okay?" Lottie placed her hand on my shoulder as I blinked back a tear. God, I hated crying. You did it once in the morning, and it was like there was a pressurised tap ready to leak inside you for the rest of the day.

"Fine." I sniffled, and gave her my best smile. See? Totally fine.

"Jay, let's play hide and seek. Mommy will come find you in a minute." Lottie covered her eyes with her hands and Jay shot me a sparkly-eyed look before running to the other side of the couch and placing a cushion over his head. It was adorable; his two little chubby legs wiggled out over the couch's edge, visible for the whole world to see.

"Talk to me." Lottie grabbed one of my hands and clasped it with hers, running her fingers over mine.

I looked into her open, honest eyes, and I wanted to hold back—I really did—but sometimes, holding all the pain on your own got too much. And being on the road with a group of forty-odd people was one of the loneliest things I'd ever done.

"I … my boyfriend died," I whispered. It was the only way I could think of to explain.

Less than a second later, Lottie's arms were around my own, and she pulled me tight against her slight frame. "Hon … Stacey did mention. I'm so, so sorry."

"It's … okay." Of course, those treacherous tears had started to fall, but at least they left their ugly, wracking chest-coughing friends at home. "Well … actually, it's not."

Now those suckers came through, and I did those ugly-cry hiccups of full-blown pain, even though I tried to stifle them down. It was just so hard not to think about why, and to wonder when it would stop hurting—because I didn't know if I could survive much longer.

I pulled away, and Lottie's forehead creased in a frown. "Do you mind if I ask how?" Even her eyes had the sheen of unshed tears over them.

I shook my head. "Motorcycle accident."

Lottie smoothed her features and reached out to wipe some of the tears from under my eyes. "Oh, lovely Kate."

I bit my lip. "He … he was amazing. An artist; an old soul kind of guy, you know?"

Lottie nodded encouragingly. "I know."

"He'd had such a hard time in life; his parents passed away when he was younger, and he'd had cancer …" I swallowed the lump that emerged in my throat. "But he was a good guy, you know? He showed me … how to appreciate being in the moment. How to really live."

We sat in silence for a few moments, punctuated only by the sounds of heels clicking through the hotel lobby, a low thrum of voices checking in and checking out.

I sucked in a deep breath. "The worst part it ... I'm starting to forget. And that hurts, hurts so, so much."

Stab.

Right in my heart.

Lottie pulled back a moment, her hands clasped firmly in her lap. She pursed her lips, as if making a decision, then opened her mouth. "Do you mind if I ask you something pretty candid?"

"No."

"Do you think you're honouring his memory by holding onto the past?"

The words hit me like a slap in the face. "I ... what are you talking about?" I spat, but the anger didn't boil in my blood like I wanted it to. "I am ... I'm hurting, okay? How can I ...? Just, don't. You're wrong."

We sat in silence for a while, Lottie looking at me, me thinking about Lachlan, Jay hiding under a pillow. We were possibly the least rock 'n' roll trio ever to tour with a band.

"Mommy ... are you still finding me?"

I smirked, and Lottie gave me a wry smile. She danced around the chairs for a few moments, pretending to look under all the cushions, inside pot plants, and even in my handbag, while I played along and offered her 'places' to look. Finally, she saw Jay and gave him a full-body tickle, resulting in the sort of giggles that stick in your heart. They sucked their way into your soul.

After his mirth dissipated, Jay locked his ocean-coloured eyes with Lottie's. "I need to wee," he whispered, his eyes wide. I couldn't help but give a short giggle again. The kid had cute pouring off him by the kilo.

Lottie took Jay's hand and I picked up my phone and bag, walking with them to the corridor that led to the hotel restrooms. "Want me to hold that?" I gestured to Lottie's handbag and she smiled, holding it out to me.

"About before ..." She trailed off, biting her lip.

"It's nothing." It's everything. "I know you meant well." But how can I let just let him go?

She walked down the corridor and led Jay into the women's restroom, and I spent a few minutes contemplating when, as a single mum, you let your little boy pee in the men's room alone.

But my brain kept turning back. Turning back to the inevitable. My thoughts churned around at a million miles an hour, but the overriding one, the one that shouted, kicked, screamed, and pulled at my hair, was hard to ignore.

It was asking what if she's right?

I leaned back against the wall and faced the foyer, but a raised voice pulled my attention back to the hallway. It was because I knew that voice.

Lee.

"We had a deal."

I froze, unsure if I should stick my head around the corner to see who he was delivering those venom-filled words to, or if I should stay right where I was.

I pursed my lips and tried as hard as I could to decipher the mumbled words by another man in the distance.

"What did you just say?" Lee's voice was heated, and even though I was so curious as to what he was talking about, I couldn't help but thinking keep it down, idiot. If any of the press here at the junket upstairs got wind of this, it'd be Scandal City.

I leaned as close as I could to the corridor without actually looking in, desperate to hear the other man's response.

"Excuse me, Miss, can I help you?"

I cursed as a staff member of the Grand Sawain Casino gave me a curt bow, his maroon-coloured top hat wobbling dangerously when he moved. "I'm fine, thanks."

"Are you sure? Because we offer a guest service centre with free Internet, coffee and tea, twenty-four hours a day, seven days a week. And added to that—"

"Fuck off!"

The words rang out clearly through the corridor, through the whole damn lobby, and people stopped walking, their heads spinning toward where I was standing and the restrooms behind me.

I followed, unable to look away, even though I knew I was about to view a train wreck.

Lee Collins stood at the end of the corridor.

On the floor, clutching his jaw, was a man I'd never seen.

SIXTEEN

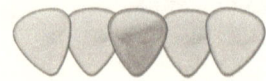

LEE

Four years, six months ago ...

I COULDN'T GET enough of her. It was like Carly was the tide, and I the ocean. She stimulated everything I was, moved me, made me want to reach greater heights.

I adored everything about her; the way she looked, talked, laughed, dressed, walked ... everything she did fascinated me.

We were meant to be.

I'd only seen her, been in her extraordinary presence a handful of times, but I already knew she captivated me.

"Lee," she answered the front door, her eyes wide, her lips slightly parted, quickly replaced with a smile. "I didn't expect you here. What a surprise."

"I hope this is okay," I said, pressing my lips together. I'd cancelled a show, said I felt sick, because I had to see her again. It had been ten days since our last coffee date, and she'd plagued my mind like a disease, rendering me unable to think of anything but her. Anything but us.

"It's ... great!" She blinked, but I saw the look. The split second of indecision that entered her eyes, and I got a clue, an inkling, that maybe this wasn't for her what it was for me. Maybe this was a one-sided affair.

No. Surely she felt it, too. We were everything more.

And I had to show her that.

I surged forward, aiming to press my lips to hers but she turned her head at the last second, leaving me kissing her cheek. Her soft, sweet scent of daisies washed over me and I slowly moved back, feeling like a grade-A dick

"Oh." I shoved my hands in my pockets. How did I get the signals so confused? We talked on the phone almost every day, and she'd begged to come to gigs whenever we were in town. "Have I read this all wrong?"

Carly bit her lip, then opened her mouth to speak and slammed it shut again. Finally, she found her words. "Lee, I really like you."

Four little words. They sounded so positive, but you'd have to be a fool not to read the subtext. "I'm sorry." I ran a hand through my hair and stared at the sky. This hurt. It hurt like a damn bitch.

"Don't be." Carly stepped close to me again, and that stupid daisy smell wafted up my nostrils. My stomach turned. I'd really thought we were meant to be together. Carly. Me. Forever. "I ... I'm not really ready for a relationship right now." She studied the ground beneath her. "There's been this guy ... Well, he's been travelling a lot for work, and so things are kind of hard. We're ... we're not really together right now."

I narrowed my eyes. She ... did she mean ... me? "Oh." I nodded. She isn't sure that I'm really into her and will stick around in the long-term. "But you think when he's ready to stay in one place for a while, you guys will be ... y'know, together."

Sunshine flared in Carly's eyes as she grinned. "Exactly."

A million thoughts raced through my mind. How long would I have to wait until we could be together? Would I have to quit the band to make it work? When was I going to see that fine body naked?

Focus, Lee. Take each day as it comes.

Carly placed her hand on my shoulder. It felt warm there. Nice.

"Don't you have a gig across the country tonight?"

There was a moment in your life when you could tell the truth, risk it all, and admit to being the total fool that you were. Risk the shame, the ridicule, and worse, the rejection of someone you not only value, but who you're beginning to hold dear. Someone you could possibly love.

"I cancelled it. For you." I took that risk. I embraced, relished it, dove in headfirst. Where Carly was concerned, nothing could be enough.

Carly looked at me, her eyes a storm of emotions all warring with each other. But eventually, it was enough. She leaned forward, this time giving me a tiny peck on the cheek. "That's so sweet," she sung in a quiet voice, her breath hot on my ear. "But next time, just take me with you."

"Ahem." A throat was cleared behind her, and I pulled back immediately. Standing in the hall was a tall man with salt-and-pepper hair, but the body of a tank. Seriously, the guy looked like there could be a stripper or a body builder hiding underneath that near seven-foot frame, and something told me—probably his ridiculously large biceps—that I did not want to fuck with him.

"Lee, this is my dad, Mike." Carly stepped back and clasped her hands, looking from her father to me.

Mike gave me a look, narrowed eyes, head to the side, and Carly gave him the world's least subtle elbow to the ribs.

It jerked him into action and he extended his hand for me to shake, which I did, with gusto. Still, it seemed like he was holding back, and I couldn't help but wonder if it was because he disapproved. Maybe no one would ever be good enough for his little girl.

I smiled at Carly. I couldn't blame him.

"Well, it was nice meeting you." I nodded, and Mike gave a wan smile before retreating back into the house without so much as a goodbye.

"You live with your parents?" I asked.

"Shut up! Bartending doesn't exactly earn me a heap of cash," Carly whispered, linking her arm through mine and walking out of her house.

"I would have thought you'd earn great tips." I smiled, but I could just as easily have said 'I would have thought your tits get you tips' because that was how enamoured I was with her in that moment. I couldn't think straight; words were no longer coherent.

"Anyway, you know the bar stuff is just while I study. When I get my fashion degree, I'm going to move out, get a real job."

"I know you will." I pulled her closer to me, and when she didn't resist, I kissed the top of her head. I wanted so badly to kiss those lips, but maybe she just wasn't ready. After having a guy be on- and off-again with her for a while she no doubt had little faith in men who were constants in her life.

Carly pulled back and we walked to the car. I opened the car door and she slid in the front seat and placed her feet up on the dash, looking across at me expectantly. "So, where are we going?"

"It's a surprise." I revved the engine and sped off down the street, a smile twisting my lips.

"Is it … a trip to maybe a sound studio, where you guys are gonna record?" Her voice was a combination of mirth and excitement. I chuckled.

"No."

Silence.

"Is it … a one-on-one with some Hollywood starlet who's gonna give me the money to start my own fashion design business?"

"Is that what you want to do?" I chanced a glance at her before passing through an intersection. She winked at me, and warmth flooded my heart. Was there anything she did that didn't make me fall?

"I think so. I've always loved clothes. One day, I want to make amazing dresses for theatre performers. You know, ridiculous things … like ball gowns."

I reached my hand across the centre console to the gear

stick, my eyes glued on the road at all times. The turn-off to the track was always hard to spot. "I think your ambition is amazing."

"You do?" Carly voiced, so soft it was like a feather.

"I do. And I have no doubt you'll get there." And I didn't, and not just because she had fashioned my dreams for the past month. It was because she was determined, this ball of energy and willpower, and I knew she'd get what she wanted, what she deserved, whatever the cost. That day at the park told me that. I admired that about her.

I wished I had more of that certainty in me.

My hands wrenched the wheel to the left and I made a sharp turn, sending the car careening as we entered the dirt track.

"Where are you taking me?" Carly laughed.

"It's a secret."

We traversed through the countryside on an orange track that was only wide enough for one car to fit through at a time. I hated to think what would happen if we met another vehicle; then again, I'd never seen anyone else up here, so I didn't really think it was a concern.

Finally, I pulled the car up at the start of a fire trail and killed the motor. Carly unclicked her seatbelt and I did mine, reaching into the back to grab a wicker basket.

"A picnic?" She clapped her hands together, and I beamed like I was Miley Cyrus in her good, wholesome days.

"That's it." I waggled the basket. "But first, we walk."

I locked the car and we started down the trail, Carly glancing from side to side with a look of slight trepidation on her face. Thick tree trunks with gnarled growths attached sprouted from the ground, the canopy a mixture of soft greens and murky khaki. Birds called to each other and contrasted the crunching of leaves at our feet.

Finally we reached the rocky outcrop I knew was there, and I placed the basket down and walked to the very edge of the rock that overlooked a cliff face, from where we had the best view of the national park. It stretched out for miles before us, a sea of green and brown interspersed with the flittering of wildlife and the rushing of water.

"It's … beautiful," she breathed. "Although, you know I would have been just as happy to go to one of your shows."

"You really like seeing us play?" I studied her, a smile playing on my lips.

Carly shoved against my chest, and hoped to hell she liked what she'd touched. "Of course I do, Lee. You guys are amazing."

"Thanks." I shrugged. "It still feels weird, this whole music thing being my job now, you know?"

"I bet."

Birds called in the distance, filling the comfortable silence that stretched between us. I stole another glance at her. Her green eyes glinted in the sun, her blonde hair floating in the breeze, the spaghetti straps of her tank not hiding the purple lace of her bra.

"So, are we eating on this picnic?" Carly asked, excitement on her face.

"Shit yeah!" I raced to the basket and opened it, bringing out the blanket and spreading it over the ground just before the rock. What a dickhead. I'd been so caught up in her looks, I hadn't realised she'd been starving.

Seconds later I had it all spread out; four different cheeses, some quince paste, strawberries, prosciutto, oysters and champagne, plus a fine white and a fine red wine. I wasn't taking any chances, here; I needed her to find something she liked.

"Lee …" Her eyes misted over, and for a shit-awful second I thought she was gonna cry, but she blinked back the moment and a huge grin took over her face. "This is amazing."

She gracefully folded to the blanket and took a strawberry, making love to the luscious red fruit in her mouth. Or, maybe she just ate it like a normal person. I was too busy fantasising about her lips to tell.

I poured us both a glass of wine after asking which she was after. She clasped her hand around the stem of red, but I didn't release it. Instead, I held tight. "Carly … it means a lot to me that you could come here this afternoon. I just … I feel something with you, you know? Something I don't feel with everyone else."

Her eyes softened and she reached up her hand, caressing the side of my face. Her hand was ice against my skin.

She propped up her elbows and rested her weight against them, settled down on the blanket, then took a sip at her wine, staring at the view in front of us. I laid by her side, staring at her.

"Lee?" she asked, and I hummed my acknowledgment. "Do you believe in good and evil?"

I paused, licked my lips. "In what sense?"

"Can a person be truly good? Truly bad?"

"Yes." I nodded once, studying her worried face. "I think people can be truly good or bad."

"But what if they try hard to fight it?" She twisted to face me, and her top flared open, exposing her cleavage.

"I think that's almost worse." I focused on those green-grey orbs, even though every cell in my body wanted me to focus on her rack. "Because if you try to fight it, you know it's bad. You know what you're doing is wrong. It's the failure that makes you worst of all."

Silence flattened the space between us, heavy as a lead weight. I needed to change the mood. This was getting us nowhere fast. "Let's play a game."

"A game?" Carly tilted her head to the side. "What kind of a game?"

"Like how we did when we first met. Things people don't know about us."

"Oh." Carly gave a light laugh. Her phone buzzed with a text, but she ignored it.

"You need to get that?" I asked.

"It's fine." She shook her head, dismissing the thought.

"So instead of things people don't know about us, I thought we'd play things we do know about each other." I stared at her, deep in her eyes.

"But we've only hung out a few times." Carly shifted her weight over to one side, and while there was mirth in her eyes, there was a guarded expression hiding behind it. She needed to relax. And I knew just how to make her do it.

"I'll start." I offered, holding my glass up as if in a toast. "I know that Carly Watts is possibly the most beautiful woman I have ever seen."

Carly's cheeks flushed red and she giggled, but she took a sip of her wine, and at least it had broken that dreaded tension that blanketed us moments earlier.

"I know that Lee Collins likes saving damsels in distress, even if he's not sure what they're doing up the damn tree." She giggled and we chinked glasses before taking another sip.

"I know that Carly Watts has the sweetest, kindest soul out of anyone I've ever met." I breathed the words as if they were fairy floss, light and intricately spun together. "I know she's going to do anything and everything she wants, whether it's working in the bar for the rest of her life or becoming a fashion designer to the stars." Second deep breath time. "And even though this is scary as shit, and she's not going to want to hear it, I know that I'm falling for her. I know that she is the first thing I think of when I wake up and the face I see when I'm singing love songs on stage." I swallowed, not daring to look in her direction. "I know that she's quickly becoming everything."

And then my everything careened into hell.

Present day ...

"WELL, CAN you get it, or not?" I stared at Hamish, one of our sound guys. He wore torn jeans, his shirt black, and he had a ring through his ear the size of a hula-hoop. Or, it had to be close.

"Yeah man, yeah. I've got it in your guitar case right now." He nodded, handing me the case, as if he were recounting where I'd pick up my fucking groceries instead of the logistics of my bribery deal.

See, I'd known our manager would be suspicious if ten grand suddenly disappeared out of the band account, and he might even ask Tony where the cash had gone. So I'd deposited the money into Hamish's account, plus a little extra, and asked for him to take the dollars out for me, telling Tony and company that I was buying a new guitar from him.

Fuck, it was confusing being a muso some days.

I thanked him and he disappeared into the busy Vegas streets, off to do whatever it was our crew did when we weren't working. I shook my head. Days like today, I wished I were them.

Three interviewers came, three interviewers went, and before too long the clock ticked over to 3:55 p.m., and I made some lame excuse about needing to step out and do something, and ran downstairs.

As soon as I entered the lobby I saw Lottie and Kate, sitting and talking to each other. Lottie had her arms around Kate, and I bit my lip. What are they talking about?

They both knew too many of my secrets.

I ducked back behind a pillar and scanned the room again, on the lookout for anyone who could be my guy.

To my surprise, it was not as I'd expected. I guess I'd been looking for someone who looked like an addict, someone who wasn't particularly well off: someone scrawny, tired and a mess, as if they were about to fall apart. Instead, the guy who jerked his head toward the men's restroom was dressed in a suit, and if Brad Pitt had a double for his red carpet appearances, this guy could sure as shit give that job a go.

I followed him down the corridor and into the restroom, where he checked every stall before moving the courtesy chair—you know, for all those times when you feel like sitting and watching someone else piss in the trough—under the door handle.

"It's the only place they're not legally allowed to film you." Brad shrugged when I looked questionably at the door. "But it doesn't stop a lot of the paps."

Somehow I had stumbled across a swindler to the stars. Oh, lucky me.

I shook my head. "The lobby in a major hotel? You thought this would be a nice discreet location?"

Brad looked at me, his lips pursed in a clear 'screw you' gesture. "Shit, I guess next time I'll try choose somewhere a little more to your liking. You'd rather your hotel room?"

Brad reached into his leather briefcase and pulled out a thin yellow envelope. I took it and peered inside, where a USB and a large photo of Kate and I stared back up at me. There was even a shot of us from that day at the water park, obviously taken with a long-range camera. It was like something from a bad movie.

"You got a kid with her?" Brad pointed to Jay, and my blood boiled.

"Leave him out of it!" I hissed, balling my fists and scrunching the edges of the photos. Brad gave a low whistle. I could all but hear him saying I was protesting too much. Shit. I couldn't just go out with Jay in public. Lottie was gonna murder me.

"Here's your cash." I handed it over.

Brad pocketed the large wad of bills, shoving them deep in his trouser pants. "It's all there?" He raised his brow.

I felt like telling him to count it himself, but instead just smiled. "To the dollar."

"Good." He moved the chair back from the door and placed his hand on the handle, ready to turn. "Just so you know?"

"Yeah?" I asked.

"Maybe you should tip me. Who knows how watertight your info will be otherwise?" Brad winked at me as he removed the chair.

"We had a deal," I gritted out, more loudly than I should have.

Brad gave a shrug. "Don't worry, your secret's safe with me …"

As the door swung shut behind him, I heard him mumble.

"Pop stars and their slutty groupies ..."

I open reached over and opened the door, speaking into the corridor. "What did you just say?"

"That your situation sucks, but the girl was clearly a fucking slut. And what a damn shame about your secret love child."

Anger welled up inside me. My body worked on autopilot, my brain rushing to catch up. I dropped the photos and bolted out the door.

"Fuck off!"

Next thing I knew, Brad was lying on the floor in front of me, out cold.

Fuck.

seventeen

KATE

THERE WAS a time when I'd thought Lee Collins was one of the nicest men I'd ever met. Now, in the space of a week I'd heard him confess to murder, seen him assault a wall, and picked him up from jail after he'd punched some other guy's lights out.

Still, none of these facts looked like they belonged to the polite, broken man sitting before me. He stared at his feet shod in those bulky Dr Martens, and ran his hands through his hair, defeat etched all over his face.

"So … you wanna talk about it?" I offered. I figured it was the least I could do. I knew about his scandal clause. I wasn't sure how much time as a band employee I had left.

"Nope."

I huffed out a breath, hair flicking off my face. "Well that's real mature."

I stood up and walked to the kitchen of Lee's suite, only to be met by a snort from behind. "What's that supposed to mean?"

"It means that you're not exactly the picture of maturity yourself." Lee's words punctured my chest like tiny swords as I sought out a wine glass. Surely he didn't mean that. Surely he was lashing out, seeking revenge—"After all, if I'd been where I was supposed to be, none of this would have happened."

I dropped the glass from my hand, letting it clatter into the sink. I stormed around the bench till I was right in front of him, my legs in between his parted ones. "What the hell is wrong with you?" I punctuated my words with a well-timed shove to his chest. "I did nothing wrong here. I wasn't the one punching guys out and dealing drugs!"

"No. But you were too busy fraternising with the other staff to make sure I stayed where I was supposed to." His tone was sullen, spoilt, and entirely unlike the Lee I knew. The Lee I thought I knew.

I tucked my hair behind my ear and studied the white ceiling. I wasn't that surprised he'd noticed me with Lottie. As he was waiting for the police, hotel security separating him and the other man, Jay had run up to him, given him a big hug, all while Lottie looked on with a disappointed look on her face before I ushered her and Jay away.

I didn't know what to say. "I'm …"

"You're sorry?" He raised he eyebrows.

I paused for a beat, taking in the facts. He had a point. I shouldn't have been with Lottie. I should have been waiting outside the conference room. But in all honestly, any grown man who needs that much of a babysitter has problems far bigger than myself.

"I'm leaving," I said, grabbing my handbag and storming toward the door.

"Good," Lee hissed. "So mature of you, Aussie."

I slammed the door to his suite behind me. It may not have been mature, but it sure felt good.

It wasn't long before I felt tears well in my eyes and I swiped my hand underneath them, trying to stem the flow. How did this happen to me? And why did I care so much?

It was just a job, and even if I was to be fired tomorrow,

my contract only had another few weeks left on it. Even if I did have to fly home in shame, I'd still have made enough money to last Dad several weeks of treatment.

So why was I so upset?

It must have been because it was hard having someone yell at you. And being away from your family.

Liar, my brain sang. I willed it to shut up.

"Kate." Michael's voice reached me and it took all my strength not to throw my head back against the wall behind me. Really? Now?

"Hey, are—are you crying?" He put his hand on my shoulder, and his familiar face, body, gesture, they all set me off into a waterfall of tears. I crashed against his warm chest and his arms encircled me, slow pats of reassurance on my back as I broke into pieces around him.

"Here, come 'ere." He grabbed my hand and dragged me away from the elevator and to another room on the same floor. He opened the door and led me into a room that was nice, but not quite as opulent as Lee's. Where Lee had marble, Michael had fake granite. Where Lee had a floor-to-ceiling TV, Michael had a floor-to-ceiling projector.

"Sit," Michael instructed and I shakily made my way to the couch while he clattered and clunked in the kitchen. Seconds later he joined me on the white cushiony material and handed me a glass full of ice and a honey-coloured liquid.

"Am I going to regret—"

"Drink," Michael ordered, and I gulped it back, gasping and spluttering at the strong taste.

"What the hell—"

"If Stace were here, you know she'd make you do it again for complaining." His eyes held a warning, but also a smile, and I couldn't help but let the corner of my lips twitch. He'd won. A little.

"So, big day, huh?" I gave a wry smile.

"You could say that." Michael widened his eyes. "I turned on my phone before. Even my parents had sent a text to say they were worried I was going to turn to a life of crime."

I shook my head. It was strange how quickly you got used to the media. "Tabloids, huh?"

"Yeah."

"Stacey worried?" I asked, tilting my head to the side.

"Hardly!" Michael snorted. "She just asked if I'd gotten a prison tatt yet."

I laughed, because it was such a typical Stacey line. Such a veiled way of checking he was okay.

"I do wonder if the record company will can the contract, though." Michael stared out the window. It was after dark now, and the lights of the city had just come into play. The lights in the city of sin. Where Coal had fallen … "Did you hear? We all had to sign a document, even me, saying we wouldn't get—"

"I know, I know." I sighed. "Any unwarranted media attention as a result of true illegal activity."

We sat in silence for a while, till I asked, "Do you think Lee really is a bad person?"

Michael's face broke into a broad grin. "Let me show you something."

He stood up and walked toward his room down the hall, pausing in the doorway. "Come on."

I joined him and found him sitting on a ridiculous gold bed spread with an even more opulently over-the-top gold bedhead encrusted with red gems. "This is … romantic."

"Ha! Vegas, right?" Michael laughed, but his attention was all on a small bag he'd pulled from somewhere. He rifled through the contents, finally bringing something out to show me.

He shoved the piece of paper toward my face and I took it from his hand, bringing it closer so I could read the words on it.

Dear Coal,

Thank you so much for evry everything.
We have moved into a beautiful house

by the beach, and you can sometimes see whales from our balcony!

You're still our favourite band and Dad listens to you all the time. If you write a new song, you should call it Matt's Dad.

Love from,
Matt McDonald

I frowned, staring at the note again. "What's this about?"

"Lee didn't take royalties last quarter. Instead, he put a deposit on a house for a fan who had cancer. We met him in hospital once, when we were there doing some sick kid charity stuff. Lee just took it upon himself to provide for Jim and his kid, Matt, when he saw how much they were struggling."

I bit my lip. It was so hard to see the darkness when actions like this showed Lee's light was shining through.

"He also gave Lottie a job, and she has a great eye for clothes, but I don't know how qualified she really is ..." Michael added. I smiled, thinking of the lifeline he'd thrown their little family. He'd saved them.

"And then there's what he did at Lachlan's funeral ..."

He only had to say the word and time stood still. Lachlan. My Lachlan.

Gone.

I closed my eyes, pictured his face, but it was hazy. I could remember him as a still photograph, but the video-images were getting more and more out of focus.

"Hey, Kate." Michael's hand was on my arm and I wasn't sure when I started crying, but I knew I was now. "S'okay."

Michael let me cry my tears, and then tucked me under the covers in his bed. I dozed fitfully, dreaming of forgiving Lee and loving Lachlan.

Or maybe it was the other way around.

Dear Lee,

You're a dickhead

Kate

I stared at the letter for the longest time before finally crumpling it into a ball and throwing it in the trash. I hated that he made me feel so everything and nothing, so a million dollars and so fifty cents, so freaking confused that it hurt, and ate at every fibre of my being.

I hated that he made me feel.

Three days later, and Tony was coming. They were the whispered words on everyone's lips, from the sound guys to Lee-freaking-Collins himself, and everyone was on edge. I'd even caught Michael ironing his jeans before I'd left his apartment that afternoon—a sure sign of distress.

When I went to call the boys out from backstage they were all huddled together, at odds with their usual separate warm-ups. Maybe they'd sensed that this could be the end. Maybe they needed to hold on to what they had.

They played their usual set to a crowd of their usual fans, although a few had to be escorted out for violence. It seemed everyone was angry these days.

The moment Tony arrived everyone stood up and took notice. He wasn't hard to miss: he was the first guy on tour I'd seen wearing a suit that hadn't been a bellhop. The band performed a little tighter, Lee's audience engagement just that tiny bit sharper, and even the sound and road crew stood to attention. I saw one of them tuck in his T-shirt.

Tony stood next to me as I watched from the side of the stage, my clipboard to my chest. After three songs, he finally spoke. "You must be Kate." His vision didn't once waver from the boys. If I hadn't been so very aware of his presence, I wouldn't have known he was talking to me.

"You must be Tony." I reversed his treatment, only I looked up at him just in time to see a fleeting smile pass over his face.

"You know, Lee pulled a lot of strings to get you this job." He clapped politely as a song ended, in complete contrast to the screaming of the fans in the crowd. "We had many candidates, but only you would do."

"Oh." I swallowed. I'd known he was doing me a favour, but I hadn't really gauged how big.

"And I can't help but wonder why, under your watch, he's been caught punching a guy and causing a public ruckus when he's never done anything even remotely like that before?"

Now Tony's steely eyes bored into me, and I shivered.

"I … I have no idea, sir." The courtesy escaped me before I could reel it back. "Tony. Sir."

"The two facts aren't related?" He folded his arm and his gaze stripped me to the bone. "Him, squeaky clean. You, new, and damage control has to be brought in."

Something stirred in me at that, and I felt the need to defend myself. "Aren't the strippers pretty new, too?"

"Yes." Tony swallowed. "They are, but they're different."

"Why?" I challenged, this time folding my own arms across my chest.

Something like trouble crossed Tony's face, and for a moment I wondered if he might be human after all. "You're unique. Lee … Lee told me that he thinks you're a smart kid. He listens to you."

The rest of the set was spent in silence, but I couldn't help repeating the three things I'd learnt from that conversation in my head, over and over again.

Lee went to a lot of trouble to hire me.

He hadn't been in trouble of any kind before; and if anyone

would know, it'd be Tony.

Lee thought I was smart and listened to me ... me.

I still thought he was a jerk. But something about that made me feel far too good.

EIGHTEEN

LEE

I SAT THERE, staring at the note I'd been writing, wishing the right words would come.

But they didn't. No amount of hope could fix what I'd started.

Dear Kate,

I am so fucking sorry. Nothing will make the way I spoke to you okay; it was just unacceptable. And I can't believe I did that to you.

But you know what? True to form, you stood up to me. You didn't take my *crap. And once again, it made me realize that I'm a dick. Because the one real person in my life, the only individual who isn't afraid to tell me how it is—the one person who understands me like no one I've ever met—is you. And I don't want to blow it.*

And that was where I was stuck. Because what else could I say? Where could I go from there?

Five sharp knocks rapped on my hotel room door and I stood up to answer, folding the letter and putting it in my back pocket as I went.

I jerked the handle and pulled the door open, then immediately wished I hadn't. I didn't know how I'd managed to avoid her for two days, but I had.

Clearly, all good things had to come to an end.

"I can explain—"

"Explain what, exactly?" Lottie spat, her arms folded across her chest, pushing up her more than ample cleavage. "Explain how you were involved in a punch-up in a public restroom, right in front of my son?"

I swallowed and opened the door wider, gesturing for her to come in. She stormed through the room then stopped at the window, staring at the strip below, hands on her hips. "Lee, I told you when I took this job, I wanted to protect him from this …" She gestured to the street below, then turned to face me. "… this way of life."

"I know." I closed the door and sat on the couch, elbows on knees, head in hands. This was all one colossal fuck-up. "I'm sorry. If I'd known you guys were in there—"

"You would have what? Scheduled your fight for later?" Lottie threw her arms out to the side, but I didn't miss the sheen of a tear glistening in her eyes.

"I got caught up in the heat of the moment. There were photos, Lott …" I trailed off. "Of Jay, and Kate and me. At the water park."

Lottie's hand flew to her lips. "What … what kind of photos?"

I looked back at the plush carpet, unable to meet her gaze. "His hat had flown off in the wind. I'm sorry, Lottie."

When I finally looked back up, her face was white, her hand still firmly against her lips. "I knew … I knew I couldn't keep him from it forever. I just thought …" And with that, she fell to her knees, her head in her hands, sobs shaking her body as if she were a baby. "He's the only good thing in my life, Lee."

I stood and went to her, awkwardly placing an arm around her frail shoulders. "I know. I know."

"I wanted to protect him from everything—from all this."

My hand rubbed her back, and I swear, I could almost feel every bone of her ribcage. I wondered if she were eating as much as she should be. It sure as shit didn't feel like it. "At least it was Kate and me, not you and me."

Lottie stilled.

Then she turned on me, menace flashing in her eyes. "How dare you try and presume that just for one moment, I'd want someone to think that she was the mother of my baby, that you were the father? Jay is mine, Lee."

I stepped back, reeling. What the hell would make her think I wanted to take him from her? I gave her this job so she could keep her kid.

I tried to formulate a logical sentence but ran out of time for words. Lottie pushed to her feet and stormed out of the room.

I flopped down onto the floor, staring at the stark white ceiling again, hoping for answer.

Fucking women.

NINETEEN

KATE

When I finally saw the boys alone at the after-party I pounced, like a moth to a flame.

"How'd it go?" I asked Michael, not wanting to meet Lee's eyes. I still wasn't sure if he was mad at me or not.

"Fine," Michael grumbled. "But we're on warning."

"What does that mean?"

"That everything can be taken away from us at the drop of a hat." Xander flashed a dark look in Lee's direction, then pushed himself up from the seat. "I'm going to the bar."

"Is he okay?" I looked between Lee and Michael.

"What do you think?" Lee snapped.

"I think you're being an arse," I replied, placing my hands on my hips.

"I think I'm going to the bar." Michael bit his lip and made an awkward exit.

"Can I talk to you for a second?" I placed my hand on Lee's arm but he shrugged it off, running a hand through his hair. "Seriously, Lee. This seems really out of character for you.

This …"

Lee glanced around furtively from left to right, then grabbed my wrist and pulled me into a dark corner beside the bar. We were in another roped-off club area, and the regular patrons couldn't see us here, behind the large palms and sound system in front of us.

"I'm not a bad guy." There was an earnest appeal in his eyes that had my heart convinced.

"It's none of my business what you do in your free time, but the things I've seen … you gave me a job to help me and my family out." I swallowed. "And I know you've done nice things. Michael told me about the guy with cancer, and …" I shook my head.

Lee took a step closer to me and brushed his hand over my arm. His touch felt safe. His touch felt warm, and I leaned in inadvertently.

"I did it to protect you."

"Pardon?" I leaned in closer, so close his warm breath brushed my neck as I strained to hear what he'd said.

"I did it to protect you."

Slowly, I pulled back, looking into his icy-blue eyes again. They drilled holes right into my soul, and I shivered. "How?"

"This guy had a photo of you helping me leave the club the other night." Lee bit down on his full lower lip, and something inside me pinged. "The way it was taken, the angle it was at—it looked like I was making out with your …"

The words trailed off between us, but I didn't need him to continue. "These things, Kate, they can blow up real quick. I didn't want your parents seeing that. I know you guys have been through a lot in the past year, and something like that?" Lee gave a small shake of his head. "The first time I got involved in a major tabloid scandal, Dad had a heart attack. It was touch and go for a long while there." He looked past my shoulder and at the bar, as if locking eye contact would make his information worse. "I didn't want that to happen to you."

"So you tried to buy him off?" I squeaked, the words getting all choked up in my throat.

"That's it." Lee raised his eyebrows. "And when I went to deliver it …" Again, Lee stopped talking, and he swallowed, his Adam's apple bobbing up and down. "The guy might have said some things about you, and they might have made me a little pissed."

My eyes grew to the size of saucers. Lee not only bought some sleazy guy off to protect my family, but he then punched his lights out because of something he'd said about me?

It was stupid. I hated violence. I didn't think it solved anything, and it sure hadn't in this situation. All it had gotten Lee was a date with a court and a heap of public embarrassment. Still, there was a tiny part inside of me that felt kind of flattered. He'd done that? For me?

"Thanks," I said softly.

Lee smiled, his shoulders relaxed. "I won't let anything hurt you, Kate." He pressed his lips together, then released. "I promise you that."

My eyes were still locked on those lips, lost in his words that sent chills down my spine. For the first time in a long time, I felt, I really felt something. I couldn't ignore the way Lee affected me any longer. I reached forward to touch his arm—

And snatched my hand back. I gave myself the equivalent of a mental shakeup. No. You can fight this.

Still, Lottie's words lingered in my mind. Is that really what Lachlan would have wanted?

"I just wanted to say, I'm so sorry, Kate. I should never have yelled at you, or called you unprofessional. I was angry and lashing out, and … let's have a drink, yeah?" Lee broke the awkward tension and leaned over the bar, calling for the bartender to bring us two beers which we then took back to the couches where everyone was sitting.

"Oh, it's the angry rock star." Xander snorted, tipping his beer back. "Wanna punch on?"

"Shut up." Lee cuffed him on the back of the head, but he was smiling. "Guys, I'm seriously sorry. I screwed up. I shoulda just let it go, or told you or the cops or …"

"Or Tony, your trusting label rep?"

I spun around. Tony was standing behind us, his arms folded, looking very out of place in his suit in the middle of what was some kind of a Caribbean-themed cocktail bar.

"Sorry again, man." Lee extended his hand for Tony to shake, and the smaller man gripped it reluctantly, then Lee sat down, gesturing for me to do the same beside him.

"You know you were never going to lose your deal over this. Honestly, we'd stand to lose more than we'd gain to let you go over something so minor." Tony turned to me. "I've got my legal team to handle all the details, but Lee will be repped by one of the best in the business on the assault charge."

"Great." I nodded. "Can you send me the details of any paperwork you need relating to the incident?"

Tony hung his head to the side, his eyebrows raised just a little. "I already have. And I've sent you contact information for Lee's lawyer. He'll be in touch with you."

"Thanks." I nodded, although I wasn't sure why he was telling me this. What did he think my job here was, exactly? I'd be gone by the time this trial made it to court. Back home in Australia.

Far, far away from Lee.

I shifted my weight on the couch, and my bare knee brushed Lee's jean-clad leg. A warm feeling rushed over me. And I hated that I liked it when his fingers, resting on his thighs, tickled my leg.

Beer flowed, and the boys found their natural rhythm again, the events of the day all but forgotten. A warm buzz settled in my stomach and I found myself staring at Lee, often. At his dark hair, so deep brown it was almost black, at his crystalline eyes, at his olive skin. He was intoxicating.

Why have I been fighting this so long?

At the end of the night, Lee took my hand as if it were the most natural thing in the world. Michael was already back at the hotel, and Xander had gone home with one of the girls at the bar.

We hopped into the lift together and Lee swiped the

number for his floor. "I'm on level—"

"Stay with me." Lee pressed his lips together.

"Lee, I—"

"Not like that." He leaned against the lift wall. "I'm sorry again for acting like a dick and yelling at you for not doing your job. You're not my babysitter."

I raised the corner of my lips in a half-smile. "You might need one."

"That's why I'm asking you." Lee grinned, and I felt it deep in my belly. "Can we just … just hang out tonight? Please?"

I couldn't say no.

Worse still?

I didn't want to.

I squashed down my guilt until it was just a tiny ball, then pressed it into an imaginary spot in my body, down my legs, in my feet. I was allowed to hang out with Lee, alone in his room at night.

We reached his suite and Lee opened the door, ushering me inside with his hand on the small of my back. I was so aware of it, of every finger imprinted on my skin.

I took in the room. The place looked magical. The lights of the city stretched out before us, and the decadent room was tastefully bathed in a warm white glow.

"Grab a seat." Lee nodded to the couch, and I did. Nerves took place in the pit of my stomach. This was no ordinary 'come and hang out' moment. I could feel it. He liked me; surely guys only punched other guys in a bribery-deal gone wrong because they liked you … right?

I shook my head at the ridiculousness of the thought, and let my imagination run wild. From the first time I'd met him, there had been something about him that I had been inexplicably drawn to, and now, it looked like Stacey was right, and he perhaps felt the same way.

Lachlan ….

Stop.

I took one deep breath and then another while Lee fixed us some drinks and then joined me on the plush white leather.

"You wanna watch a movie?"

"Sure." I nodded while Lee flicked through the channels and I pretended not to stare at the muscles that defined his arms, the way his lips gleamed against the glow of the television, the way he somehow smelt like a mixture of bourbon, pine, and something exotic I couldn't quite put my finger on.

Lee settled on a channel and rested back into the couch. I relaxed too, unsure if I should scooch up closer to him or stay where I was, very much on my side.

"You can sit a little closer." Lee laughed, then turned his attention back to the TV. I inched along the couch until once more we were close, and even still, my body wanted to keep going, wanted to crawl into his lap and stay there.

His hand reached across, and landed on my knee. I studied it; his big, warm fingers, the callouses touching my skin. "Thanks for staying."

I opened my mouth, but I didn't know what to say. I wanted to ask him to take his hand off my leg, a leg that wasn't his to touch.

I wanted to ask him to never let me go again.

The entire movie, Lee watched the screen. I watched Lee.

For the first time in seven months, my heart beat for a whole new reason.

TWENTY

LEE

Four years, five months ago ...

SEEING CARLY, even without our relationship getting any more physical, was still one of my favourite things to do. Seeing each other didn't happen often enough, but we made the most of our time, and I even flew her out to a gig once or twice when the absence was too much. She loved seeing us play. Said it gave her a thrill, being backstage while the others watched from the crowd.

And I'd do anything to thrill her.

"Hello ... anything going on in there?" Ryan gave my shoulder a punch and I smirked.

"Sorry, mate. Million miles away." I couldn't wipe the stupid grin off my face. In two hours time, I'd be with Carly, after she returned from the "wine lunch" she'd told me she was going on. In my hotel room. Alone.

"I bet. That new girl you've been seeing?" he asked, a knowing look in his eyes.

"Sure is." I took a swig of my beer. "She's ... God, remember what you were saying that first day we met?" Ryan nodded. We now caught up once a week at least, whenever I was in town. He'd even been to dinner with our parents. "I'll never forget how you raved about your woman, said she just changed everything for you."

"She's special." Ryan smiled.

"Well, that's how I'm feeling now," I confessed.

"I … I bought a ring, Lee." Ryan's face darkened with gravity. "I'm gonna ask her to …"

"Congratulations, brother." I clapped him on the back and ordered another round of drinks, which were promptly settled in front of us. "That's awesome news!"

"Yeah. I'm really happy." Ryan took a swig of his drink.

"What do your folks think?"

Three seconds.

That was all the time it took for me to realise that what I'd just said was not a good idea.

"Your parents? Or my shit-kickers?" There was acid in Ryan's voice.

"I … I mean your folks, man." I tried to keep the cool in my tone.

Ryan sucked in a breath and picked up the hotel room key with the number 1304 on it I'd left sitting on the bar top, flipping it over and over in his hands. "When I was ten, I went to hospital with my ma." He continued his nervous fidgeting as I watched. "He punched her in the gut so hard he cracked a rib. Only it resulted in internal bleeding."

I shook my head. "Ryan …" I thought of all the blessings in my life, how lucky I had been. If they'd had me first, I could have been the one in that situation.

"She dropped her wedding ring down the sink. The beating was to remind her to be more careful next time," Ryan growled the words. I touched his back but he flinched away, shooting me a murderous look. "Don't act like you understand, bro. You don't."

"I don't." I shook my head sadly. "I'm just … I'm sorry."

"I watched him hurt her for years. Sometimes we'd go to the hospital, other times we'd just stay home. She had the largest collection of makeup I'd ever seen. It was the one thing he let her spend a lot of money on; I guess 'cause it helped to hide the scars."

Ryan's voice shook, and I didn't know what to say so I ordered another round of beers. His was near empty already.

"So no. No, I didn't tell my parents about this, 'cause mine don't bloody know the meaning of the word marriage." Ryan took a swig of the old beer, knocked it all back, then started on the new one.

I took in a deep breath. There but for the grace of God …

"When are you gonna pop the question?" I asked, figuring changing the subject might be the better option.

"Tomorrow. I've been out of town for a few days, so I'm gonna surprise her. Tomorrow, I'll rock up and we'll go out to lunch. Just a picnic or something, nothing fancy." Ryan shrugged. "I don't know, I'm not great at this romantic shit. Hey, maybe I should play her one of your songs!" He laughed, nudging me in the ribs.

"You play?"

"Yeah. A little. Not too great on the guitar, mind, but I gotta tell you, she loves your band, all right. That new album of yours has been on her iPod for weeks."

"Bartender," I call the guy over. "Can I get a bottle of Veuve to go, thanks?"

Ryan looked at me, his chin pulled back to his chest. "Lee …"

"You can take it on your picnic." I shrugged. "On me, of course."

"I hate handouts. I'm not some charity case you need to—"

"Chill." I placed my hands on Ryan's chest. He'd moved up close in front of me, so close I could see the red spidery veins running through his eyes, could smell the hit of weed he must have had before coming into the pub.

Would that have ever been me?

"It's an engagement gift," I tried. "A pre-emptive one." Ryan still didn't look convinced, and frankly, he seemed a little on edge—had been all afternoon—so I called the bar guy back around. "Can you make that two bottles, please?"

Ryan looked at me questioningly, and I shrugged. "See? It's nothing. Thought I'd get one for my girl, too."

The smile he gave me was one of the first genuine grins I'd seen out of him since we'd first met. "You know, I reckon I could grow to like this whole having-a -brother business."

I clapped him on the shoulder. This time he didn't pull away.

I stumbled into the hotel lobby. My feet were thick, much larger than I remembered them being. Was I wearing clown shoes? What the hell was wrong with—

"Hi." Carly waved at me from next to the lift, and I grinned.

"Carrrrrrlyyyyyy," I greeted her, throwing my arms around her and attempting to lift her off the ground, instead stumbling backward into a wall.

"Lee." She giggled and gently pushed me away. A few people in the foyer turned to look at us. "Are you … drunk?"

"Shh!" I whispered, droplets of spittle coating the tip of my finger. She was right. Carly was always right. She was so much smarter than me.

That was why we were meant to be.

The elevator doors pinged open and we tumbled inside, then I pressed the button for the thirteenth floor.

"You are a mess." Carly giggled as I swayed when the metallic box lurched. "What have you been doing all afternoon?"

"Having beers with … my brother," I slurred. The doors opened and we walked down the corridor to my room where I started rifling through my wallet, then my pockets, looking for the key.

"Your brother …" Carly frowned.

"Yeah … I've told you 'bout him before." Finally I gave up, and turned to Carly with what I hoped was a plaintive expression on my face. "Can you please run down to the front desk and ask for another key? I lost it." I handed her my ID in case she needed it, and Carly gave a slight roll of her eyes but disappeared down the hall, allowing me to slump to the floor against the door, softly murmuring to myself.

Carly … we're meant to be.

Present day

MY EYES were stuck shut, and there was a warm body pressed up against me. I rested my head back against the armrest and smiled. This. We must have fallen asleep on the couch and it felt so nice, so warm, so right to be lying here with Kate that I decided to let it continue for just a moment longer. Just until she woke up.

Only it seemed my body had other ideas, my arm wrapping around her waist, cinching her in tight against me. She groaned and pushed back into me, and I felt her round ass against my cock that was already keen for some morning action.

I leaned closer to her and whispered my fingers over her neck, pulling her hair to one side so I could nibble up it, soft licks, kisses and sucks of her silky-smooth skin. She sighed and it egged me on, my other hand inching farther up her side, the swell of her breasts teasing at its restraint. I kissed just below her ear and it tasted so good, and smelt like apples. Her chest heaved, and—

Her chest.

Heaved.

She wasn't awake. And I shouldn't have been there anyway.

Reality came crashing back in and I darted my arm to the side and somehow vaulted over her, as if jumping girls were an Olympic event. I stood there, my hands pressed against my body, my eyes wide with horror as the woman I'd basically groped in her sleep looked up at me with question in her eyes.

"I … I didn't mean to take advantage of you," I stammered, shaking my head rapidly. It was the first thing I could think of to say.

"You weren't." Kate sat up and brushed her hair out of her face, her legs sliding over the couch till they were on the floor in front of her.

I ran my hands through my hair and turned away from her, rubbing my eyes. "I'm sorry."

Silence.

"You came onto me." Kate's voice wobbled as she spoke the words, and I gritted my teeth together, determined to stay strong. I had to stay strong. For Kate.

Soft footsteps padded toward me and I knew she was standing right at my back. Two small hands roped their way around my waist and I turned to look at her, unable to refuse her softness, her raw emotion. "Lee ... I slept with you."

I couldn't help but smile. "In the most literal sense of the word."

She shook her head. "For me, that's a big deal. I haven't done that with anyone since ..." The words trailed off and once more I gave myself a great big pat on the back for being the world's biggest idiot. Yes, somehow I had managed to fall, and fall hard for a girl. I was breaking the rules, rules set because I didn't deserve to be happy, and Kate didn't deserve an asshole like me. She'd lost someone amazing; she needed someone special.

I placed my hands on her waist. "Kate, I ..." The words got stuck in my throat. I flicked my gaze down to her lips, staring at those rosebud pink full gems that shone up at me. Kate slid her tongue slowly across her bottom lip and I couldn't take it anymore. I had to have one taste.

Just one.

My arms snaked around her waist and I pulled her to me, crushing her lips with my own. It was a kiss full of passion, desire, and her soft, sweet lips were like honey to me, singing a song of redemption and affection all at once.

She parted her mouth and I darted my tongue in, duelling with hers as my hands roamed up her back, pulling her tighter to me, so tight that her breasts pressed against my chest. I fisted her long hair in my hand and she gave a little moan as I tugged against it, biting down on my lip and causing my dick to twitch in my pants.

I wanted her; I wanted her so badly that it hurt. I wanted to take off that dress, so I lowered my hands to the hem and started to reach up. I wanted to see her here, naked. I wanted to explore her body with my fingers and my mouth, making love to every sweet inch of her.

I froze.

That.

That was the problem, right there. I didn't want to go making love to anybody. Not after I'd promised. Not when I didn't deserve it.

I wrenched my lips from hers and released my grip on her body, my hands falling to my sides.

"Lee …" Kate looked up at me, studied me, and the innocence in her eyes? The hope she had kindled there? It broke my fucking heart.

"Sorry." I raised my hands to my head and laced them over my crown, staring up at the ceiling as if it might have a logical explanation for why I'd so suddenly pulled away after being so very clearly into it, into her.

Kate took a small step forward and stood on tiptoes, pressing her sweet lips to mine again, and I groaned, then stepped back, my hands now on her shoulders, keeping her at a safe distance.

I couldn't do this.

I wouldn't.

I stared at my feet, hoping they'd somehow get me out of this awkward situation, but they were not moving, and neither was Kate.

Until she was. Then she was a nervous flurry of activity, all at once gathering her belongings, pulling her dress down, trying like hell to get out of there as quickly as she goddamn could.

"Sorry, I should never have …" She trailed off, because we both know it was just as much me as it was her, if not more so.

I wanted so badly to step forward, to pull her into my arms, to tell her I wanted this. Because seriously, a part of me did. She was so refreshing, so honest, so real that I would love to try and see where things between us could go.

But I couldn't.

Promises were promises. And I wouldn't let mine be broken.

Instead, I watched Kate finally get her shit together and leave the apartment, her heart and her head very clearly scattered in the room behind her.

But I was still standing.

I was always still standing.

Even if I fucking hated it.

I'd been lying on my bed for hours, staring at the ceiling, hoping for an answer. None came. I opened and closed the letter I'd started to Kate the day before, hoping a solution suddenly inspired me, but none rose to mind.

The bottom line was, I had to make a choice. A choice that should have been easy. A choice that was really not a hard decision at all.

I would do anything for the ones I loved.

And keeping them safe was paramount.

TWENTY-ONE

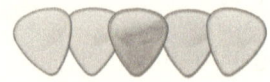

KATE

WHEN SOMEONE you had feelings for rejected you, it made you do stupid things. It made you ignore the big, important things in your life, such as what am I going to do in one week when tour ends and easier to focus on the trivial, day-to-day stuff, such as why the hell wouldn't he keep kissing me when it was clear his mouth was the tequila to my salt and lemon?

Then it made you feel guilty. It made you feel as if you'd betrayed the guy you loved, because pushing down my feelings, pretending Lachlan didn't exist anymore wasn't a solution, and I'd cheated his memory by attempting to find something more with another guy.

It made you drink a bottle of wine, and then down a tub of Ben & Jerry's ice cream. Because, der.

"Stace … I'm a bad person." I sighed. I didn't even have the energy to cry anymore. All I had was a whole heap of sadness weighing on me, pressing down on my soul.

"You're not, sweetie, you're not." She smiled through my screen, and I hugged the couch cushion closer to my chest. "I know the grief can be tough sometimes like that, but I know you'll be okay. It's like they say at work."

"The pet psychic place?"

"Hush, good advice is good advice. The point is, they always say that when someone is gone, their memory lives on in the spirit of others. You're just … ah, forget it. This isn't helping, is it?" Stacey asked, and I couldn't help but give a small smile. It wasn't, really, at all.

"I just … the feeling of loss. It's overwhelming. Some days, I'm totally fine, and I just go about life as per usual. It's those times when I can be attracted to Lee, when I can just … just be normal," I said, trying to put my feelings into words. "And then other times, other days, bam! It's like the world is a really horrid place and I become crippled with guilt and just this hurt, this hurt that rips at my insides and eats me alive. It's like today, when Lee … rejected me." I shuddered. "Sadness breeds sadness. And now all I can think about is pain."

Stacey worried her lip as something flashed across her face, a fleeting strange expression.

"I sound like a crazy person, huh?" I gave a single laugh.

"No, it's not that …" Stacey trailed off, and glanced around her room, as if she were checking no one was in it. "Kate … I get it. I know exactly what you mean; those feelings … God, the way you said it just sums it up so perfectly."

"Stace?" I frowned. As far as I knew, Stacey hadn't experienced any death in her family, or from any of her friends.

"I … I didn't tell you this …" A tear dropped from Stacey's eye and crashed on her cheek.

"Babe, are you okay?"

She shook her head and continued. "When you were going through everything with your dad … I was pregnant."

My jaw dropped. I saw it on the little Skype window. "Pregnant? To who?"

"Some guy … my sister's boss, apparently." She waved the comment off. "I … I thought the baby was everything. It was going to fix me. Save me from a life of nothing."

"But you drank at schoolies!" I protested.

"Took the shots, spat them in the water bottle."

"Ha!" I laughed. Wow. That was seriously good planning. "What about at dinner that night, with Dave and …"

"Didn't actually drink or feel like I had to fake it. Our night was cut short, remember?" she asked. And how could I forget? That night had been a total disaster.

"I was careful, Kate. I did all the right things. That's why I took the job with the psychics; I wanted to earn some cash, so I could make sure my baby had a place in the world. That I could treat it right." She sucked in a deep breath and looked down. When she looked back up at me, tears had already fallen down both cheeks, and her bottom lip wavered. It was all I could do to stop myself lunging for the computer and holding it close to my chest. I wished I could comfort her in person. "I lost the baby, Kate. And it was the worst thing that's ever happened to me."

"Oh, hon." I reached out and touched the computer screen, as if that could somehow translate to a physical touch.

"Sto-op touching the scre-een," Stacey sobbed through a small laugh. "Your hand looks we-eird."

I giggled, and we both smiled at each other, Stacey still wiping away her tears. When we'd finally calmed down, I spoke again. "Why didn't you tell me? I get why at the start, but what about when you lost it? Didn't you need someone to talk to?"

"It was the day after Lachlan …"

Stab.

There goes that pain again.

"My point is I get it, Kate. It's so silly, my baby was never born, but I had our lives all planned out. I even knew what kind of pram I'd be getting. And now, some days, I'm fine. Everything is sunshine and lollipops, all freaking good, and then others?" Stacey shuddered. "Other times, each breath I take is laced with shards of painful memories. Of missing thoughts. And even though you want to stop, you have to keep breathing."

Even when breathing was hard. Even when air clogged your throat, made each inhale a struggle.

"But it doesn't change the fact that you didn't do a bad thing, sweetie," Stacey said. "Kissing Lee is good for you; it'll help. Maybe not right now, but soon."

"Thanks," I whispered. Maybe one day ...

Stacey and I said our goodbyes, and just as we were about to disconnect the call, she left me with some words of Stacey wisdom.

"Just because you move on doesn't mean you have to forget."

TWENTY-TWO

LEE
Four years, five months ago …

WE FINALLY got into the hotel room and I broke open the Veuve, foam spilling over the carpet. Carly giggled and pretended to lick the spill up, which only made me want her even more.

"How was your day?" she asked, propping herself up on her knees on the floor of my room.

"Good." I nodded. "Real good. I'm … a bit drunk." I moved till I was kneeling directly in front of her. She was so alluring, so irresistible.

Tonight was the night.

I was going to make my move.

"Yours?" I asked casually, as if I hadn't just pictured her naked, imagined how good it would finally feel to be inside of her.

"Well …" Carly looked from side to side, as if the bed might be listening. "Don't tell anyone, but me too! Me and-a-friend drunk a bottle of wine each at lunch, and now …" She swayed and looked at the carpet. "Now I'm licking expensive champagne off the floor."

Carly cracked up laughing and I joined her, till we were both holding our sides in mirth. I handed her the bottle from the table above us and she took a swig, then passed it to me. I took a swig and handed it back, and soon the bottle was near empty.

I shook my head. Carly was still sitting opposite me on the floor, hands on her knees. The sun streamed through the window, glinting off her golden hair, her green eyes shining, and I wondered if maybe drinking during the day was not the best idea.

"You're a rock star," Carly said. I guess I said that aloud. "You can do what you want."

I smiled and passed the bottle to her again, a tiny amount of liquid still pooled in the bottom. "Last drink is yours, Carly."

She took it and tipped the bottle up, swallowing the liquid down, her throat bobbing with the movement. When she put the bottle down, rivers of sparkling dripped from either side of her lips.

And that was when I couldn't take it any more.

I gently edged my way forward, licking the champagne from her chin up to her lips. Her skin was soft, and she smelt like this delicious combination of daisies and wine, and God, I wanted to drink her up.

When my tongue met the corner of her lips she stilled, and I stilled, and for one interminable moment I sat on the edge of not knowing. Of not knowing if Carly, the girl of my dreams, felt about me just the same way that I felt about her.

All in.

I ran my tongue along her lower lip, tracing her plump, delicious mouth. She shuddered under my touch. I placed my hand along her jawline, cupping her face, looking her in the eye, but she didn't meet my gaze.

"Lee …" She trailed off.

My heart burned. I knew just how hard this was. She was right. There were no words. No words except—"I love you."

I pressed my lips to hers and kissed them, those sweet,

delectable lips, and after a moment she met my kiss, parted her mouth and allowed my tongue entry. She tasted like candy and champagne, and as I ran my hand up her back, pulling her close against me, as close as two people could possibly be, I knew one thing.

We were meant to be together, Carly and me.

Two mouths should never meet as perfectly as ours.

Our bodies rolled into one, and soon Carly and I rolled beneath the sheets, her giggling as I traced my tongue up her neck. Her naked body writhed beneath mine and I slipped my hand between her legs, feeling how ready she was for me.

"I love you, Carly," I said into her hair, and she stilled, froze beneath me.

"Hmm?" She pulled back to study my face.

"I love you, Carly Watts. You are just … I want to be with you forever." And we would be, Carly and I. We were meant to be.

Carly wrapped her arms behind my head and raked her fingers through my hair, pulling my lips down to crash over hers. Her tongue danced in my mouth and I moved myself so I was positioned to slide into her, feel her surrounding me, making me complete.

I pinned her arm down above her head and then moved my hand to cup her breast, caress her nipple, and then give it a little flick until it was a stiff peak beneath me. She gasped, thrusting forward to meet my touch. "Make love to me, Lee, from Coal," she breathed, and I slowly lowered myself into her, losing myself between her legs until we both stilled, lost in the ecstasy of our union.

I looked down. Carly's green eyes blazed up at me, her blonde locks splayed over the pillow on the bed, and emotion swelled in my heart. "I love you so much."

Something akin to a tear glossed Carly's eye, but then she rolled her hips, and I had no more time to look at her eyes, think about emotions, or anything greater than the here and the now, and the way our bodies were joining together.

We moved faster, sweat helping our bodies slide in

perfect unison against each other until she pushed against my shoulders, rolling me sideways so she could be on top. I loved this; loved her riding me, looking down at me with so much emotion behind that gaze.

"God, Carly!" I yelled as I climaxed, pulsing inside of her, feeling her clench around me.

"Lee …" She panted, her heavy breath matching my own.

Neither of us heard the door open.

Neither of us saw him until he was right beside us.

"What the fuck." It was a low growl, deep and filled with menace. Worse, it was a growl I most definitely recognised.

Carly stilled.

I froze.

"Carly, get dressed and get in the car," he ordered, and Carly's face whitened as she jumped off me, scrambling to find her clothes.

"Ryan I—" she started.

"Shut up," he snarled, his stare fixed on me.

I pulled the sheets up to cover my body, hiding my nudity from his intense gaze. All the pieces of the puzzle fell into place. Carly's on-again, off-again boyfriend. She hadn't meant me.

Her initial hesitation to meet my kiss, despite our intense chemistry. The look on her face whenever I'd speak about him.

Because Carly and I weren't meant to be, after all.

Carly was meant to be with someone else.

My brother.

Fuck.

Present day

Dear Lee,

I get it. You're not interested. That's totally fine. I didn't take this job so we could be together.

But you know what? What you did
to me the other day sucked. You
hit on me. You kissed me, Lee.
You kissed me. And to then make
me feel like this worthless piece of
nothing?
I'd thought you were better than
that. For a split second, I'd thought
you really cared, but someone who
liked me would never have done
that, and you know what? I deserve
better. I deserve someone who will
fight, be proud to be by my side.

Kate

Another night, another party, only this time it was
different. This time, I was sitting alone with Benny while I
pretended not to be watching Kate dancing with Lottie, not to
be watching Kate doing shots with Michael, not to be watching
Kate laughing and touching Xander's arm. At that, I frowned.
He was no good for her. Xander wasn't that kind of guy.

"You all right?" Benny asked me, I gave him a wan smile.

"Yeah, man." I nodded. "Just tired …"

"And a little bit in love with that girl over there?" He tilted
his head in Kate's direction and I wanted to kick myself.

"I don't really …" I trailed off and tilted my head back. It
was Benny. He knew.

"'Fraid so." Benny smiled, not unkindly. "Look, I figured it
was a thing. You buy the woman trainers, you send her secret
love letters—"

"Dude, they're not love letters." I slapped his chest. I

thought of the one I still hadn't given her, where I more or less told her how I felt. "Besides, it doesn't matter how I feel. I can't—I can't do relationships right now."

"Because of what happened with …?" Benny trailed off.

"Because …" I paused, then decided to do something different for a change. To tell the truth. "Because, yeah. I ruined three relationships. And I don't deserve to be happy."

"Oh, come on!" Benny laughed, slapping me on the arm. "That's the most self-pitying bullshit I've ever heard."

"It's true." I shrugged. "I don't deserve to be happy. And even if I did, there's another … well, I don't know. All I know is it's complicated."

Benny narrowed his eyes but didn't question me further. "Well, I think you're not trying hard enough."

"Believe me, I would if I thought it would amount to anything."

Benny leaned closer to me, and a serious look washed over his face. "Could you see yourself ending up together?"

I thought about it. Thought long and hard. Because no, I couldn't really see that. I was going to die alone. It was something I'd resigned myself to a long time ago.

"You need to decide if she's worth it, Lee. Because the look in your eyes tells me she is." Benny leaned back in his seat and I looked across the room again, searching for Kate. I couldn't see her anywhere.

"You're a lost cause, brother." Benny laughed as I moved from side to side, trying to seek her out.

Then I spotted her. In the corner next to the bar, Xander by her side. His hand was on her lower back; she laughed at something he said, touched him on the chest.

He looked up at me.

And he winked.

"I'll be right back." I excused myself and flew to my feet, striding across the room with one person in my vision. How the hell could he do that when he knew, he had to know how I felt about Kate? Granted, I'd never said so much, but he knew how much time I'd been spending with her, had heard me tell him not to touch her before, even if I'd been stupidly off-my-face. My blood boiled and when I'd finally pushed my way over to them, I was ready to ignite.

"What the hell are you doing, Xan?" I folded my arms across my chest, staring him down.

"Um … what the hell is your problem?" Xander pulled his lips back, a questioning expression on his face.

"You know Kate is off-limits." I nailed him with a firm glare.

"Dude, we were talking." Xander frowned.

"Talking, my ass." I shook my head, and I knew I sounded like a crazy person, but I just couldn't stop. "You winked at me, for crying out loud."

"Oh, shit, did I? I winked! I broke the cardinal rule of brotherhood and winked at you. How the hell dare I?" Xander mocked.

"You can't just treat her like one of your whores," I spat.

"Um, guys, I'm right here!" Kate muscled her way between us and placed one hand on each of our chests, turning to me. "This is ridiculous. Lee, Xander wasn't trying to hit on me." She turned to Xander, looking him in the eyes. "Xander, Lee—"

But she didn't get to finish that sentence. She didn't get to finish because Xander, the double-crossing bastard, swooped in and kissed her, jerking her body against his with both of his hands, her tiny waist pressed up against him.

"Xander!" Kate shrieked and pushed away.

It was a good thing, too. She moved, allowing me just enough time to lay a solid punch, right in Xander's jaw.

I was getting good at this whole violence thing these days.

TWENTY-THREE

KATE

XANDER STAGGERED back, grasping his jaw. A small speck of blood spilt from the corner of his split lip, and I swear my eyes fell out of my head.

"What the hell?" Xander yelled. I looked around. The club had fallen silent, the dance beats in the background the only noise as people stared at us, at the spectacle that was Coal falling apart.

"I told you not to touch her, and you ignored me," Lee shouted, his chest rising and falling with each heavy breath he took.

"What does it matter to you?" The words fled from my lips, and I wished I could take them back almost as soon as they had. "You don't like me, Lee. For whatever reason, I'm not yours."

Lee's lips thinned out to a line as fire raged in his eyes. "You think that's the case? You really think that I hired you, hung out with you, protected you from the paps, fucking kissed you, but I don't like you?"

The words rocked me to my core. "I …"

"She told me everything. You made her feel like shit. What was she supposed to think, dude?" Xander hissed.

"Exactly," I snapped. "You don't like me, and if you do, you have a fucked-up way of showing it."

My pulse thudded at my wrist, each beat causing a minor ache, and I turned on my heel and stormed out of there, past the security guards at the entrance to our section, down the stairs, past the general club-goers who all stared at me, as if I were every bit as famous as Lee and Xander and Michael. And I guess, in that moment I was. Phones clicked and flashes went off, but all I could do was keep marching, all the way out front until I flagged down a cab and rode back to the hotel.

It wasn't until the door clicked shut behind me that I realised all the anger I'd held in my body had somehow dissipated, leaving me this hollow shell of emotion.

Alone.

Confused.

Tired.

The knocking on my door had gone on for more than thirty minutes. I'd had three calls from reception, asking me to keep it down, but I didn't know how to make him go away. I couldn't.

I just didn't know what to do anymore. I couldn't handle this harassment all night, and we had to fly out to New York in the morning for the last set of gigs and media appointments. The schedule was both long and gruelling, and I shouldn't have been awake. Lee shouldn't have been awake.

But the problem with heartache was it liked to screw you around like that. It didn't stick to a schedule; didn't show up and leave on cue.

And that was why, even though I knew I had feelings for Lee, even though I'd kissed him, wanted to be with him, my throat swelled with a lump so big I just had to let it out, and all the guilt and sadness I'd squashed down over Lachlan came tumbling out. Tears welled in my eyes and slowly fell to my cheeks, and I shook my head and tried to hold onto Stacey's words. Moving on doesn't mean you have to forget.

"Kate! Please!" Lee yelled again and kept up his rhythmic assault. I turned on the TV, as loud as it would go.

After a while, the beats stilled, so I turned down the volume. Maybe he'd gone to bed. Maybe now I could finally get some sleep and hope that tomorrow, somehow, this whole thing would be resolved, and—

"I don't know what I believe either."

His voice was so soft I could barely hear it. I bit my lip, debating my options before padding over to the door and sliding down it, picturing Lee on the other side doing the same.

"I think—I used to know there was a Heaven. And I didn't know for sure, but for me, I always thought Heaven would be Hell for the bad people, y'know? 'Cause there wouldn't be anything there to keep the sinners satisfied."

Lee laughed, a sad and hollow sound that echoed through the hall. It echoed through my heart. "Then I realised that sinning isn't such a strictly defined thing. No one wants to commit a sin. Just because you're a bad person doesn't mean you don't enjoy the same things good people do. And no one wants to ... no one wants to be evil, Kate. There's always another side."

I sucked in a breath, and rested my head against the hard, cold wall.

"I think ... I think there has to be something. If there's not, this whole thing is just too depressing, right? A freaking joke." Lee snorted. My heart sunk. "And I sure as hell don't know what that something is. I don't have the guidebook. I don't get to speak to those who've passed, and I sure as hell don't want to, and I don't know that I believe anyone who says they do."

Silence stretched out between us, blocked by a thick wooden door, while I took in his words. I needed for there to be something. I wanted it so badly it hurt.

"I'm not saying there's definitely a god; I'm not saying there's a good place, a bad place, or even an in-between place." Lee let out a heavy whoosh of air. "I'm just saying that there has to be a place. And I know that when you get there, you spend your life with the people you love."

I licked my lips, the taste of salt from my tears so strong. "How do you know?" I paused. "And what about the dinosaurs?"

Lee chuckled, and a small part of my heart smiled. I tried to stop it blooming, but the stupid thing grew buds like a darn frangipani in spring. "I don't know, Kate. But if you don't believe in something … what's the point in anything?"

If you don't believe in something, what's the point in anything?

The words struck a chord deep within me, resonated against something I already knew. They argued against what Lachlan had taught me: to seize the day, take a chance, and live each moment as if it were—

That was a sentence I couldn't ever finish. Because he'd had his last moment.

And I wonder if you got those seized moments back.

My phone buzzed on my bedside table but I ignored it and reached my hand up and twisted the doorhandle, inching it open slowly. Lee fell backward momentarily then righted himself with the palms of his hands. We sat there, him staring at me. Me staring at him.

"I don't know if I'm scared of what's after, terrified of the future, or mourning the past." I swallowed. "I just know that when my life flashes before my eyes … I want to see the best moments. I don't want to see a girl who's broken, who cries herself to sleep, who wakes up short of breath in a freaking panic."

Lee stretched out his arm and cupped my face, his thumb stroking over my chin. I melted into his touch, his embrace, and let him hold the weight of my head. I let him hold my world.

Seconds passed, and I wrapped my hand around Lee's

arm, pulled him closer until he was inside the doorway, on his knees, facing me. "Kate …" He shook his head, a cloud marring his eyes.

But this was about seizing the moment. This was about having no regrets. And I knew that if I didn't do this now, I always would have one.

I grabbed the collar of his shirt and pulled him closer to me, pressing my lips against his. At first they met a strong line, hard and unyielding, but seconds later his lips parted and I felt his warmth, tasted his sweet, delicious breath and felt his strong, captive hands pulling me closer to him, wrapping themselves in my hair.

My own need met his as I snaked one hand underneath his shirt, parting lips only to yank his top off, desperate to feel his skin, his muscles, his body against me.

"You're." Kiss. "Not." Kiss. "Embarrassed." Kiss. "I." Kiss. "Took my shirt off?" Lee punctuated his sentence with affection, and I laughed, pulling back to look at that lean body, those strong, defined arms. I ran my nails up his chest, scraping them over his pecs as I went.

"Well, technically I took it off this time." I grinned wickedly. "But I think I'm going to have to join you at your game and raise the stakes." I ripped my shirt off over my head, throwing it behind me.

Lee swallowed. His Adam's apple bobbed as he looked down at my chest.

"What's the matter?" I asked, reaching my hands behind me. I extended one leg and tapped the door so it moved to close. "Lee Collins, famous rock star, hasn't ever seen a pair of boobs before?"

My bra fell to the floor, and lust shone bright in Lee's eyes before he closed the gap between us and met my lips again, his fast and hungry, determined to capture me. Our tongues met and danced in one another's mouths, an explosion of desire-fuelled energy.

"Kate." Lee's hands worked up my sides to cup my breasts, and he moved his mouth down to suck my nipple, his tongue teasing it, working it into a peak until my body yearned for him, swelled into him.

I reached for his pants, my hand rubbing over the hardness I felt inside, and I tried to blindly undo the button, eager for more, desperate for more.

Eventually Lee reached down to aid me and together we removed his jeans and briefs, leaving just him. I wrapped my hand around his dick and he stiffened from his head to his toes as he bit his lip. "Kate ..." he gasped.

I pumped once, down then up, and he shuddered. Relief coursed through me. As I enjoyed the feeling of him swelling in my hand, Lee traced his fingers over my thigh, pushing my skirt up until he was close to my core. He traced his fingers over my panty-line, and this time it was my turn to shudder in anticipation. He teased back an edge and his finger slid against me, teasing me, exciting me, and tension wound itself into a coil as I yearned for more, yearned for more of his touch. I pumped my hand over his hard length faster, and he hovered over me, our kisses desperate and ravenous, designed to consume each other in this crazy lust we'd created.

"Kate," Lee said, a pitch of tension in his tone, and I groaned into his mouth, biting down on his lip and then releasing it as his actions sped up, too.

"I want you inside me," I whispered.

He stilled.

"Is that the best idea?" Sweat glistened on his forehead.

"I want this, Lee. I promise you, I'm thinking clearly, and I want this."

And I did. I wanted to have sex, right then, right there, with Lee Collins. He was sweet, caring, sexy, and we connected—really connected, in the sort of way I'd only ever felt akin to one other person before.

Lee pushed himself to his feet and extended his hand for me to take. I wrapped my fingers in his and he pulled me to standing, leading me toward the bed.

This time, our kisses were slowed, magical, and alive with the promise of something more than just lust—something deep, something dangerous. He unzipped my skirt and it fell to the floor until I stood there in only my panties, all but naked before him.

Lee stepped back, looking at me from head to toe with a smile on his face and bewilderment in his eyes. "You're so beautiful, Kate."

Then I stepped back, lying on the comfortable mattress, and he covered my body with his heavy weight. It felt so nice to be underneath him, so safe, so secure, but so exciting at the same time. Our bare skin thrilled against each other, such a gorgeous feeling of being so close to at one.

Lee caressed my body, his fingers tracing patterns over every inch of skin and I burned, tingled, and felt in ways I'd never felt before. Heat pooled between my legs, and I shifted my hips, rubbing against his erection, to ready to feel him inside me.

"Have you got …" Lee paused and licked his lips.

I froze. What the hell was he talking about? Did I have … sexier underwear? A pair of handcuffs? A video camera? "Am I … am I doing something wrong?"

Lee's forehead wrinkled in consternation. "We need protection, Kate. Like a condom."

"Oh! Of course." I nodded sagely. Kill me, kill me now. Of course a condom. Like, the thing people use when they're about to have sex. "No. I don't."

Lee pursed his lips. "Shit."

He pulled back and started opening and shutting drawers in the bedside tables, but all he came up with was a copy of the bible. Most un-sexy.

He disappeared into the bathroom and came back triumphant, a foiled packet in hand. "Thank God for well-stocked complimentary bathroom selections."

I smiled, but bit my lip. In the heat of the moment I'd been fine, but now? Nerves chased each other through my body, a whirlpool of activity that had all my senses on high alert. This was going to hurt; everyone said it did. And God, what if I didn't do it right?

Lee ripped open the foil and rolled the condom over his length, covering it in the thin white material. It looked big. Too big to fit in … me.

"Kate?" Lee leaned forward and hovered over me, resting his weight on his arms. His face was so warm, gentle and caring, and his body so damn sexy that I felt my shoulders relaxing just a little. "It's okay."

And with those two simple words, it was. He pressed his lips to mine and we kissed, a kiss of promise. Of things to come.

His hands trailed down my body and rested between my legs where he teased me, played with me, until I wanted more, so much more. "God, Lee."

"You're so beautiful, Kate." He stared deep into my eyes, and I melted, my whole body turning into a big puddle of goo. "Are you ready?"

I paused. This is really happening. "Yes."

He eased his way in, pushed inside me. It was slow at first, and I buried my face in his neck, not wanting him to see the face I was making, the sting I was fighting. But inch by inch, he lowered himself, until finally he was all the way inside me and he stopped, still.

"You're so tight," he whispered, and I paused in my oh-hell-am-I-going-to-make-it pain to give myself a pat on the back. Well done, vagina. You're all right by Lee's standards.

Then, I started to move. Slowly at first, building to a gentle rhythm, Lee stopping every few moments to ask if I was okay. But soon we got faster, and while it didn't feel great, it stopped stinging and I started to enjoy it. Heat pooled at my core and tension built as he hit that spot, over and over. Sex with Lee felt nice; sex with Lee felt amazing.

Or it did until the whoosh of the door swinging open made me freeze; made us both freeze.

"Do you want to go out for a …"

It was one of those moments where the world slows down, and you remember things in slow motion. Me, kicking the door to, and obviously not getting it caught in the latch. Me, ignoring the subtle buzz of my phone as it had vibrated against the bedside table.

And now, there was Lottie.

And she didn't look impressed.

TWENTY-FOUR

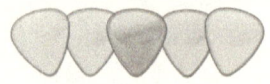

LEE

Four years, five months ago ...

I'D RUN after them out to the parking lot, but by the time I had gotten there—allowing a minute for me to pull on some pants—they'd gone. Ryan's car had sped down the road, dust flying up under the wheels, and I'd slapped myself on the forehead and cursed, kicking a power pole, which did absolutely nothing to resolve the situation, but did create a nasty sting in my foot.

Now, I stood with my hand poised, ready to knock on Carly's door. Ready to face what hell had just occurred and try, try to stop the aching in my heart, the dull ache that reminded me that she had lied. We weren't meant to be together at all.

I gave three sharp raps and stood back, waiting for the door to swing open.

When it finally did, her father answered, his brow furrowed. "You're here for ... Carly."

"Yes, if I can please, sir." I nodded.

The man shook his head and shrugged, gesturing down the hall. "She's outside in the courtyard, talking to her Ryan."

He emphasised those last two words, and I felt about an inch tall. No wonder he'd acted strange the first day we'd met; he knew she had a boyfriend, would have seen the resemblance, and he knew I didn't belong.

I didn't belong with Carly.

"Thanks," I said, and started walking.

Suddenly, my arm was jerked back and I froze.

"You musicians … you're all the same," he hissed in my ear. "You so much as try to hit on my baby girl and I'll eat you alive."

I paused. It didn't seem appropriate to tell him just how far that ship had sailed.

When he said nothing further I kept walking, sliding open the balcony door and slamming it shut behind me.

"Some nerve you have, showing up here." Ryan stormed up to me and shoved me in the chest, catching me unawares and sending me backward till I slammed my body against the glass door.

"I want answers." I used my foot to propel myself forward. He wouldn't intimidate me. He couldn't intimidate me.

"You knew I was going to marry her, bro—you knew—and you fucked her anyway?" Ryan's face was red, and he looked up to the sky as if it had all the answers.

I could tell him that it didn't. I'd been searching there for the past hour, desperately seeking a solution, but all I'd found was a weird form of insignificance, as if my life were meaningless. I was nothing. When it came to the galaxy, I was the smallest motherfucker around.

Maybe that was why Carly had found it so easy to rip me in pieces. Maybe that was why she didn't care, hanging out with me, making me believe, all while she was seeing my brother. Because she knew.

She had to have known.

"Carly." I stared at her with hurt eyes. "Why …?"

Carly sobbed, her arms wrapped around her waist and I could see the pain she was in from her shaking body, her tightly shut eyes. I stepped forward to try and offer her some comfort but Ryan stepped in front of me, giving me another short push back. "Dude! Don't you get it? She's my fucking girlfriend."

"She's mine, Ryan! We've been hanging out, talking on the phone every day for weeks," I spat, the words flying out my mouth before I could think them through. "She didn't even mention your name to me; not once."

I still couldn't figure that out myself. Why hadn't she mentioned him?

"I did!" Carly screamed. "I told you there was this guy, and he was out of town a lot, and ..." Her words dissipated into a stream of sobbing.

My heart stopped. That line hadn't been some cute way of telling me to stick around.

That line was about my brother.

"I ... I thought you were talking about me." I almost whispered the words. Ryan snorted.

And yet still, I knew that she was going to choose me. Carly and I had such amazing chemistry. We were meant to be together ...

Now, though, those words weren't filled with the usual solace I found in them. Now it was less of a sentence, more of a question.

"I'm so, so sorry," Carly choked. "I didn't mean to ... to do any of it."

"It's okay, baby—"

"It's not okay!" Carly pushed Ryan away, and his face was as red and as hurt as if she'd slapped him. "It's not okay. Ryan, I love you—you were my—"

"Don't." His voice was small, but I heard it. Oh, I heard it. Right through my bones. "Don't say were."

"Haven't you ever been confused about what you wanted?" Carly held her palms up in the air. "I was drunk. I made a mistake, Lee. I'm sorry."

It should have been enough.

But it wasn't.

Every time we'd laughed—a lie.

Every moment we'd shared—a lie.

Every secret we'd told—a lie.

And now, the time we'd made love—lie, lie, lie.

Because it wasn't making love. It never was if your woman was with someone else.

Especially if that someone was your brother.

I turned on my heel and stormed out of there, ignoring Carly's pleas for me to stay, Ryan's shouts for me to go. I opened the door to my car and was just about to hop inside when a flurry of footsteps raced to my side. I spun around just in time to receive a huge clock in the jaw from my dear, estranged brother, and then everything went black.

Four weeks later ...

It hurt. The pain roiled around in my gut, and I couldn't get her out of my mind. I'd texted Carly; I'd asked for time, just a few weeks for me to sort my head out and for Ryan to cool off. If she wanted it, of course.

As for me? I so badly wanted it all, but I didn't have the first clue as to how to get it.

I sang the songs at the gigs we played with little to no recollection of my voice hitting the notes. I was in another world, another time. I was waiting for things to settle. Waiting to see Carly.

And then I did. In the very front row of a concert in Seattle.

After our last song, I signalled to the security guards to bring her back-stage, and waited in our dressing room. After a heap of ribbing, the guys finally left, all nodding a 'Hey, Carly' as they passed her on the way out. The door finally closed, and it was the two of us. Carly and me.

"You've talked about me to your friends," she said, resting against a table in the corner and folding her arms. "Good things, I hope."

I smiled, a huff of air expelling from my lungs. "I haven't told them you're with my brother, if that's what you're asking."

A flash of hurt darkened Carly's eyes, and she shook her head. "I'm sorry for hurting you, Lee. I … I fucked up. I just … I liked you, a lot, and … and …" She started to cry, and as much as I wanted to hate her, wanted to tell her to get the hell out of my dressing room and go back to my brother, I couldn't. This was Carly. My Carly. I still wanted her as mine.

And somewhere, deep down inside of me, I wasn't ready to let that go.

I closed the three-step gap that separated us and pulled her to my chest, her sweet floral scent infiltrating my nose. I rubbed one hand up and down her back, the other wrapped up in her hair.

"Everything's so hard," she cried against me, her tears mingling with my sweat. "I've made a big mistake."

"Shh," I hushed, holding her tighter. "It's going to be okay. Nothing you've done can't be fixed, okay? We're in this together. I'm here for you."

Carly pulled back and looked me in the eye, her green orbs shining with fear and something else, something I couldn't quite put my finger on. "No. There's something I have to tell you. Not just Ryan. Something I haven't told him; I can't. Not until I know. Something big."

I sucked in a breath. What else could she possibly have to lay on me now?

Present day …

"You DIDN'T knock?" I scrambled off Kate, covering her with the sheets and grabbing the comforter to hide my nudity. Not that it really mattered. Lottie had seen it all before.

"You're fucking each other?" Lottie's eyes widened, her voice octaves higher than normal. I walked around her and slammed the door shut. I had a feeling this wasn't going to be good.

"Was that photo that almost leaked deliberate? Are you trying to play happy little families?"

"What photo?" I frowned, keeping my voice low, level, a direct contrast to Lottie's screech.

"The one you said that paparazzi guy had. The three of you! Is this all a game to try and take my son—"

"What is going on?" Kate asked. She clutched the sheets close to her neck, her neck gaze flicking from Lottie to me. She looked so frail, so scared that I wanted to hold her tight, make everything okay.

Lottie, however, clearly felt none of my empathy. "You're doing this to me, to us, but you haven't told her?" Lottie laughed, a bitter laugh that ran cold through my bones. "Oh, this is good. So you've chosen Kate, some random from Australia—"

"She's not random," I spoke through gritted teeth.

"So you've asked her to be your girlfriend?" Lottie asked.

I chewed my lip. I didn't look at Kate. I couldn't. "No."

"You're going to choose her over Jay?"

And there it was. The big guns. I knew she'd pull them out sooner or later.

I looked to Kate. Her knees were pressed tight to her chest and she clutched at them, holding them close to her. "What are you guys talking about?"

"I … I don't want to discuss it." Lottie's voice was quiet. "Lee did something, something I'd asked him not to do. I made a mistake; I made a huge mistake, but I never knew just how ruined I really was. Just how much I'd fucked up." Lottie shot me a look that screamed murder. In that moment, she reminded me of that day, that day long ago when she'd yelled at Ryan in the courtyard. Only now she went by Lottie, instead of Carly, another version of her formal name. Now I was bound to her. "I fell pregnant."

TWENTY-FIVE

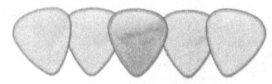

KATE

"WHAT?" I squeaked. What the hell was going on? A minute ago I was mid losing-my-virginity and now I was in the middle of some argument to rival in volume those in housing commission out in Sydney's west.

"You want to tell the whole story?" Lee thundered. He grabbed his pants and, after throwing the condom in the trash, pulled them on then strode over to Lottie's side, looking down at her, his face fierce as a storm. She matched his prowess, arms folded, chest puffed out, and something like lightning striking her face alight.

"People make mistakes. How many times do we have to argue this?"

"Then why is it one rule for you, one for everyone else?"

"Enough!" I yelled. The two of them spun to face me, and I straightened my spine. "Okay. Lee … you have a son?" My voice was so high, I was sure the neighbourhood dogs would have been howling.

Lee's face softened and he rushed to my side. "I don't really know, I—"

"How do you not know?" My mind spun. "Is it Jay?"

Lottie and Lee both fell silent. Well, this was awkward.

"Jay could be Lee's, or he could be his brother, Ryan's. We don't know." Lottie finally broke the quiet, and I blinked.

"You do have a brother." I levelled Lee with my gaze, and he winced. "Had." I added in quickly. "And you could be … you could be Jay's dad?"

This to me seemed the least believable part. How could Lee, Mr Puts Family First Lee Collins potentially be the father to a child he hadn't embraced as his own?

"It's possible, yes." Lee conceded, and I rested my forehead against my knees. Lee and Lottie had slept together? My mind whirled, and my stomach churned. Weird tension between them. Lottie letting Jay hang out with Lee, a freaking rock star. Hardly the best choice of babysitter. I was an idiot.

"How do you not know?"

"Because she wouldn't tell me. Probably because she wanted to go open her legs to another—"

"Can it, idiot," Lottie snapped. "Look, are you going to keep her? Is she going to be your girlfriend, or what?"

I looked from Lottie to Lee. Lottie radiated menace, and I didn't know that I'd ever seen her look so mad. Did she still hold a candle for him? "I'm sorry you're seeing this …"

I trailed off because it quickly became apparent to me that neither of them was listening. Instead they were locked in a silent battle of wills, staring each other down, emerald eyes locked to icy blue.

Right then, right at that moment is when I saw something break in Lee. Something deep that went right to his core. "Lottie, get out." His voice was quiet, barely a whisper.

She paused and chewed her lip, then spun on her heel and flounced from the room, slamming the door in her wake. It was just him and me. Me and him.

"Start." I pulled the sheet farther up my body, as if having some material between the man I thought I'd had feelings for and me would help protect me from whatever bullets his words contained.

"I met Lottie when we'd just hit the big time." Lee swallowed, and his eyes got this faraway look. "We were young; eighteen, and I fell head over heels for her. I thought we were meant to be." He pinched the bridge of his nose and slumped over his knees at the end of the bed, defeat and utter exhaustion written in his posture.

"We started seeing each other, hanging out all the time, and then ... well, a few months earlier my parents told me I had an adopted brother. We'd met a few times, and he'd had a rough life. Family who had abused him."

I shivered. I couldn't imagine ...

"One day we met up, and he told me he was going to propose to his girlfriend. We got drunk. I met up with Lottie, went to my hotel room and we ..."

"You don't have to fill me in on every single detail," I snapped, shaking my head.

"I'd left my key at the bar. Ryan thought he was being a good brother by returning it to me. Little did he know ..."

"You were banging his girlfriend?" I guessed. Lee nodded. Hmm. It was at least a good thing he didn't know she was taken. Even if that was a damn small silver lining in the grand scheme of things.

"So Lottie got pregnant, and then ... did you really kill him?" I tightened my grip on the sheet. My stomach rolled and I felt physically sick. How had my night gone from deciding to take a chance, from living in the moment, into this worst possible version of that?

"I ... Lottie got pregnant. We didn't know who the baby belonged to—me or my brother. She didn't really know what was going to happen—with us, or with her and my brother. I thought she wanted me, though. I really thought she wanted me."

"You went back," I guessed.

"I don't know what I was going to do. I ..." He turned to face me and his eyes were rimmed with red. "You have to understand, Kate. I didn't know."

"What happened?" I reached out my arm to touch his shoulder, but he flinched, and I pulled back to my chest as if the simple action had burned.

"Ryan withdrew. The stress of it all, competing with his famous brother who already had it so much better than him ... He started to do a lot of drugs ... hell, I think he already dabbled, but things turned pretty serious, pretty quick." Lee stared off into the distance, his eyes glossed over.

It was in that moment that I knew.

I wasn't the only one with a past that haunted me. I just didn't know if Lee was ready to let go of his to be with me.

TWENTY-SIX

LEE
Four years, four months ago ...

"You sure he wants to see me?" I asked Mom for the tenth time, and she nodded. Her face was terse with strain, and I knew this was hurting her just as much as it was hurting me. Since that day at the hotel, Ryan had withdrawn not only from me, but from Mom and Dad, too. They'd lost the son they'd finally gotten back.

I got out of the car that was parked outside Ryan's house, and when I say house, I was being generous. Ryan lived in a trailer, an old beaten-up white number that was parked in amongst thirty of its lookalikes. I only knew which one was his as Carly had told me.

Carly ...

It still hurt to think about her, but I straightened my spine. I had to do this. I had to face them both. I had to fight for what I wanted.

I walked toward the trailer and rapped on the door. Seconds later it flew open, and there stood my brother.

He was shirtless, and sweat coated his body, as if he'd been working out. He wore baggy pants that sagged around his waist, and his hair was matted, clumping up around his face. The whites of his eyes were spidered with red, and he smelt like smoke, and sweat, and meat.

"You came." He folded his arms across his burly chest, looking me up and down. "Get in." He jerked his head in the direction of the trailer and I edged my way past him. He didn't move an inch, making me brush up against his body. I wasn't a small guy; I worked out, but Ryan made me feel like a damn ant.

Stepping inside, I looked around. The trailer wasn't too small, a bed at one end and small table with bench-style seating at the other, opposite a cooker and a small sink. Carly sat on the bed, her hands in her lap. Her arms shook. She was a mess.

"At the table, Collins, not next to my wife," Ryan snarled, and I blinked.

"Your wife?" I looked at Ryan then at Carly. Sure enough, there on Carly's hand was a ring, glinting away in the light. "You ... you got married."

"Yep. Road tripped it to Vegas, got hitched, and came home." Ryan grabbed a bottle of bourbon from the shelf and poured some into three dirty glasses he found by the sink. "That's why I invited you here. To celebrate family." He sneered, then handed a glass to me and one to Carly, then lifted his own up in the air. "To love!"

I couldn't take my eyes off Carly. Off the woman I'd thought was mine.

She didn't meet my gaze. She stared at the floor instead.

Pain roared through my body in a tidal wave, ripping and tearing at my insides, coating them in its thick substance. I'd thought ... when she'd come to see me, I'd thought ...

Carly lifted her glass to her lips, and I froze.

"Carly ... you shouldn't have that." I nodded my head toward the drink, and she finally widened her eyes and looked at me, an expression that clearly read shut up on her face. That was when it hit me; I knew she was pregnant. But did my brother?

"My wife can have whatever she wants." Ryan rubbed his big hand across her back and she took a small, nervous sip of the booze, swallowing it down with reluctance. "And she wants me, Lee. She could have had either one of us, but she chose me."

I leaned back against the seat. She'd chosen … him? But hadn't told him about the baby? "Carly, can I talk to you outside for a minute?"

One minute Ryan was leaning up against the bed next to Carly, the next he was in my face, his hand gripped around my shirt collar. "You don't get to talk to my wife alone. Ever. You got that?"

His eyes were wild, and I knew that there was a lot more going on here than just booze and maybe some kind of depression. He was on some serious drugs.

The smart thing to do would be to walk away, to let these people out of my life for good. But one voice wouldn't leave my mind. What if that was my baby growing inside her?

Losing Carly was already ripping me in two, but a baby? After what Mom and Dad had been through, giving up their son and having him turn out … like this?

I couldn't do it.

I wouldn't.

"Carly, you need to see reason, babe," I said, ignoring the hand that slowly tightened around my throat. My breath became thick, and I choked out the words, "Think about what I can offer." I widened my eyes. It was as close to saying for you and the baby as I could come without actually letting the words escape my mouth.

"Oh, Mr Famous Rock Star, with all your money," Ryan sneered, shoving me back against the bench seat so my skull snapped against the wall behind me. Pain shot through my head, couple with an ache in my lungs from the reduced airflow. "Did you know that I lost that contract I was gunning for? The job I told you I'd almost got? It's because I was late to work, after having my heart ripped in two by my brother."

Sick worked its way up my throat, and I swallowed, Ryan's hand too tight around my windpipe. How had this all gone so horribly wrong?

"We were perfectly happy until you came along; we'll be perfectly happy again when you leave," he finished, jerking my head back one final time before letting my throat go. I gasped for air, coughing.

"Is that true, Carly?" I stared at her, but once more, her gaze was drawn to the floor at her feet.

"I love him, Lee." She finally looked up to meet my eyes.

"But I thought we had something," I choked out. All those times we'd spent together. She'd fallen from a tree.

"I've … we've been together, on and off, since I was fourteen." Carly looked up at Ryan, and he smiled down at her. "Things aren't always perfect, but … I love him. Life with you, all that rock 'n' roll stuff … it was always just a fantasy. Just pretend. It would never have lasted."

Bam.

Kapow.

There it was, like a sucker punch straight to the stomach. Falling in love wasn't like being wrapped in silk, gently caressing your body. It was being restrained by it, the thick material clogging your pores until you were covered in sweat, writhing to break free.

Sadness washed over me in a hurry, big and strong, and then it curled into a whirlpool in my stomach and came rushing back up. This time, it wasn't so sad. This time it was furious.

"Well shit, thanks for leading me along," I spat, pushing to my feet. "Did you ever think that maybe I actually cared for you?"

"Dude, you shouldn't have gone after someone else's girl." Ryan gave my shoulder a small shove.

"I didn't know she was someone else's girl," I yelled, my voice hoarse and on the verge of breaking. Fuck, it hurt. It hurt so damn much. "That's how much she cared for you, Ryan. So much so that she went on a heap of dates with me, not once mentioning your name."

"I thought we were just friends, Lee." Now Carly was on her feet, walking toward us with shaky steps. "I had no idea you were doing this grand romance thing. I even told you I had a guy! Usually, when boys like you, they try and make out with you, or get in your pants. They don't take you on picnics."

"Oh, and sleeping together? That's what you do with all your friends?" I raised my eyebrows.

"I made a mistake, Lee. Once. I'd been drinking, and people make mistakes. I'd take it back in a heartbeat if I could. A heartbeat."

I'd take it back in a heartbeat.

My heart.

It was empty.

Blood poured into it. It pumped it all out, and with it, it washed away all feeling. All desire to care, to love, to put myself out there because what was the point? What was the point when things like this could happen, and the one you thought was your forever could stab you in the gut?

I staggered to the door, pushing past Ryan who watched on with his arms folded, a sneer on his face. "Looks like you don't get it all, Lee," Ryan yelled as I walked to the car. Mom watched on through the window, worrying at her lip. "Hi, Mother! Shame you were such a slut you accidentally got pregnant as a teenager!"

I froze and spun around. His middle finger was raised in the air. I looked back at the car. Mom's face was ashen.

That was when I did it. That's when I gave Ryan the gun, handed it to him, and while I may not have pulled the trigger, I damn well could have.

Fury raced through my veins, and I said the most spiteful thing I could think of.

"Oh yeah? You know who the real slut is?" I spat. Carly came racing to the door, pulling at Ryan's arm, trying to get him back inside. "Your wife's pregnant, bro." I poured scorn into the endearment. "And there's a pretty good chance it's mine."

Present day ...

KATE LOOKED at me with confusion in her eyes, her brow furrowed, her hands still holding her legs to her chest. "So you told him Carly was pregnant. And then?"

I frowned at her, my palms facing skyward. "What do you mean and then? That was it. It tipped him over the edge."

"And you got in a fight?" She screwed up her nose and tilted her head to the side.

"No." I shook my head. "No, Kate. No." I gingerly sat down on the edge of the bed, my lips pursed together. "He committed suicide."

Kate slowly reached out her arm and placed it on my shoulder. This time, I didn't flinch away. I needed the comfort, even if it were only small. "He did that, Lee. Not you."

"It may as well have been me." I shook my head. "I slept with his girlfriend. I could have gotten her pregnant. I had the perfect parents and childhood whereas he grew up abused, watching his mother beaten half to death. I made him lose his big work break. He sent me this letter ... Carly sent me this letter ... she told me. I may as well have been the one to blow his brains out."

Silence coated the room, a thick, terse silence that I didn't want filled. I would never, ever forget my past. I couldn't.

"When you first told me you'd killer your brother ... I'd thought that was unforgivable." Kate sighed. "But this ... this isn't the same thing, Lee. You made a mistake. Carly made an even bigger one."

"Please, leave her out of this," I begged, then immediately regretted it when I saw the hurt flash across Kate's face. "I'm sorry, I ... she's had a hard life, you know? And I ... I owe it to her to at least try and make things a little easier. I owe it to Jay."

Kate didn't say anything, but her expression said it all. Anger, pain, hurt ... they washed over her in waves. Without saying a word, she spoke volumes.

Without saying a word, she made me feel like a total dick.

After a few minutes, Kate grabbed her clothes, the sheet

stretching from the bed behind her, and slipped them on. I didn't know why she bothered to hide—she was truly beautiful naked—but I guess she'd seen enough exposed tonight to not want to expose anything further.

She was too good for me; she was too unique. Too special. And after what she'd gone through with her two exes, what she was still going through with her father ... she wasn't meant to be with me. I'd been an idiot for thinking otherwise.

The best thing I could do was erase her from my life for good.

Especially if I ever wanted to forge a relationship with Jay.

"I'll organise a severance cheque for you." The words tumbled out of my mouth and caught Kate frozen.

"What?" she asked, her hands behind her back as she did up her bra.

"You're leaving, aren't you?" I tilted my head to the side.

"Lee, this doesn't change anything. Unless you don't want me here." Kate slipped on her shirt, but there was fire in her gaze, a fury that had been missing before. "You can't seriously think I would walk away because of something that happened five years ago?"

I shook my head. "It's not ... it's not just that. I can't be what you want. I ruined Lottie's life. That's why I don't ..." I trailed off.

"You don't do serious relationships because you feel guilty for ruining hers?" Kate looked at me with wide eyes, then threw her hands in the air. "Unbelievable."

"Not just hers, Kate. I ruined her relationship with Ryan, sure. I ruined her relationship with me. And then Mom and Dad? They broke up over this, Kate. The pressure was too much," I said, no concern for volume. "But Lottie was pregnant, and she wouldn't let me come near her, or the baby. She disappeared, shut me out for three long years! She told me I'd ruined her life. I don't deserve to be happy."

"Three years ago, Lee. You've not gotten anyone pregnant since, right? Lesson learnt. What's holding you back?" Kate asked. Her cheeks were red and her hands shaking with rage.

"What isn't holding me back? I ruined her life; I ruined everyone's lives, Kate. I owe her," I said. "And now I want the chance to make it up to her. To the both of them."

"So you won't be with me because you're too scared to take a chance, because you don't deserve to be happy or because you think I'm gonna fuck you over?" Kate spat the words out.

I froze.

Each syllable hit me in my soul like a shot from a gun.

Kate snorted. "I guess not being able to answer is answer enough."

With that, she stormed toward the door, handbag under her arm. "I need to … I need to go …"

"Kate," I called as her hand touched the exit. I didn't want her to leave. I liked her; hell, I liked her so much. She couldn't go.

But she couldn't stay.

Lottie had already told me she wouldn't let me have anyone else. Tonight was proof enough of that.

Because even if we didn't always like each other, we were meant to be together, Lottie and I.

Kate looked at me expectantly, and I so badly wanted to take her in my arms, to tell her everything would be okay. Then I remembered Lottie's face when she'd found us together earlier. Then I remembered Jay. My son or nephew, Jay.

"It's your room. I should go." I stood up and grabbed my shirt, walking out the door.

I didn't make eye contact with her as I passed.

I couldn't.

TWENTY-SEVEN

KATE

THE PROBLEM with heartache is no two wounds feel the same. One can cut you, fester, infect, slowly destroying you from the inside out. It can loiter and eat away at your soul, bit by bit, day by day.

Then you can learn to trust again. You can fall, and you can think you have it under control, that things will be different, but then the knife strikes once more. And while you think you've already experienced the worst pain possible?

You haven't.

And the second wound hurts like a bitch.

I sat in my room, tears falling from my eyes, wondering why. Why did Lee have to be so caught up in his past? I wasn't even sure what it was he was afraid of. Did he owe her, in some sick way? Had she made him vow never to be happy, since he'd ruined her forever? I shook my head. Surely no one could be that self-involved.

Still, there was only one sure way to find out. I grabbed my handbag and marched down the hall till I got to Lottie's door, hammering my fist against the wood, demanding to be let inside.

"Lottie!" I yelled after no one answered. A man down the hall stuck his head out from his door, shushing me, but for once in my life I didn't give a damn about what other people thought. I just wanted some answers.

I kept banging and the door swung open, and an irate Lottie stood with folded arms in front of me.

"What?" she hissed. "I have a kid trying to sleep in here."

"Whose?" I raised my eyebrows. "Lee's or Ryan's?"

Lottie rolled her eyes, and stretched her hand out, gesturing for me to come inside. I stormed past her and sat down on the couch. "Lottie, I thought we were friends."

"So did I," Lottie shout-whispered.

"So why are you so mad at me?" I asked, my voice an even tone.

"I … I'm not," Lottie muttered, studying her feet. She walked to the fridge and poured herself a big-arse glass of wine. She didn't offer one to me, and I didn't ask. "I just …"

She sighed, and ran a hand through her hair. "When I took this job, I had to sign a contract saying I wouldn't form a relationship with anyone while on tour. And I asked that Lee … m Lee wouldn't do anything either. Not in front of Jay."

I frowned, and bit my lip. "But it still doesn't explain why he blames himself so much. Says he doesn't deserve to be happy."

"Kate, I was twenty-two. I was young, confused … I did a lot of stupid things. Things that now I couldn't dream of." She shuddered, as if the memory made her blood chill. "When Lee told Ryan about the baby … Ryan lost it. He changed, doing drugs—he was a different person, Kate." Tears glazed over her eyes and she blinked them back, biting on her lip. "I said some things I regret. I told Lee it was his fault. That he should never have confronted Ryan like that, that he didn't deserve to be happy, and that I would be watching to make sure he wasn't." A sob choked out from Lottie's throat, and I wanted to hug her, but I stayed right where I was. "Kate, I didn't know he'd hold onto that forever. But my life, raising Jay was so hard … my pride wouldn't let me get in touch and tell him otherwise."

We stood in silence for a few moments, me trying to digest all I'd learned, and Lottie drinking more wine. She had a sad, forlorn expression on her face, and a part of me just wanted to give her a hug, let her know that everything would be okay.

"Why did you do it, Lottie?"

She looked at me, and those green eyes of hers drilled into mine. "A lot of reasons." She shook her head. "I loved his band. I was borderline obsessed, although I managed to keep that hidden." She clasped her hands together. "Ryan was away a lot. We were always on and off, but he'd been doing—doing drugs, and in Lee … I guess I saw an out. I saw the boy I'd fallen in love with, but the lifestyle of someone I desperately admired. And just for one afternoon, I wanted to experience that."

Emotions waged war within my body. I just wanted to blame her. It would be so much easier to make this all her fault.

But somehow, I couldn't.

Everyone makes mistakes. Even if sometimes those mistakes change your entire life.

"Why haven't you had the paternity test?" I asked in a softer voice, stepping in closer.

She gave a bitter laugh. "I don't want to know. I couldn't handle it if he were Ryan's …" Lottie's eyes got this wistful, faraway look. "And I couldn't handle it if he wasn't." She sucked in a deep breath. "When I came on tour, I told Lee maybe, in time. But just … baby steps. I want him to get to know Jay first. He's my everything."

"You can't hold him to this, Lottie." I frowned. "It's a promise he made a long time ago. People change."

Silence washed over the room, and Lottie drained the rest of her wine. She placed the glass in the sink. "I miss my Ryan."

I stood and walked over, rubbing small circles on her back as the older woman cried against my shoulder.

"I made a mistake," Lottie sobbed. "I was angry, and … aside from their circumstances, they coulda been the same person. Without Ryan … without anyone, with Jay on the way … it was so, so scary. I don't have close family, a support network like you do. Until you've lost your everything, you don't know what you'd do to get a little part of that back."

Her words resonated within me, and a part of me wanted to agree with her. If Johnny had been very similar to Lachlan then maybe, maybe I would have tried to work out something with him.

No. I wouldn't have.

Because sometimes, second best isn't enough. Sometimes, you just have to face your fears and move on.

Lachlan taught me that.

I walked back to my room. I was a mess. My feet were heavy to lift, my limbs ached, and to my shame, so did in between my legs. I wanted to regret what we'd done, what hadn't meant enough to Lee, since he wasn't willing to fight for it—for us—but I didn't. Was anything ever perfect in this world? Was anyone's first time like it is in the movies, complete with a bouquet of flowers and an orgasm to boot?

I was still furious Lee had left. But it was his reasoning that made me mad, not the fact he did it after sex.

I threw myself down on the bed and stared up at the ceiling. How had this all gone so horribly, horribly wrong? And how the hell could I make it right?

That was when it struck me. I couldn't. Only Lee could decide to take that chance, and at some point, he'd deemed me not worth the effort. Not worth taking Lottie on, trying to sort things out.

A big fat tear trickled down my face, and even though I was quick to swipe it away, another followed in its wake. I hiccoughed, and it seemed to unleash a dozen more, and then I was crying, full-blown in tears over everything. I wasn't enough for him. The only guy I'd thought was worth it; the only one I was willing to move on for …

I'd ruined everything.

More tears came, and even though I knew it wasn't true, even though I was really starting to believe that Lachlan would want me to move on, it didn't make the hurt any less real. I grabbed the TV remote and threw it at the wall, the loud thud giving me cause to smile.

"How dare you?" I screamed. "How dare you die and leave me to deal with shit like this?"

My breath came in short, fast gasps, and the air cloyed my lungs, making it hard to breathe. I wanted to run, to put on my shoes and just try and exhaust the pain out of myself, but it ran so deep it crippled me. I was a shell.

I didn't know who or what I was crying for. I was crying for Lachlan, for Lee, for how I wasn't anything worth it. I wasn't a risk worth taking, and even though I knew it wasn't his fault, I couldn't help but wonder if Lachlan had thought I wasn't worth staying alive for?

Eventually, my sobs subsided and I was able to get my breathing under control. I went to the bathroom and washed my face, shocked at the girl staring back at me in the mirror. I was a patchwork of red and white, my eyes an intense greeny colour, and my lips puffy.

I'd thought that the pain, the grieving would have an expiry date. I gave a small smile thinking of something Stacey had told me back in tenth grade. "According to Cosmo magazine, it takes exactly half the amount of time you were dating a guy to get over him."

I smirked. By that logic, I should have let Lachlan go in month one. Less than that, almost.

But there was something special about him, my brain argued. And it had a point. There wasn't any handbook for grieving. You couldn't allocate a fixed time and pattern to it.

Pull yourself together, Kate. I widened my eyes, trying desperately to convince myself. "You are strong."

But sometimes, life doesn't give us time to pull ourselves together. It doesn't give us time to be strong.

Because seconds later, my phone rang. I walked to where it sat, plugged in to charge on the bedside table, and picked it up. Blocked. Hmm …

"Hello?" I asked.

"Kate," Mum gasped. "Kate, please, please come home?"

"Mum? Mum, what's wrong?" I asked, my dialogue an overture to her symphony of choking in the background. My heart thudded in my chest, pounding against my ribcage as I prepared myself for the worst.

"It's your father. He's had a stroke."

TWENTY-EIGHT

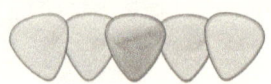

LEE

Four years, four months ago ...

TWO LETTERS. One stamped, with a date. The other hand-delivered.

Lee,

I'm not an idiot. I know what you can offer. And I want the best for Carly. She's ... she's special, man.
But I can't stand by and watch you be together. I know she married me, but who knows how long it'll take until she wants you again? Where's the comparison? We look the same ... but you're a fucking rock star. And if that baby's yours ... There's no way I can see that. It just hurts too much. That's not to say that I'm not fucking mad at you, because I am. You got

everything: the good parents, the
upbringing, the proper education, then
you got to be in a band with a huge
record deal, and have my girlfriend
too. Hell, knowing my luck, that kid
inside her is yours as well. I wouldn't
be surprised if I had shithouse sperm.
Did I ever tell you about the time I
met Carly? I'd seen her at school—
she went to the girl's only one, across
the way from mine, and I couldn't get
her outta my mind. I snuck out at lunch
one day and picked flowers from all
the fancy la-di-da houses down the
street, then surprised her with 'em
when classes were over. She'd said it
was a cheap trick; that I wouldn't be
able to keep it up.
I brought her flowers every damn
week we were together, Lee. Don't
for a second think I didn't deserve
her, because I sure as hell did. We had
something. I drink, I know I do, but
fuck, it's the only way I've been able
to cope lately. I'm not a loser. I treat
her right.
You, though? If she was that special
to you, you woulda fought harder.
You wouldn't have let her marry me.
Well, the joke's on you. You have
to live with this now. You have to
support her, and the kid. Because I
sure as hell won't be able to from
where I'm going.
I'm not afraid of dying. I know this
is the only way that kid has a chance
of living. Fuck, a trailer home ain't

no place to raise a boy—I'm sure it'll be a boy—and even if it is, who's to say Carly won't one day decide she wants back with you again? I can't put my kid through anything like what I went through. I want my kid—my kid deserves something good. A solid chance.

A chance I sure as shit never got.

So make sure you look after them. Both of them.

Because I'm bowing out.

Ryan

You knew it was never a good sign when you finished a show and your parents were waiting backstage. Mom and Dad hadn't been to a show since that fateful night when they'd told me I had a brother; right before my life changed.

A shiver ran down my spine as I walked toward them, handing my guitar to Hamish on the way past.

"Mom, Dad. So glad you guys came." I gave them both a hug. Dad clapped his arms around my body, a full embrace. Mum carefully placed her hands around me. Awkward. Distanced.

"Wanna … wanna go talk in the dressing rooms?" I asked.

"Yes." Mom nodded.

We walked through the corridor in silence, and even though the boys and I had been sharing a room that night, I found a private room a few doors down and led my parents into it. Whatever they were here for wasn't group conversation material.

I closed the door behind them and leaned against a table in the corner. "So what's going on?"

Mom looked at Dad, then at the floor, then at me, then

back at the floor. Then finally, she spoke. "Your father and I ... we're getting a divorce."

My eyes widened. My heart stopped. "A divorce?"

But these were my parents. My always happy-in-love, still-holding-hands-on-date-nights parents. It was the love I'd always wanted to have; what I'd been so sure I'd someday get. And my dad needed someone. Someone to take care of him. They couldn't be ... getting divorced?

"What?" I asked, because it was the only logical thing I could think of asking.

"These ... events recently, they've put a lot of strain on our marriage," Mom said, hurt flashing in her eyes, and I bit my lip. She didn't say the words outright, but it was clear.

I'd done this.

I'd ruined their love.

"Dad ... are you okay?" I frowned.

Dad looked at me, and his eyes shone with tears. I couldn't think of the last time I'd seen my dad cry. He just wasn't the type. "Son ... it's too ... too ..."

"We watched our son kill himself, Lee," Mom burst out, full-blown crying. "He killed himself, and it was all because we re-entered his life."

She didn't say it, but the subtext was there. It was because I'd re-entered his life. They were living with the guilt of being the creators.

"If we hadn't given him away ... if we'd tried harder ..." Mom sobbed.

"You couldn't have tried harder!" I protested. "You were kids. Babies yourselves! How could you raise a human?"

"How could you destroy one?"

The words hung in the ether between us. Mom clapped a hand to her mouth, shock widening her eyes. "I didn't mean that, honey. Honey, I didn't—"

"It's fine." I brushed her away as she stood to embrace me. "It's nothing."

Only, it wasn't. It was everything.

I'd killed my brother.

My parents blamed me, too.

"Things have been ... tricky." Dad nodded slowly. "And we're h ... having some time apart."

"Right." I nodded. "Got it."

"I wish ... are you sure you can't work things out with Carly?" Mom tilted her head to the side. "That's our grandbaby she's carrying."

"I've tried calling, but her phone's always off." I shrugged. It was something I thought of daily. She might have chosen Ryan, but surely she'd need some support.

"Keep t ... trying, son," Dad said.

"I don't know what else I can do!" I protested.

"You need to fix this. You have to," Mom said. "We want you to know that we love you very much, Lee." Hurt was still fresh on her cheeks.

"I love you, too." My reply was automatic. Like a rifle. Like a machine gun.

I'm a killer like that.

Dear Lee,

He's dead, Lee. I walked in and found him hanging from the back door of the fucking trailer. Do you know what dead people look like? How their skin is cold to the touch, how when someone suffocates with a tie—a fucking necktie—their lips turn purple and their face, instead of white, it's blotchy? Red and white?
I sure as hell do.
And I wish to God I didn't.

The sick thing is, the really sick thing, the first thing I wanted to do was call you, to ask what I should do. But, you wouldn't have helped me. You're the one who got me into this mess in the first place. If you had just kept your mouth shut ...

But you couldn't do that, could you, Lee? You had to win. You had to have the final say. More than that, you had to ruin what we had. I know we were both drunk, but didn't you think for one moment that if I'd been interested in you, I would have made a move sooner? I feel like you took advantage of me, Lee. And now my life is ruined.

Mom and Dad won't take me back; not while I'm pregnant. I still have my job, thank God for that, but how long can you survive pouring beers for while you're pregnant?

Don't try and contact me again. I want nothing to do with you. I don't give a damn if you can offer me financial support, or a bleeding shoulder to cry on—I don't need your brand of toxic presence in my life.

You know what Ryan said to me the night before he did it? "If

only you'd never met."
It's a sentiment I echo wholeheartedly. You killed my husband, Lee. And I hope you never find happiness again.
This time eight months ago, I had it all. The only thing I didn't have was the privilege of saving a cat from a tree.
Now, my life is ruined.
Maybe I'm better off joining your brother.

Carly

I called her phone, and got no answer. I sent her text messages, emails, but nothing. She didn't respond. And that was how I found myself out the front of her family home at the first opportunity I got, desperate to see her, to make sure she didn't do anything stupid.

I knocked on the door, three firm raps, and waited. Each second ticked past like it was an eternity.

Then the door swung open and her father was there. His expression changed from questioning to murderous in a heartbeat, his eyes livid, his lips a terse line.

"What the hell do you want?" he hissed.

"Is … is Carly here?" I swallowed, knowing full well she wasn't.

"No. You good-for-nothing scumbag, get the hell off my property."

He turned to walk away and started to close the door, but I wedged my foot next to the doorframe. I had to help. After I'd ruined so much, I had to at least try to save this.

Because what if Carly died, too?

I couldn't handle that.

"Please, just tell me where she is," I begged. He looked at me, really looked at me, and shook his head.

"It's idiot musicians like you …"

I stayed outside his house all night. I tossed and turned in my car, only waking when the policeman knocked on my window and told me to move on.

Ryan had died. Killed himself, because of what I'd done. I'd only just found my brother, and I'd managed to ruin his life in five short months.

Mom and Dad had broken up, begging me to find Carly and fix things—a promise I just couldn't make.

Carly had left me. She was on her own, raising a child, kicked out of home, her life in pieces.

I couldn't do anything right. How could I fix this when I couldn't get in touch with my absolution?

It was then I made up my mind. I'd do as Carly said. I didn't deserve to be happy, and I couldn't risk ruining someone as wholeheartedly as I'd ruined her again.

Love wasn't for me.

Love was for suckers.

And love would never be real. Not anymore.

Present day …

I SAT ON my bed, staring at the letter. Opening it, reading it, closing it. Each time the words seemed to twist in my brain, making things seem as they were not. I'd pushed her away. It was for the best; I still had to protect Lottie. The day she'd changed her name from Carly, the day she fell pregnant with that little boy … that was when she became my responsibility. And I couldn't risk losing her and Jay again.

I thought about Kate. Kate, sweet Kate, making sure I was okay when I drank too much. Kate, determined Kate, standing there in her underwear to prove a point. Kate, thoughtful

Kate, discussing the meaning of the world—life after death, and everything in between. Kate, listening Kate, the only one who knew my biggest secret.

The only one I trusted.

Kate, sexy Kate, naked and giving, giving herself to me …

I knew what I had to do. We were going to have to talk. I was going to have to try and make things right.

I left the letter lying on my nightstand, open so I could read it once again before I went to bed. So I could try and work out if there was any hope. Dear God, I wanted there to be hope.

Dear Lee,

I've had to leave. I'm sorry it's so sudden, but my dad—he's had a stroke. I'm taking the first plane out to Sydney this morning, but I've already spoken to Tony and given him my transfer notes, and he has a new girl on the way already. She'll be knocking on your hotel doors tomorrow morning at nine a.m., getting you up for your midday flight back to NYC.

Thank you so much for the opportunity you've given me. I've learnt a lot. I know it's not a job that you offer to everyone.

I want you to know that I think you've got to make a choice with your life here, Lee. I'm not saying between Lottie and me; you've made the answer to that question abundantly clear. But are you willing to close yourself off from love forever?

You need to forgive yourself, Lee. Don't make the body count behind you include your own.

Lachlan (yes, the guy who died) once told me that life was all about taking chances, about pushing the boundaries. I didn't realise it, but until I took a chance with you, I'd been holding back. I was clinging to a grief I still felt, but I wasn't giving it a chance to pass. I wasn't trying to accept the future. Maybe that's something you need to think about, too.

Thanks again for everything, Lee. I wish you all the best.

Kate

TWENTY-NINE

KATE

I HATED HOSPITALS. The smell of them, bleached and sterile, the beeping of machines, the quiet hush that floated through the corridors.

Today I hated them even more.

Today, this hospital held my dad.

I stared at him from the doorway of his room. He was hooked up to a whole bunch of machines, some beeping, some pumping fluid into his body, some taking liquids out. His face was almost grey, and from the way Mum sat beside him, his hand clutched tight in hers, I knew this wasn't good.

I kept staring, the emotion building up inside me until I couldn't take it anymore. Leaving my suitcase in the doorway, I ran into the room, a small sob erupting from my throat as I reached the bedside.

"Mum." I stretched out my arms and we collided. She pulled me close to her chest, her nails gripping my back so tight. I felt her ribs, each one separate and digging into my arms and I wondered how long he'd really been unwell, how long she'd really been this worried.

"Kate." She pulled back and looked at my face, tucking a strand of hair behind my ear. "You look awful."

I gave a half-hearted laugh and shrugged. "Well, no sleep, followed by twenty-plus hours on a plane will do that to you."

"I love you, darling." She clutched me to her again, and I relished in the embrace. It was nice to feel safe. Warm. Home.

After a few minutes we pulled apart and I walked over to the bed. Dad's eyes remained shut; his body still. He looked so lifeless; so unlike the father I used to know, or even the father he'd become with the disease. "How is he?"

Tears flushed Mum's eyes but she swallowed them down, managing to stutter out the words. "He's …" She shook her head and her shoulders began to tremble. I rushed to her side, patting her back. "It's not good, sweetie. The doctors …"

Time slowed down. My pulse thudded at my wrist and I became acutely aware of every other one of my senses. The smell of Mum's sandalwood perfume. The clip-clap of feet from the nurse down the hall. Blood rushed in my ears as panic gripped me like a vice, rooting me to the spot.

The stilling of my heart.

"They don't know if he'll make it."

There. Those seven words.

All of a sudden, everything paled in significance compared to what I was about to lose. My father. The dad I'd only just learnt to accept, to appreciate, could be on the verge of death.

A new wave of hurt washed over me and for the eight millionth time in the last two months, I tried to shake it off. But this pain was exactly like the ocean. You dove under the wave, you surfaced, and sucked in the clear air. But the salt? It stuck to your skin. It festered in your wounds, and as soon as you were in the clear, off the beach, it was gonna sting.

You knew it was gonna sting.

"When … what …?" I shook my head, unsure exactly what question I was trying to ask. When would they know? What was his condition? What could I do? If he was going to die, when?

All the questions seemed ridiculous when faced with the situation in front of me.

"I'm going to get some coffee, dear. Would you like one?" Mum asked.

"I'll go with—"

"It's better you stay." She nodded. "Now, coffee?"

I shook my head and she squeezed my hand on the way out.

I inched my way over to the bed and sat down in the hard plastic chair. My brain ran over the thoughts on repeat. He was here, but he wasn't. This was my dad, but it wasn't my dad.

Pain slogged me in the gut and I wrapped my arm around my waist. It crippled me and I grabbed his arm, finding it way too cool to the touch for my liking. "I can't lose you too," I whispered.

I bit my lip and made little circular motions on his hand, wondering if they were any comfort, if he even knew I was here. I remembered hearing somewhere that people in comas liked it when you sang to them. Or was that talk? Could you do the wrong one?

Considering my singing voice was well below par, I thought I'd give talking a go.

"Dad … how you doing?" I asked, then immediately shook my head. Idiot. "I tried to send you an email, you know. I tried so many times …"

He lay there, still, and I wished the words came more naturally to me, wished they weren't always so damn hard to find.

"I'm scared, Dad," I whispered, lacing my fingers through his and clutching his hand with all my might. The beep of the heart-rate monitor lulled me into a sense of security, and I managed to find some more truths in my mixed-up head. "I'm scared that I'll lose you again; and I already feel like I've lost you twice."

He didn't move, or reply, not that I really expected him to, but God, seeing him lying there, so vacant, so checked out scared the shit out of me. I dug my nails into his hand, hoping

I could somehow shock him out of his state. The monitor doubled up for a beat, then beeped its way back to normal. Damn it.

"The truth is, you can't … you can't die now." My voice was tiny, and I leaned closer to his hand, laying my cheek against it. "Dad, I … I need you here. I just spent two months overseas, and the six months prior I was practically in a coma myself. Damn it. I couldn't stand it if I lost that time we could have had together. I can't lose you."

Tears leaked from my eyes and snailed their way down my cheeks, and I brushed them away with the palm of my hand. I didn't know that I'd ever felt so desperate, so much desire for something for so long.

People lost their loved ones all the time. I'd lost Lachlan. Lee lost Ryan. Johnny lost his whole family.

But I didn't want to lose again. God, please don't make me lose again.

"Don't die, Daddy."

Two hours later, I walked out of emergency, bag wheeled behind me, and I caught the train home. Mum stayed at the hospital to be by Dad's side. She wanted to be there always. Just in case …

It wasn't until my head hit the pillow that I realised. I realised that I must believe in something after all.

Who else was I praying to if I didn't?

"So you just left?" Stacey turned the handle of her coffee mug from side to side, her jaw basically on the floor.

"I did." I nodded.

"Shit." She looked around, and I joined her in the observation. We were back at Sideways, but with different people looking after it, everything about it had changed. Sure, things were the same; the décor hadn't changed, and some of Lachlan's art still hung on the walls. But the service was brisker; there was an Employee of the Month star chart hanging behind the cash register, and a small sign next to the coffee machine that read The best kind of tip is a smile. It was very un-Johnny. Hell, it was very un-anyone-but-Mary-Poppins.

"When will you know more about your dad?" she asked in a quiet voice, so low I leaned in a little closer to reply.

"We don't know. The doctors are monitoring him ... but he's just not ..." I pressed my lips together and brought my hand to my nose, my index finger and thumb pressing against my bridge. "Sorry, sorry."

"It's okay, sweets. It's okay." Stacey sat there in silence as I tried to compose myself. God. What was I going to do if ...

"I just ... Stacey, I c ... can't." I wiped a tear away and my shoulders shook as another onslaught of emotion overtook me. My dad couldn't die. He just couldn't. I checked my watch for the time. Only twenty minutes till I had to leave to see him. Mum and I had decided shifts were the best way to go, so someone could be there if he woke up.

When he woke up.

Right?

More tears flooded me, and I brought my hands to my face, hiding from the world.

"The sun'll come out ... tomorrow ... bet your bottom dollar that tomorrow ... there'll be sun ..."

I stopped. What the hell?

"Just thinkin' about ... tomorrow ..."

I looked up. Stacey was singing. Singing, some crazy musical tune to me. Out of key.

"What are you—"

"Clears away the cobwebs and the sorrow ... till there's none."

Now people from nearby tables had turned to look at us.

"This is gonna continue until you start smiling," Stacey warned me, and a tiny smile played on my lips. "Stacey ..."

"When I'm stuck with a day ..." Stacey got to her feet, her voice louder now. "That's grey! And lonely!" This note she howled, yodelling across the café. "I just stick up my chin, and grin, and say … oh!" The note was so high, it crossed the line between singing and canine communication.

That did it. It broke me, and I burst into laughter as a guy in a black shirt and an apron came over to ask her to please keep it down, as she was disturbing the other patrons.

By this stage, Stacey and I had dissolved into fits of laughter, and she joined me back at the table, sticking her tongue out at one lady who was still giving her a disapproving look.

"Thanks, Stace." I smiled at her. She just got me. She knew how to make me smile.

"It's cool." She shrugged. "So long as you know that when you want to be sad, I'm here for that, too. I just …" She narrowed her eyes at me. "I thought you could use a laugh. After all, we're at Lachlan's café. Looking at the positives is what his life was about."

We sat in silence for a few moments more, drinking our warm beverages and people-watching.

"Stace … I'm so sorry about …" I bit my lip. "… your baby."

A cloud flashed over Stacey's eyes, but it was gone almost as soon as it had appeared. "It's … it's fine." She gave a sad shake of her head. "It's … I know it's nothing like what you went through with Lachlan, but it still hurts, you know?"

"I do." I reached across the table and took her hand. "Do you think you'll try have a baby … again?"

"One day, for sure." Stacey nodded. "Honestly, I felt so complete when I thought of being a mum. But I need more time to let go of this one first."

Her words rang through me. I knew exactly what she meant.

"What are you going to do about Lee?" she asked me. "Do you still have feelings for him?"

I studied my own latte, the milky-brown colour that filled the glass in front of me. "I do. But …"

"Lachlan?"

"Not … not really." I pursed my lips. It actually felt good to admit it. "God, Stace, I still miss him. I miss him like crazy, and

I still have feelings for him; I think I always will. I just … it's like I have room inside me to care for someone else now, you know? Room to … move. And the guilt I felt, when I thought I was replacing him, forgetting him?" Stacey gestured for me to go on. "That's kind of … it's not there as much anymore."

Stacey nodded sagely and reached across the table to give my shoulder a squeeze. I knew that Stacey understood.

"Lee doesn't have that room to care yet, though. I think he's still in love—maybe with the idea of being in love? I'm not entirely sure. All I know is that he can't move on until he lets go of the past." I pursed my lips together.

"Five years, huh?" Stacey took a sip of her chai latte. "You're a hell of a lot more emotionally connected than he is."

I smirked, and we shared a moment. A moment where for just one teeny, tiny snatch of time, we weren't hanging out to discuss all the things going wrong with my world. "So, tell me about you and Michael. All good?"

"Sure is." Stacey widened her eyes. "I've just about finished this semester and am thinking I might fly over and surprise him next time he goes on tour, y'know? I mean, after he comes back next week."

"You have the money to do that?"

"Abso-freaking-lutely." Stacey gave a smug smile. "I've gotten in touch with my spiritual side, Kate."

"Oh, please." I rolled my eyes.

"Seriously! I have strong psychic abilities. I've been taking clients, and let me tell you, pet psychics do good business."

I shook my head, but I laughed. Her enthusiasm was kinda contagious.

Then I paused. "Stace, can I ask you something?"

"Anything."

"Do you believe in an afterlife?" I studied her as she tucked a lock of her short dark blonde hair behind her ear, biting her lip.

"I … I don't know exactly what I believe, but I know there's something." She slowly nodded, her hands twisting around her mug. "I'm not kidding, Kate; I really do have communication with spirits. I could try and talk to Lach—"

"Gosh no!" I interrupted, eyes wide.

"Thank God you said that, I was so worried," Stacey blurted out, and I smiled. "Seriously, though, I do believe there's something. We don't just cease." She stretched her hand across the table and took mine in it. "And even when we're gone, our memory lives on—"

"In the memory of others," I finished for her, and we smiled, but there wasn't any mockery behind it. This time, it was genuine.

THIRTY

LEE

Four months ago ...

"IF YOU ask me, this is just a bullshit excuse to see some strippers."
Xander slapped my back.

"Man, I told you, it's not like that." I gave a light laugh.
"These girls just need a break. I bet some of them are just
doing this 'cause of the money."

"And some because they lurrrve getting their tits out."
Xander laughed, and I smirked along with him. Hiring
dancers to add some extra appeal to our act had been Tony's
idea. Making them strippers had been mine. If I could just
change one person's life for the better ...

"Hi there, handsome." A topless waitress winked at
Xander as we walked past, headed for a table near the front.
Xander's legs followed me but his eyes stayed firmly fixed on
the woman. I shook my head. At least it was dark in here, and
the club was closed. We'd entered through a secret elevator
from the upstairs hotel; no media would know we were here.
Hell, they'd even dimmed the club lighting so the girls on stage
wouldn't know we were who we were. It was just the way Tony

liked it …

Xander and I sat at a small table down the front. Seconds later, Boobs placed two beers in front of us, and a bottle of top-shelf bourbon with some glasses and ice behind that. "Can I get you anything else to drink?" She batted her eyelashes.

"I wouldn't mind sucking on your—"

"We're good." I shot Xander a murderous glare, but he just laughed it off.

"We'll have our first dancers out in three minutes for you. They'll do an intro number, then you can see their solo performances. And if you'd like any private numbers …" She didn't need to say anymore. Even if she hadn't mentioned it, we would have known. When you're at the top, you rarely need to ask for special favours. It just seemed to go with the territory.

"So what do you think of Michael?" Xander asked, taking one of the beers and knocking back a sip.

"He's cool," I said. "I can't believe it's been … God, almost five months already. That flew."

"Sure did." Xan nodded. "Personally, I can't believe how long it's been since you've been laid."

"Dude, give it a rest …"

"All I'm saying is, it's not natural. I'm all for the single life—I don't think you're wrong for not wanting a relationship—but you know you're allowed to indulge in some pussy, right?"

It was my turn to take a sip of beer. It was nothing I hadn't heard from him before. "You know I'm not interested in anything serious."

"I don't know exactly what happened with Carly, but you gotta let it go, man. It's time."

I was standing, hovered over him, before he could get another word out. "You don't know anything about what happened with Carly," I hissed. It had been four years, but the pain was still there. Somewhere in the world, I had a nephew or a niece, a son or a daughter. And I had thrown that away. Right around the time when I'd killed my brother and ruined my parents' relationship.

Xander looked up at me, took another sip of beer. His eyes

were dead calm as he said, "The show's started."

I heaved in a deep breath and turned around, sinking into the slouched leather seat. Girls strutted onto the stage, some twirling around poles, some moving their bodies in time to the music, their hands running up their legs, over the bodies. One woman in front of us threw off her top and it landed on my lap, her tits jiggling as she spun around the pole, making the sort of crazy shapes with her legs that left little wonder as to how flexible she'd be in bed.

To her left was another girl, her back to us. She was in nothing but a G-string, shaking her ass from side to side as she swirled those hips, around and around. She reached behind her back and unclipped her top, turning toward us as she got ready to throw it over her shoulder.

The first thing I saw were her boobs. Big, voluptuous, and round.

The second thing I saw was her face.

Carly.

I took a long sip of my bourbon, letting the smooth liquid numb my insides, numb my brain. When I saw her face, I ran. I went to the men's room, and didn't come out, and I don't think she saw me. Her eyes had this horrible glazed look, as if she weren't really here, but on another planet. Although maybe, considering what she was doing, that wouldn't have been so horrible after all.

When the dance was over, I'd asked our waitress for a private show with her. Any second now, Carly was about to walk into this seedy, mirrored room with the sticky black lounge, the satin sheet-clad bed, and the floor-to-ceiling mirrored walls and strip for me.

Only, I wouldn't be letting her strip. Hell no.

The lights dimmed and a sexy bass beat thrummed through the room. My back stiffened as I stared into my glass. Surely she'd start the strip with more clothes on than she had on stage … right?

One sexy leg scissor-kicked through the doorway, then another, spinning around so Carly entered the room backward in just a G-string and a bra, closing the door behind her.

"You wanted a pri—" Carly gave a seductive wink over her shoulder. "Oh my God!" she screeched and ran to the bed, grabbing the sheets from it and wrapping them to cover her midsection. "What the hell are you doing here?"

"Me?" I stood up, slamming my drink down on the table. "What the hell are you doing here?"

Carly seemed to cower in on herself for a moment before straightening up, puffing her chest out in defiance. "I'm making a living, Lee. Not all of us get to be rock stars." She sucked in her bottom lip for a moment, then let it out. "Not all of us get a happy ending."

The look in her eyes was somewhere between fight and flight, as if she wanted to stay, to let me know just how badly I'd screwed up—as if I didn't remind myself of that every single day of my life—but it also spoke of how desperately she wanted to flee.

"Carly …" I sat back down, sinking my head into my hands.

"Lottie."

I snapped my head up. "Lottie?"

"Lottie. You …" She shook her head. "You may not have known, but my birth name was Carlotta." She nodded, swallowed, her throat bobbing with the movement. I hated that a tiny part of me still responded to that. Still found her so attractive. Was that why I'd found it so hard to commit, all these years? "I changed my name. I'm not the girl you knew anymore."

My knuckles cracked as my fingers dug into my palm.

"I didn't know." I shrugged, but I felt lame. Stupid. They say ignorance is bliss, but ignorance is also careless. Dumb.

How had I not known her real name?

"I looked for you …"

"I know." Carly studied the floor, her toes poking out

beneath the red silk sheet that was draped around her body. "I made myself hard to find."

I stood up and crossed the room, took the four steps to be right in front of her. There was no more hiding. No more running. "Why?"

Carly looked up at me, and her emerald-green eyes, they weren't emerald anymore. Now, they were jaded. "I was angry, Lee. And I said some things … horrible things … things I regret. Things I am so, so sorry for." She looked back at her feet, but when her gaze met mine again, fire burned behind it. "I needed you. And I didn't want to need you. Not when you didn't care enough to fight."

"Fight?" I spat, my hands to either side of me, palms facing the ceiling. "Fight? You didn't give me a chance to fight! You just ran!"

"Not then, before. When Ryan first found out … you disappeared on tour. I know, I screwed up—believe me, I know. But I couldn't help thinking that if this was a real thing, if we were meant to be together, wouldn't it have been easier?"

I turned and ran my hands through my hair, my mind spinning.

"Lee, I'm so sorry." Carly's voice cracked. "I had a lot going on back then, my emotions were haywire, and …"

I spun on my heel. "The … baby?"

Light flared in Carly's eyes. For just a split second, she was that girl I used to know. "He's amazing, Lee."

Three words. That was all it took to change my life forever. "He?"

"Jay. Lee, he's … he's an angel." The reverence in her words shone.

Everything, all the guilt I'd carried around like a weight during the past four years, it lessened. Because this could lighten my load. This could be my salvation.

This could be my son.

"Do you …" A lump took over my throat, making it hard to form words. "Have a picture?"

Carly smiled, and nodded. "Yeah, but, you know …" She

glanced down at her sheet-covered body. "Not on me."

I gave a short laugh. Because what else could you do at a time like this, but laugh?

It was at that moment that I made up my mind. I'd found her. I could fix this; could make it right, just as I should have all those years ago, just as my brother's letter had requested, just as Mom and Dad had wanted me to. For them. For Ryan.

"Come work for me," I blurted the words out.

Confusion crossed Carly's brows. "I won't be a private dancer—"

"Be our stylist. Work in fashion, like you always wanted. Come and live on the road with me and the band, with little Jay in tow."

"Ha!" Carly snorted. "And we'll what, all live happily ever after?"

Her words were like salt on my wound. After how much I'd wished, how much I'd tried to atone for my mistakes all these years … that line was too much. "It's not a fucking fairy tale, Carly!" I roared. "I just want to try and make things right!"

"You can't save everyone, Lee Collins," Carly seethed. "And some of us just aren't worth saving."

She folded her arms and sat on the bed. I folded mine and sat on the chair. Sure, I was still physically attracted to her, but in that moment, I knew. I would always love Carly, but I would never be in love with her again.

"I haven't had a real relationship since you left." The words were soft, spoken directly to my hands. "I haven't had peace. Please … please, let me try and make this right. Let me be … let me be a dad, or an uncle."

Silence swept over the room, swallowing me. Here I was, four years on, finally finding Carly, only to lose her again. My one chance to make this right. My one chance to try and find redemption …

"Okay."

I blinked. Did she just say …?

"But no telling Jay, no paternity test, no girls, no media drama—nothing." Carly took a step closer to me. "Not until

I'm ready."

I swallowed. So I wouldn't be a dad, an uncle. I wouldn't see other girls.

But I was getting that chance. The one I'd always wanted.

"Welcome to the tour, Lottie."

Present day ...

"WE NEED to talk." I studied Lottie from across the table. It was breakfast, the day after tour finally ended, and I'd arranged to have it brought to her room for her and Jay to enjoy. I'd say and myself, too, but my stomach was knotting itself up. Four years was a long time. It was a long time to walk away from.

"I thought as much." She took a sip from her glass of champagne and orange juice as Jay ran his toy truck over the tower of pancakes in front of him.

"Look, Mom." Jay smiled a big, toothy grin at Lottie, and I found myself grinning, widening my eyes as he kamikazied his truck off the stack and let it drop to the floor, no doubt a chunk of maple syrup landing with it.

"Wow." Lottie dropped her jaw. "That's one outta-control truck."

"Like the trucks Lee said he'll show me at the monster trucks." Jay nodded, and I grinned.

"Sorry," I muttered in response to the glare Lottie was shooting at me.

"So talk." Lottie smiled, ruffling Jay's hair. I still felt like an intruder in their little family duo, and I knew things would take time, but I wanted more. I wanted more than this role of 'Mom's employer'. I wanted to be his relative. I couldn't have this half-life anymore.

"Lottie, I … I know we have sort of an understanding …" I articulated the word with care. "But I can't keep doing this."

Her glass hit the table with a solid thud. Her smile dropped from her face. "So you're letting us go." It wasn't a question.

"No." I shook my head. "Not at all. But I … I can't do what you asked. I can't have 'no girls.'"

Lottie's face crossed in confusion. "No … girls?"

"Yeah. No girls." I affirmed.

"What are you talking about?" She pulled her head back in puzzlement.

"First it was that letter. Lottie, I couldn't … it was my fault. I didn't deserve to be happy." I pushed my hands over my forehead and through my hair. "No. I didn't think I deserved that. I think … I think I could, now. Maybe. I've paid my penance."

Lottie sat in silence for a few minutes, then poured herself another drink. I took a bite of the toast in front of me, but it was cardboard, porous in my mouth.

"It was a mistake."

The words were so quiet. I leant forward in my seat to hear more.

"I was wrong, Lee." Lottie swallowed, only in that brief moment, she was Carly, the vulnerability shining in her eyes. "I was young, and I was stupid, and I just … I fell for two guys. And then I bled for them. Because neither was the right choice."

Tears started to fall from her eyes, and the part of me that always wanted to protect Lottie, that always wanted to save her, tried to run to her side.

But I couldn't be that guy anymore.

Some people needed to save themselves.

"Lee, I'm so s … sorry," Lottie sobbed. "I'm sorry for Ryan. For not l … loving you. And for the letter. I am so, so sorry for the letter."

The words were like an absolution to my soul. Like the weight had been lifted. Like the guilt from my past was being eased. "But what about when you said no girls? Back at the … strip club?"

Lottie frowned. "Around Jay? He's just a kid, Lee. I didn't want him to be meeting his father, or his uncle, and a host of whores you were keeping around, too."

"I don't have who—"

"I know now, okay?" Lottie sighed. "But I didn't then. And I have to admit … when Tony made me sign that contract, saying I wouldn't see any other guy—"

"Tony did what?"

Lottie frowned. "Made me sign the contract."

"What contract?"

Lottie took a deep breath. "You need to speak to him about it. Basically, it said I couldn't be in a serious relationship. Now, I guess it was in case I spilled the beans. Then, I thought it was because …" She looked at her feet, shifting in the thick carpet.

Realisation dawned, as bright as the desert sun. "Then you thought it was because I wanted to get back together."

"Is it going to sound completely ridiculous if I say yes?"

Her big, emerald eyes blinked, and I stood, walked to her side, and hugged her, held her tight for every time I hadn't held her, for everything we hadn't had before.

Holding her felt like my past. Holding her felt like family. Holding her felt like letting go.

"I'll do whatever you need, Lottie. I want to be a part of Jay's life. I know you said you needed time, but is there any chance we can look at getting the test soon?"

"No." Lottie's voice was firm, hard.

"Never?"

"Not until we've settled in a little more." She topped up and took a tentative sip of her drink, which was now noticeably more champagne than orange juice. She always was one to live life on the wild side … "Lee, just give me … give me a year. I know I was the one who screwed up. I totally get that. But if it's … if Jay is …" She shook her head, and I knew. I knew what her deepest fear was.

That Jay would be mine. And then her guilt would weigh even more than my own.

"We'll wait." I nodded. Where family was concerned, I had all the time in the world.

Lottie and I sat in silence for a while, punctuated only by the sound of Jay's truck crashes that filled up all four walls of the living room. God, I loved that kid. And I loved even more the idea that one day, I could be in his life more.

"So … have you booked your flight?" Lottie raised one side of her lips.

"For what?" I already knew the answer. A blind man would be able to sense it.

Because once my guilt had lifted, I'd been able to see the truth. That in a way, Lottie was right. I needed to fight for what I truly wanted.

Because Kate was worth every punch, every blow to the jaw. Every hurt I had to endure. Everything Lottie could throw at me.

"I'll see you later, little buddy." I grabbed Jay as he careened past, his car skating over the top of my chair.

"You coming back soon?" He batted those stupidly long kiddy eyelashes at me.

"A few weeks," I conceded. I looked up at Lottie, and she was smiling. A big, proper, genuine smile. Maybe the first I'd seen her have.

"Good luck, Lee Collins." Something shone in her eyes, and my heart swelled. This was the right thing to do. It was the only thing.

"Where you going?" Jay persisted, tugging on my jeans as I stood.

"I'm going to fight for what I want," I said, and I smiled, knowing truer words had never been spoken.

I was going to catch a plane.

I was hoping to catch a girl.

THIrTY-ONe

KATE

I SAT AT the bed, holding Dad's hand, counting the little blips on the monitor. It felt so trivial, such a nothing activity to pass the time, but I had to do something. I needed to occupy my brain with something more than he's not going to wake up. Because that's what it said, a lot of the time.

Doctors and nurses came and went, checking vitals, monitoring machines. One even asked me if there was any change, and I'd felt like yelling at him. Yes, he woke up, did the polka, and now he's back out of it again. Shame you missed it! I knew they were only doing their jobs, but still. A little logic wouldn't go astray.

"Gosh, what is there left to fill you in on …" I mused, staring at his skin. I'd gotten used to the slightly ashen colour now, the cooler than normal texture. His body wasn't shutting down, apparently; his circulation was just low. Weird what you took to be a good thing when you were in a situation like this.

"Well, Michael's due home any minute now, so Stacey's going crazy with excitement," I said, acting like Dad knew what I was talking about. "She even had a—" I stop. Out of it or not, it still felt weird telling my dad about my best friend having a bikini wax. "She had a, um, haircut." I nodded. "And she wants Michael to, um, see it. And maybe …" Hmm, what could I say here? "Maybe check the area"—with his penis—"for, uh, any spots the hairdresser might have missed."

"Aside from that, nothing new to report, today." I shrugged. It was day five of coming to the hospital, day eight of Dad's coma. I wasn't an idiot. I knew there wasn't much hope.

But it was human nature to want to believe the good, to hold on to that tiny bit of positive and hope like anything that it twisted in your favour. Because if you didn't have hope, what did you have?

"I applied for a few jobs today," I threw in, just to fill the empty space. "Nothing too exciting, mind. Something in sales, which sounds horrid, but at least it'll earn good cash. Another job in admin."

Silence stretched out between us, interrupted only by the workings of machinery, and my mouth dried. This could be the last time …

"I … I haven't heard from Lee," I choked out. God, that night had sucked, but it seemed so trivial now. Nothing compared to this. "I mean, right now it's not really a … a priority for me …" A tiny sob escaped me and I tried to reel it back in. It felt like all I'd done this past week was cry. I was surprised I had any liquid left inside me to shed.

"I can go if you'd like."

I froze. What?

"I should have … Kate, I should have figured that I'm the last person you want to see right now."

I turned in my chair, slowly, carefully. But my ears heard correctly. There in the doorway, leaning against the metallic frame, was Lee-freaking-Collins.

A sports bag rested on the floor beside him. His dark hair was ruffled, and he had a five o'clock shadow darkening his chin. But he was here. In Australia.

In this hospital?

"How did you know where—"

"Stacey," Lee answered before I had time to finish the question. "She met Michael and me at the airport."

I shook my head. She'd messaged me this morning to ask what I was wearing today, mentioning that dressing nicely was good for keeping up positive vibes. I snorted. More likely she wanted me to look hot for Lee. How had I fallen for the vibes line?

My heart swelled with hope, and a tiny part of me wanted to just run and throw myself into his arms, but I schooled myself still instead, and sat there staring at him, a what I hoped was defiant look in my eye.

"What are you doing here?"

Lee walked toward me, looking to my father and then meeting my gaze once more. "What's going to happen?"

"You're ignoring the question."

"You're not listening to what I'm asking." Lee gave a cryptic smile, and I rolled my eyes. "Kate, I'm here. I'm here, putting my heart, my everything before you. You're … you're nothing like anyone I've ever met before, and I want to know, hell, I need to know. What's going to happen? With us?"

My heart pulsed in my throat, and my stomach churned. What on earth was happening? How was Lee Collins here, in the same country, in the same hospital as me? It didn't seem real.

There had to be a catch. "Did you talk to Lottie?"

"Yes." Lee's voice was clear, and I knew he wasn't lying. "But that's not why I'm here."

"She gave you permission?" I widened my eyes.

"She gave me the truth." Worry clouded Lee's normally clear eyes, and I tried not to reach out and touch his arm, but it was so darn hard. "And made me see that … I can't save everyone, Kate. And at some point, I have to save myself."

Lee walked to my side and stood by my chair, his eyes locked on mine, crystal blue meeting hazel-green. "Kate, everything you said was right. I still … I still feel guilt about Ryan's death. I don't think anything will ever make that go away, no matter how hard I try." He let out a rushed puff of air. "But I need to live my life. And I've been thinking … I can't work out a way to do that without you in it."

This time, my heart started doing Zumba from my stomach to my throat, giving me a good old-fashioned internal workout. What was he saying? Was he going to try—did he want to—

Then, Lee did something that stopped my thoughts right in their tracks. He lowered himself, down to his knees.

Oh. My. GOD.

The Zumba became replaced with a mimes session. My heart was doing its best impression of a still life, somewhere up in my throat.

"Kate." He looked at me with all this feeling shining from his eyes. "I love you."

Emotions welled within me, and I wanted so badly to say yes, to kiss him, to make this happen, but—

"It's too soon!" I blurted out. I couldn't keep it in any longer. "I mean, I do, I really like you, and you have no idea how happy I am that you're here, and I would love to date you and God, I'd even consider moving in with you, but—"

"What are you talking about?" A frown crossed Lee's brow, then a few beats passed and he looked down, then back up at me, and laughed. "Um … since you were sitting, I thought I'd kneel so we were on eye level." He bit his lip, laughter dancing in his eyes. "Did you think …?"

Oh. My. DOUBLE GOD.

This had to be some kind of horrible dream, the type where the next thing you know you're naked in front of a hall full of people. "I wish my clothes would come off," I mumbled, pulling at my shirt. Nope. Still firmly on.

Lee gave a suggestive wiggle of his eyebrows. "I'm sure we could—"

"Not in front of my dad." I frowned. Comatose or not, I still wasn't going to have anyone making sex references around him.

And that's when my heart stopped. The machine attached

to Dad's arm started beeping like crazy, frenetic angry noises, as if it had just been plugged in after resting in a stale state.

"Get someone!" I screeched at Lee, and he rushed out of the room. I hovered over Dad's head, his face impassive, but his body jerking every few seconds, his little finger twitching, his face spasming.

This was it.

He was going to die.

My dad was dying.

Hurt welled in my body, up through my veins, and I started to cry. I grabbed his arm and begged, pleaded for him to stay, for anything but—

"What's happened?" One of the nurses from earlier came rushing in, the doctor right behind her.

"He's dy—"

"Let's get a team in here, stat!" the doctor yelled, and within seconds, the room was a hub of activity, people coming and going like ants in a farm.

My throat clogged up and I surged forward. I had to be with him. He couldn't go like this.

"We need you to step out in the corridor." A woman in scrubs touched my arm, gesturing to the door.

"No!" I cried.

"He's coming to." She smiled kindly.

Three little words.

I love you.

We are good.

Happily ever after.

He's coming to.

They changed everything. They made it all better.

Lee and I walked out of the ward. I was numb, in a state of shock.

"He's …" Lee pressed his hand over my shoulder, and I looked up at him and smiled.

"I think so." From the window in the corridor my eyes were glued back to the bed, where a host of people were now checking monitors, shouting medical terms and generally looking important. But I didn't care. What I did care about was his hand. That little finger … it kept twitching.

He was going to be okay.

"I …" I froze. What was I thinking? "I gotta call Mum." I grabbed my phone and dialled her number, unable to keep my eyes from the prone figure on the bed that maybe now, was coming back to life.

I hugged my arms around my middle while we talked, and I smiled, I smiled so wide that my cheeks hurt from holding it that big. It felt like for once in my life, everything was working out.

Maybe I would get a happy ending after all.

THIrTY-TWO

LEE

Two days later …

LOOKED AT the gorgeous girl sitting across from me, and I smiled. It still felt too good to be true. To incredible to be real. She was sitting there, having greeted me at the door to her parents' home when I'd finished rehearsing with Michael, telling me that she had ready the most amazing pasta dinner I'd ever eaten—who even knew she could cook? When did she have time to learn those skills?

Of course, that wasn't what was really amazing about it. She could have made me toast and I'd still be the idiot sitting across from her with the lovesick grin on his face. Because that was what she made me do. Smile. All the time.

"That was amazing." I pushed back from my chair and stood up, grabbing her plate and taking it to the sink. "And for all your hard work, I'll now be a gentleman and wash up."

"Well … about that …" Kate made a face, and I tilted my head at her. "What do you define as hard work?"

I narrowed my eyes. "Kate …"

She reached over and pulled out the drawer containing

the bin where a takeout container marked La Fiamma Italian Eatery was clearly visible. "To be fair, I never said I cooked it, specifically …"

She hadn't. I had presumed. But the idea of punishing her was far more fun than letting it slide.

I grabbed the tea towel from next to the sink and held it up, flicking it out so it whipped her gently on the ass as she turned around. "Ow!" she shrieked, clutching her behind.

"Trust me, I'm just getting started." I gave a wicked grin and she screamed as she ran to the other side of the table. I chased her, darting from one side to the other, trying to predict where she would make her escape. Both of us had these super goofy grins on our faces, the kind that up until now, I thought only happened in chick flicks.

Turned out life could be like that, too. Because right now, I felt as if I were living in one giant big happy cliché.

Kate darted to the edge of the table and made it to the stairs before I could catch her but I followed, tea towel in hand. She giggled and squealed the whole way, and I swear, better sounds didn't exist. They simply didn't.

I took my time when I reached the landing, then I took the ten steps to her room slowly, with care. I was gonna make this punishment good. She was gonna—

Kate stood in the doorway to her room in nothing but her bra and underwear. Red. Lacy. See-through.

I was a dead man.

"Put the tea towel down, Lee," Kate ordered, and it fell from my fingers like a feather. I think my jaw might have joined it somewhere on the floor, as I took in her creamy-white skin, her delicious curves, the way her hooded eyes looked at me as if she wanted me to do all the bad things I was thinking of doing to her right this second.

I stepped closer and wrapped my hands around her waist, my fingers skating over her smooth skin as my lips met her neck, sliding up and down it, taking delicious, sweet tastes. "You know this is a bad idea," I mumbled in between nibbles of her ear, even if my body disagreed with me.

"Relax." Kate rolled her head to the left, exposing more of her neck to my amorous lips. "Mum's going to be at the hospital with Dad for another few hours. And we don't have to Skype Lottie and Jay until tomorrow."

I grinned as I continued my trail of kisses, working my way across her jawline to her mouth. Because yeah. Lottie and Jay were Skyping with us the next day, and coming to visit us next week. Lottie had asked to fly in from the States the day after I'd left, and I'd booked the first flights I could find. Maybe, the four of us could be one weird, dysfunctional family.

It was just a start.

But it was a damn good one.

I reached my hand around Kate's back and fumbled with the clip of her bra, determined to let it loose. She froze and fisted my shirt in her hands, pulling me closer and slamming the door shut behind me.

"Let's not waste any time," she hissed right before her lips met mine in a passionate frenzy. Our mouths parted and all the tension that seemed to constantly hang between like a wire fizzled and sparked, resulting in a passionate explosion of our two bodies.

"Kate," I groaned against her lips, finally getting that stupid, idiotic bra off and freeing her breasts. I cupped one, teasing her nipple, relishing when she arched into my touch. Yes. This.

She grabbed the buckle of my belt and made short work of it, unbuttoning my fly as if she'd been doing it all her life— had she been doi—I banished the thought before it could eventuate. This was Kate. Kate was my girl. And Kate and I, we had no secrets. We told each other everything.

Soon we were flesh on flesh, bare skin on bare skin, and it felt like everything and the only thing all at the same time. We were the universe, and we were small, in it together.

I crushed her against the bed, pinning her hands in place above her head as I kissed down her arm and her neck, lowering my mouth to graze her nipple.

"Lee," she moaned, and I sucked a little harder, relishing

in her give.

She pulled one arm free from my grasp and her hand wrapped around me, stroked me, until I was so hard I worried I would burst before this was over, before we'd even gotten to the main event.

I stopped and pulled back, looking at her once more. I shook my head.

"What?" she asked, a half-smile playing on her lips.

"You are without a doubt the best thing that's ever happened to me."

I knew it was the best thing I could have said. I could see the effect my words had on her, the pink raising from her chest to her cheeks.

"Will you get a condom already," she groaned, but I knew she was happy. I'd learnt it from Michael; ignoring or downplaying a compliment was just the Australian way.

I turned and grabbed my jeans, extracting my wallet and a condom from within. Before I put it on, I leaned back over her and joined my lips to hers again, pressing up against her as our lips bruised each other, and our tongues duelled.

I ripped the packet open and rolled the condom on, not breaking contact with her sweet, sweet mouth, not for one second.

"Please, Lee," Kate breathed, her chest rising and falling rapidly. "Please, make love to me."

And I did. I lowered myself until she clenched me tight, her body embracing me as her own. I shuddered, the feeling almost too much to handle, almost too great to bear.

Slowly, I started to move, and her body responded to my actions, much more readily than it had the first time. I reached my hand down and gripped her thigh, wrapping it up and around my lower back as my other hand found her nipple, and soon her body started to convulse and shake around me.

That was all it took to undo me. That and the woman I loved, screaming my name as she fell to pieces.

When our bodies stilled, she lay against my chest, her brown hair fanned out over my arm, her breathing laboured.

"That was …" She sighed.

"Good?" I breathed.

Kate lifted her body and pounced on me, her mouth possessing mine like a witch. "We work, Lee Collins," she said, a big grin on her face. "We're just … we're meant to be."

And I smiled.

Because we were. Maybe I was meant to meet Lottie, meant to have her in my life. But maybe it was because that was what had stopped me from trying to have serious relationships sooner. That was what made me put family first.

Maybe all of this was meant to be, so I could be with Kate. And we were going to live happily ever after.

THIRTY-THREE

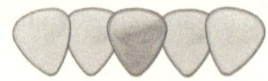

KATE

I SAT AT the grave, a bunch of flowers in one hand, a cup of coffee in the other. He would have wanted that. Lachlan was a big believer in the importance of caffeinating.

"Hey," I said to the stone, as I had almost three months ago to the day. God, how things changed. How much difference time could make.

"So, I wanted to come and formally tell you that I'm seeing someone." I bit my lip. "But I brought you flowers, so you know, things aren't all bad."

A light breeze whispered the trees, and a bird swooped low overhead. I smiled, certain he'd have appreciated my sentiment, even if it he wasn't here to receive it.

Or maybe he was.

I didn't know.

"I still miss you, Lach." I bit my lip. The acrid taste of blood filled my mouth as I continued with the pressure. I needed the release. "I miss you like … God, I just miss you."

I'd thought I could hold it together, but I was wrong. Big,

fat tears ran down my cheeks, and I swiped them away with the heel of my hand, trying to get my emotions under control. "But the thing is … the thing is, I can love you. I can love you forever, and ever, and ever, and I never have to stop."

And I would. Because nothing would change this brilliant man who was now six feet under. Nothing would change his memory, and the impact he'd had upon my life.

"I can love you for eternity, Lachlan." I took a deep breath. "But I've found room to love someone else. And it doesn't mean I'm going to forget, or that I'm deleting you from my life. You'll always be a part of me."

I placed the flowers on his grave and looked up. Lee sat in the car, looking at me, his eyes full of emotion. That was my future. That was where I was headed.

"Just because I've moved on, doesn't mean I'll ever forget."

I knelt down and gave the cold concrete a soft kiss, then I dusted off my knees and walked toward the car. Toward my future.

Toward my Lee.

EPILOGUE

LEE

THE PROBLEM with life was that things didn't always fall into place or work out the way you'd planned. And try as you might, you couldn't always control the things that were going to happen—even if you had Tony on your side, watching over your every move.

I'd spoken some harsh words to him about making Lottie sign that document, but I knew why he'd done it. Having her spill the secret of Jay's real identity could have been dangerous to us—what he didn't understand was that it would have been just as dangerous for them, and that Lottie would do anything to protect that little boy. The little boy I was getting to know more and more every day, even with Kate in my life.

Because family was important to me. It always had been; it always would be. It was why I'd stopped at the jewellery store, picking up a little blue box from Tiffany's on my way to lunch.

I walked into the cafe, scanning the tables, until I spotted them. They were seated at opposite sides of the table, and I wondered if there was any possible way they could put more distance between each other while still sitting 'together'.

"Mom. Dad." I bent down and kissed Mom on the cheek, then turned Dad's chair so I could give him a hug. He took me in a weak embrace, but it felt good. Being here felt better than it had in a while.

"Good to see you, Lee." Mom nodded.

I passed her the little blue bag. "Here."

"Lee!" She smiled, but shook her head sadly, pocketing the gift instead of opening. "You didn't have to …"

I shrugged. "I wanted to."

Silence wrapped itself around our group, punctuated by laughter from a little girl trying to push what looked to her grandfather in his wheelchair at the next table.

"I know I've said it before, but I'm so sorry about … about what happened with …" Mom trailed off, and I shook my head.

"It's in the past, Mom." She'd apologised before, but this was the first time I didn't still feel a slight sting.

Maybe I hadn't really ever needed her apology.

Maybe I'd needed to forgive myself.

I looked around the other patrons of the eatery outside the nursing home. Families were smiling. Children were laughing. I gave a smile and relaxed back in my chair, my hands behind my head. I was trying to make amends with my parents, even if we weren't falling into best buddies overnight. My relationship with Jay was getting stronger every day, even if Lottie still hadn't agreed to the paternity test. Time. I knew she just needed time.

The band was going well, and Tony had presented me with a new contract to sign for another three albums. And I had this girl … the girl of my dreams waiting for me back in my hotel room.

For the first time in forever, I belonged.

KATE

THE PROBLEM with life is it rarely wraps things up in a neat circle. Some things come, and some things go. Sometimes things stay in your life with no real resolution, waxing and waning as the years go by until you wonder if they'll ever really leave your life at all.

For me, that was Lachlan. Sometimes I'd all but forget. I'd be so happy, so caught up in Lee, in his adoration, in the way he looked at me, touched me, loved me—it would be all-consuming.

Then I'd see the picture Lachlan drew for me, hanging on the wall in the garage at Mum and Dad's. Or a social media notification would pop up from his brother Johnny, who sometimes still posted from Lachlan's account when times were tough. And sometimes, it wouldn't have to be anything at all—just a feeling that would wash over me and take me from one hundred per cent functional to crippled with need, guilt and devastation, all at once.

But I'd learnt to live with that. And thankfully, so had Lee.

After all, things hadn't tied themselves up with a little bow for him, either. While Lottie had come around a little, Lee still wasn't able to convince her to get the paternity test. We spent our lives together but apart; Lee bought an apartment across the road from their house, where Lee lived and I heavily visited when he wasn't on tour. And Lottie didn't come on tour anymore, what with preparing Jay for school. But we still got to see Jay whenever we were around. And strangely enough, Xander seemed to hang around there a fair bit, too.

While I loved Lee dearly, I kind of had other things on my mind as we stood outside the obstetrician's clinic that day, four months later. Right now, there was a very different baby I was excited to see.

"You ready?" I asked Lee, wrapping my fingers through his.

He gave them a gentle squeeze, and he smiled down at me. "Ready as I'll ever be."

We walked through the doors of the clinic, ready to see an ultrasound, the first image we'd ever get captured of Stacey and Michael's four-month-old foetus.

"It's really happening," Stacey whispered in my ear, giving me a bone-crushing hug as she met me in the foyer. "We're going to be parents!"

I didn't know, but she and Michael hadn't been using protection when they were doing the naughty. They weren't trying to fall pregnant; they just weren't trying not to, either. And I knew this was something they wanted. And that they'd give their everything to it.

"Hey, Dad." Lee pumped Michael's hand, a wicked grin in his eye. "So I hear pregnant ladies are insatiable in bed …"

"Dude! That's the mother of my child you're talking about." Michael slapped him across the stomach, and Stacey and I shared a smile. Her cheeks glowed red; she was the epitome of a healthy mother-to-be.

"Allison?" A man called from the doorway, and Stacey gave a small squeal. "That's us."

She gestured for us to follow her down the hall and we did, past several doors until Lee jerked me to one side, into the safety of an alcove that contained a whole heap of cleaning supplies. "We'll catch up," he called over his shoulder, and I heard Michael make some joke about us screwing in the baby-maker's clinic. Because, really.

"Kate … this is …" Lee grinned, and I couldn't help but smile too. He had that affect on me. "I know we're only new, and we're still working everything out, but … maybe in a year, do you want to think about making a little Kate?"

His eyes were so full of hope and excitement that they shone. Heat rushed to my cheeks. "How do you know it won't be a little Lee?" I teased.

"Because if it has any common sense, it will be as much like you as possible," Lee nodded wisely. "And if I pass one thing on to my protégé, I sure as hell hope it's some smarts."

I giggled and cupped his cheek in my hand. "Lee, I'm still only nineteen. I'll be twenty soon, but … I need to do a whole lot more living before I have a baby." Lee's gaze flickered down the hall to where Stacey had disappeared, and he opened his mouth to speak but I butted in. "And don't you dare say that Stacey's doing it, so I should do it too, because you know that's being ridiculous, and that we're not the same person."

Lee closed his jaw with a snap, and I grinned. "Besides, don't you want to do things together first?" I trailed my hand down the side of his face, his day-old stubble brushing my knuckles. "Travel the world … experience new things … maybe get a dog …"

"Maybe get married." Lee's eyes weren't hopeful. This was a statement from him, and it wasn't the first time he'd brought it up, either. He knew I was waiting; I wanted to finish the correspondence degree I was doing in event management, and wanted to do some good ol' fashioned dating first, since we seemed to spend most of our time together. I spent a lot of my life in the States with Lee, and every third week I'd fly home to Australia and spend some time with Mum and Dad. And each day I learned more about them. I appreciated them even more.

And I prayed to God to thank them for being a part of my life.

Still, even though we fit like gloves and had made things work, marriage wasn't on the immediate agenda. But it was neatly filed in my head under Things That Even Though I Knew I Wasn't Ready For, I Was Excited For To Happen. One day. Not too far away.

Because that was the problem with love. Sometimes you fell, and you fell so hard that it was like the rug had been pulled out from under you, leaving you crushed, crippled and breathless on the floor, changing the way you saw the world, the way you did everything. It made your heart ache. Consumed all your thoughts.

But it also made you be more yourself. Brought two souls together.

Bringing them home.

And that was the true problem with heartache. That sometimes, even though Lee had wanted to find one, there

wasn't an ache at all.
  Not for us.
  Not ever.

THE END

THANK YOU, BEAUTIFUL PEOPLE!

To anyone who has read ANY of my Crazy in Love books, I couldn't be more thankful to you. I so appreciate you sticking with me through this series, and learning more about Kate and Stacey's journey. Writing book three in this series was the hardest thing I've ever done. I just so hope I haven't disappointed you.

To those who have emailed or messaged me, telling me that The Problem With Crazy really struck a chord somewhere within them—I can only hope The Problem With Heartache was the third book you were hoping for. And I adore you for taking the time to contact me.

Of course, there are a host of technically awesome people who made my book shiny, and I have to say I adore KILA Designs and the genius of Kim for creating this cover, Marion, my beautiful editor for helping my words grow, and Emily, my amazing formatter. You're all so lovely for putting up with me!

If it weren't for the support of some amazing bloggers, you probably wouldn't have read this book, and I truly need to thank a whole host of them! I don't want to name names and forget people, but ones that instantly spring to mind are Lustful Literature, Book Harlots Review, Novels in Heels, Glass Paper Ink Book Blog, Vrsha, and a heap of AWESOME others. I feel so blessed anytime one of you reads my work. If you are a blogger … I LOVE YOUR FACE!

Kylie from Give Me Books, even though you're a blogger, you get your own category because you are just so giving, and willing to let me message you with stupid questions all the time. Thank you for being rad (and for making me choose a release date. That was a good idea).

My awesome beta readers: I could NEVER release a book without you. Thank you for bringing me to tears, making me laugh, smile, and pouring me a virtual glass of wine when this whole thing got too much. Jennifer Ryder, thanks for taking the time when I know you were flat out. Kristine Barakat, damn it, woman, you always make me smile with your passion and enthusiasm! You made me iron Carly out, and grow her into a real person. I will always appreciate that. Stacey Nash, you read in record speed, you found the flaws, and you made me add the feels! Simone Nicole, you suggested the feels wherever Stacey didn't (seriously, do you guys think I'm heartless?), you read the whole darn thing twice, and you were there to talk me off the cliff (every time). I love you all.

I am so blessed to have a beautiful group of friends around me. Bucket-loads of gratitude and love go to A if for F@#king Awesome, The Story Queens of Aus, Aussie Owned and Read, and McStellar's Number Achievers.

SYDVEGAS! I adore all you gorgeous women! You're just there for me all the time, and I can't think of any other people I smile at, laugh with, cry alongside and talk to so often. If our relationship isn't normal, it's the best level of dysfunctional I've ever had.

Finally, sometimes I exist outside of my head, and I see real-life people. Thanks so much for your awesomeness Mum, KMac, Mitch, Andy, Marg, Jeff, Lisa, Scott, Paul, Chloe, Hayden, Delle, Trace and Anna.

And to my Peter. Because we actually were meant to be together. And there isn't anything heartbreaking about that.

ABOUT THE AUTHOR

Lauren K. McKellar is a writer and editor of fact and fiction. She loves writing and reading, and hopes her books make you feel all the things—or some, at the very least.

Lauren loves to write for the young and new adult markets, blogs with Aussie Owned & Read, and is published both as an independent author and through Escape, Harlequin Australia's digital-first imprint.

In her free time, Lauren enjoys long walks on the beach with her two super-cute dogs and her partner-in-crime/husband.

Connect with Lauren

Website www.laurenkmckellar.com
Facebook www.facebook.com/laurenkatemckellar
Twitter www.twitter.com/LaurenKMcKellar
Goodreads goodreads.com/laurenkmckellar
Tsu tsu.co/laurenkmckellar

And if you'd like to join my street team or my e-newsletter don't hesitate to email me at laurenmckellar@gmail.com

OTHER BOOKS
BY LAUREN K. MCKELLAR

Finding Home
The Problem With Crazy (Crazy in Love #1)
Eleven Weeks (Crazy in Love #2)